AIRSHIP 27 PRODUCTIONS

El'aris
© 2020 Wayne Carey

Published by Airship 27 Productions
www.airship27.com
www.airship27hangar.com

Interior illustrations © 2020 James Lyle
Cover illustration © 2020 Ted Hammond

Editor: Ron Fortier
Associate Editor: Jonathan Sweet
Marketing and Promotions Manager: Michael Vance
Production designer: Rob Davis

ISBN: 978-1-946183-86-6

Printed in the United States of America

10 9 8 7 6 5 4 3 2 1

BY WAYNE CAREY

CHAPTER ONE
RETURN

Why had he come back?

As the shuttle settled to its landing pad in a wash of dust, Anthony Michaels glanced out of the view port beside him. A typical spaceport. Hangars and storage buildings dotted the flatness. Huge transports and cargo haulers, with company logos painted on pitted hulls, and battered merchant craft squatted on their struts, arranged in obscure patterns. In a secluded corner stood the private yachts, sleek and polished. Another passenger shuttle lifted off toward one of the orbiting space liners. This could be any planet. Why did it have to be this one?

He thought he would feel different, let the past stay buried; just get the job done. Now that he looked over the surface of El'aris, he felt the heat of memories. So many years had passed; he thought it wouldn't matter any more. He had sworn he would never set foot on this planet again, where his friend Jon Perry had died, but here he was. Surely enough time had gone by to heal wounds. Yet...

Everyone had a price, especially him. He needed work, and this was a job. Just a job.

Michaels nudged the snoring giant next to him.

"Come on, Geoff," he said.

Thatcher jerked awake, peering through narrowed eyes beneath heavy brows. "Huh?"

"We've landed." He squeezed out into the aisle and pulled his pack from the overhead compartment.

Thatcher rubbed his dark mahogany face and smoothly shaved head with a massive hand.

They made their way down the aisle to the aft exit as the steward popped open the hatch. Warm air washed through the cabin, chasing away the staleness of recycled atmosphere, carrying in scents typical of all ports.

He slung his bag over his shoulder and stepped through the hatch.

The white dwarf was brighter than he remembered. He squinted while his free hand searched for the shades in his jacket pocket. His fingers rummaged through a variety of odds and ends: electronic lock pick, scanner debugger, pocket laser, old gum wrappers. Once he had the shades in place, he studied the man waiting in front of a long black limousine. He was a lower executive type, wearing a silk suit that probably came from Deenar Four. Not the best, but expensive. A solid gold Elneebian wrist chronometer. A signet ring with the distinctive company triangle. No hidden weapons. The car was a wheeled variety, one of CentraTech's most luxurious. The glossy black surface reflected the stained white hull of the shuttle. Blackened windows concealed the interior. No registration plate. Only the company's name and the number five.

With Thatcher towering over his back, he stepped down the ramp to the tarmac.

The young man at the car stepped up, hand extended. "Mr. Michaels? I'm Stev Vindal, representative for Deltan Technologies."

Michaels turned his sour expression into a bright, boyish grin. "Anthony Michaels at your service. And my associate, Geoff Thatcher."

"A pleasure," replied the company man, his smile threatening to split his face. Perfect teeth. Perfect hair. Born to rule from behind a desk. "Welcome to El'aris."

He motioned them toward the car and away from the other passengers descending the ramp.

The car door slid open. They climbed into the cool spacious cabin, Vindal sitting opposite them. The car sped off without a sound.

"Why exactly are we here, Mr. Vindal?" Michaels asked. "Your company contacted us, paid our expenses, and made vague promises for an extravagant pay. Why?"

The corporate rep leaned back in the soft leather seat. He flashed a reassuring smile. His teeth sparkled. "Our Regional Chief Executive Officer will explain. I'm not authorized to give you any information. We're due for the meeting in ..." He consulted his chronometer. " ... fifteen minutes. I understand you've been on El'aris before, Mr. Michaels. Ten years ago, during the consolidation."

"Eleven years." *And it was a war.*

The car left the spaceport buildings behind. Shiny, modern, technical. Eleven years ago, their drop ships had landed on flats leading to the Tadamij Ocean to the east. They had burned their way through brush and young trees, getting their troop carriers to the crude native roads leading south. Now, their limousine glided over a flawless paved highway, passing vehicles traveling north.

"Eleven years," Vindal echoed. "El'aris is a perfect study in economic aid. Here is a planet, lost and completely isolated from the rest of the galaxy for hundreds of years after its colonization, the Human colonist subjugating the native race, eventually pushing them to a distant land. If Deltan Technologies hadn't assisted the Tz-en in regaining their world ...

El'aris has made quite a name for itself in the Arm in the past decade. This is a very rich planet. We've done quite a lot for it."

"What about the planetary government?" Michaels asked.

"The Tz-en are still the ruling group, ever since the consolidation. They're still the minority race, but they control all aspects of the government and the military. A great deal of merchants and trades people are El'aran."

Through the forward window, Michaels saw the new glistening bridge that spanned the marshy delta of the Arijon River. To the south, the spires of Jhamrahl touched the deep blue of the sky. His mind dropped back to the time when their troop transports had pushed through the marshes, on their faulty hover repulsors. He and Perry had been side by side in one armored attack vehicle, with fifty Tz-en warriors, when they first saw the capital of El'aris at this distance. Thousands of Tz-en warriors followed behind, with a dozen other off-world professionals. Jhamrahl had been the first target. A dawn raid. The rising sun had turned the wetlands blood red, a premonition for the day.

"Because Deltan Technologies funded the consolidation," Vindal continued, "the Tz-en gave our company first trading rights. We helped open this world to galactic commerce. Without us, El'aris would have fallen back into the hands of the El'arans, and the natural riches of the planet would be lost for centuries more. Wait until you see what our company has helped to accomplish. You've seen the spaceport. Technologically, it's one of the most advanced in the Arm. It needs to be, with all the transports passing through each day. A lot of commodities are sent off-world. Raw ore, produce, manufactured goods. Jhamrahl, the capital, has expanded in the past decade. It isn't the same city. You'll notice that as we pass through it. Look."

Michaels followed his inviting wave. The Tadamij Ocean glistened blue-black to their left, gently touching the white sands of a shore dotted with sprawling new buildings. Hotels, he realized. Casinos. Shops. Eleven years ago, a few fishing huts witnessed their approach to the city. Those had been unceremoniously blasted out of existence by overzealous Tz-en soldiers, an act that had alerted the city five kilometers away. The city was a cluster of delicate spires and towers and peeked domes, painted with elaborate geometric designs, no protective wall, no defenses. He remembered the change in Perry's eyes when the first of those domes had crumbled under a particle shell. Throughout the whole battle, he had fought without the old smile, the old enthusiasm.

He absently heard Vindal babble about the Tz-en before the war. How they were forced to live on the smaller, northern continent on the opposite side of the planet. Today, that frozen wasteland catered to visitors who enjoyed arctic sports and frigid scenery in its modern resorts.

"I've been there," Michaels said. At times he had wondered how the Tz-en could survive the harsh weather. He had never seen any of their villages, though. Only the makeshift camps where he, Perry, and the other off-worlders trained them in modern weapons and tactics. He never had the inclination to socialize. They were fierce soldiers, but a severe climate bred that kind of person. They were barbaric, lacking skill and discipline. The off-worlders had provided the training and leadership, along with contemporary weapons. With off-world aid, the Tz-en rose from poverty and subterfuge to take control of the planet.

The old quarter unrolled to the right of the highway. He took in the glistening domes.

Vindal beamed. "Tourists love this section. Romantic cafes, exotic hotels, many of which haven't been updated just to give that uncivilized flavor."

"Thanks for the holiday tour, but we didn't come here for a vacation." He hoped his voice carried enough sarcasm.

"Of course not, but there's nothing I can say about why you were brought here. Ah, we'll be there soon." He craned his head around.

The car took an off-ramp, which shot it out of the city and toward the flats to the south. Within minutes, Jhamrahl lay behind and green fields spread out on either side. Michaels looked hesitantly past Vindal toward their destination. Years ago, a major portion of the invasion had taken to the narrow streets of Jhamrahl, securing the city from its meager defenses, while he and Perry had led their troops to the palace of the M'ji.

He gave an involuntary shudder as they approached the estate. He could hear Perry talking about it, reciting their plans of entry and expounding on the beauty of the mansion.

"We've restored it near enough to its original state," Vindal said as the car neared the surrounding high walls.

They had blown away the main gates with a particle shell, taking thirty meters of wall on either side, as well as the contingent of ceremonial guards. The limousine drove up to a new gate, an intricate web of black iron. A perfect replica, from what he could remember. A few items were new, like the visual scanners and sensor units. The guard contingent was different. Four Tz-en carrying energy carbines.

"I'm afraid you'll have to leave your weapons at the guard station, gentlemen. Only security are permitted to carry weapons on the estate."

The driver stepped out and opened the passenger door. Vindal climbed out first. As Michaels followed, the heat blasted him.

Michaels gave a wry grin. "You realize that either of us can kill just as easily without weapons."

"I'm quite aware of that, Mr. Michaels. You wouldn't be here if you had to rely on a blaster for your livelihood. The company has its rules, though, and we follow them, no matter how insignificant they may seem. Yihn will take care of your belongings."

He motioned to a Tz-en warrior, who stepped from the archway of the security station in the high wall. Michaels stopped short and stared briefly. He hadn't seen a Tz-en for a long time. Tall, slender, wrapped in muscles like steel cables. The black leather uniform contrasted with the whiteness of his skin. The long gaunt face held its aloof expression, while the round pale blue eyes behind tinted lenses focused suspicion on every movement. Like most of his race, his coarse white hair grew long and straight, held at the back by a leather thong. When the warrior grinned, without any suggestion of humor, he exposed twin rows of sharp teeth and elongated canines. Michaels had almost forgotten how their appearance affected Humans. Perry had said it had something to do with pheromones. He had seen a lot of weird races in his travels. Some ugly, some repulsive. He had never come across anything like the Tz-en. At the best of times they reminded him of animated corpses. At the worst times, like during their fighting frenzies, they were nightmarish ghouls.

Reluctantly, Michaels and Thatcher relinquished their packs and weapons to the care of Mr. Yihn. At least the bundles were sealed against tampering or scanning. With an insecure feeling of nakedness, he got back into the car with Thatcher.

The car rolled through the opened gate, under the cold stares of the sentries.

The driveway wound through gardens overflowing with blossoms from various worlds. The trim lawns, shrubs, and trees gave the impression of a delicate park. Along the curve of the pavement, an El'aran pruned fruit trees. Another directed a water spray onto a bed of bright red flowers. Vindal rambled on about the variety of plants translocated from throughout the Arm.

"The palace is popular with the tourists," he said as they pulled to the wide marble steps leading to the main entrance to the old palace. "There are scheduled tours, usually after normal business hours, Frankly, they can be distracting."

The gleaming white walls no longer bore the scars of battle. A tall domed tower stood at each corner of the square, surrounding the larger dome on the center structure. The spiraled peak of the central dome reached into the sky higher than the sentinel towers. Two of those towers had been leveled eleven years ago. Blast marks had dug deep into the masonry of the high walls, and particle shells had exploded a cavern through the main entrance. Michaels could see the courtyard beyond, littered with charred bodies. He could hear the screams of the Tz-en in the blood-lust mixed with those of their El'aran victims. The Tz-en had gone wild. He and Perry couldn't control them. Perry had wanted the M'ji and his family taken prisoner. Instead, every El'aran on the estate was butchered. The magnificent structure had been laid to ruin. Only the central dome had escaped blasting.

"So," Michaels said, pushing away the memories, "the Tz-en rebuilt this place for their government."

"No, Mr. Michaels. Deltan Technologies purchased the estate from the Tz-en. *We* rebuilt it. In essence, it's our branch office and the residence for most of this sector's more influential executives. Quite a comfortable place, as you will see. A lot more tech installed than for the previous owners, but then I believe it remained pretty much the same for ten generations of M'ji."

As they left the car and started up the steps, Vindal glanced up at the high wall with its arched windows. "The quality of reconstruction still amazes me. I've seen holos of it after the last M'ji's death. Quite a mess."

Michaels glared down at the man. "Perry wanted the palace captured. We didn't need the M'ji becoming a martyr. The Tz-en went into a killing frenzy. They leveled the place, disregarding orders. There were a lot of needless deaths and destruction."

Vindal smiled amiably and shrugged. "The M'ji's martyrdom didn't seem to extend the hostilities. Besides, it was their conflict. They could have darn well leveled the place if they had wanted to. You and your associates were here as advisers." He trotted past Michaels toward the tall double doors of black marsh wood at the top of the steps. A Tz-en with a shouldered carbine stood at either side. At their approach, the guards stepped aside and the doors slid open with a protesting hiss and rumble.

Hydraulics automatically opened the four meter high heavy door panels. The original doors had been elaborately carved with images of the planet's history, some images recalling the old colonization. He had never gotten a very good look at them before the cannon had blasted them away, but he recalled the finely detailed artwork that had covered the dark wood. The replacements were plain and smooth. His reflection glided across the polished surface.

The archway led immediately into the courtyard, which displayed more luscious vegetation on a smaller scale than the gardens surrounding the estate.

People strolled across the courtyard, mostly Humans wearing rich suits and dresses, carrying satchels or cases, busy with personal data tablets or talking on com links, each one in a hurry to get on with their business. Michaels and Thatcher, in their fatigues and unshaven faces, were properly ignored, not just invisible, but non-existent.

Vindal led them into the main building and down a long, wide corridor. On either side stood pedestals displaying sculptures from various cultures. Michaels never had an eye for art, but he recognized a few of the masters. The small statues ranged from simple nudes to heated conflicts to intricately worked animal life. There were a few busts of important looking people, none of whom he recognized though one did resemble his grandmother. On the walls, spaced between the pedestals, hung framed paintings and tapestries. He guessed that these representatives of the galactic art world were all originals, each worth a small fortune.

Vindal walked briskly down the hall, past intersecting corridors, directly to a reception desk beside a large double door. The woman at the desk nodded acknowledgment to Vindal, worked a keypad, and activated the door. Michaels took a moment to become oriented. The end of the hall didn't look the same. When he had seen it before, the door had already been blasted away. No receptionist or desk had existed, only the charred and bloody remains of palace guards. Beyond the doorway lay the throne room of the M'ji.

As they passed through, his mind flashed with the ghosts of the past. Screams and shouts echoed. Figures raced among the supporting pillars. Blast beams and bullets sizzled through the air. Tz-en and El'aran bodies lay scattered as the royal guard fought fiercely to their last man. Perry had burst upon the scene too late to stop them. The El'arans weren't used to wars. Minor skirmishes, maybe. Their army had been a glorified police force. Their weapons had been crude. No blasters. No particle guns. Just swords and pistols. The Tz-en butchered them.

The throne room was hollow now. It seemed larger. The circle of pillars standing out from the wide, round wall. The great dome rose high overhead, split with narrow vertical windows that flooded the chamber with bright sunlight. As they walked across the tiled floor, their footsteps echoed in the emptiness. Michaels gazed up and stopped short. Thatcher bumped hard into him.

The entire surface of the dome carried an elaborate painting in brilliant colors, brought out in the illusion of three dimensions by the sunlight through the vertical windows. Had it been there before? He seemed to recall something, but he hadn't paid attention at the time. He had been a little preoccupied. How could he have ignored it, though? It was magnificent. The central point depicted the creation of the universe by the enormous hand of the Creator. The stars spiraled outward, springing from the hand, turning into planets. One large blue world opened up to blend into the oceans that touched the green forests and flowering fields. Wildlife began to walk the forest as the scene circled the dome. The picture expanded with larger, exotic creatures. The oceans seen through the trees overflowed with life. The spiral ended with perfect physical examples of a man and woman, their nakedness modestly obscured by some small flowering vegetation. They stood together, over the dais that had held the throne, with their hands and eyes raised up toward the Creator's hand.

"Mr. Michaels?"

Vindal's whisper echoed. He urgently motioned them on.

The throne of the M'ji no longer stood on a dais that curved along the far wall. The dais itself was gone. Instead, a long table of glossy black, its shape reminding Michaels of the company's triangular logo. Its blunt apex held a place for a high-backed leather chair that could easily face the three chairs on each side of the table or the open area of the chamber in front. At each seat, a keypad and monitor were inlaid in the polished black wood.

As they stood in front of the empty table in silence, waiting, Michaels allowed his mind to wander again, drifting into the resurrected memories. Echoes of the battle returned, and he could see the young M'ji with his pistol in one hand, sword in the other. His men died valiantly around him as he fought against the surge of Tz-en warriors and their blasters. In their frenzy, many of the Tz-en forgot their weapons and attacked by clubbing or with bare hands. They put aside their training and weapons and became savages, overwhelming the El'arans. Had they kept their heads, the fight would have been over in seconds. As it was, it still lasted only a handful of minutes. When he and Perry had entered, Perry dove into the rear flanks of the Tz-en. He shoved and beat and shouted. No one heeded him. The M'ji's head was blown away before he had gotten half way across the chamber. The M'ji's wife was overpowered and disarmed. By the time Perry reached the dais, her torn body lay beside her husband's on the dais steps. The thrones were overturned and broken into splinters. The Tz-en moved on in search of more victims.

Perry had stood over those two bodies for a long time. Michaels had tried to get him to move on, follow the warriors, make sure the palace was completely taken. But no, he just stood there, looking at the woman's dead eyes.

Michaels rubbed the sweat from his palms onto his fatigues.

The door behind the table opened.

A large man stepped in and held open the door. He wasn't a Tz-en, but Michaels caught the trace of at least one weapon hidden beneath the suit jacket. His square face definitely did not belong to any local. He was an off-worlder, and his clothes weren't the expensive, executive type, but he wasn't a professional like Michaels. Probably part of the company's internal security force. His brown eyes ran over Michaels and Thatcher, catching every detail. Then he gave an almost imperceptible nod.

Michaels counted off five men as they walked through the door one at a time. At least two were Michaels' age, while two were younger by various years, and the last much older. Even the younger ones had creased brows and cynical expressions. Each man wore a suit higher in quality than Vindal's. A woman followed them, her own strong features masked in severity, making it difficult for him to determine her age. Three sat in seats on the left branch of the table, three on the right, and each activated their respective terminals.

"The board of executives," Vindal whispered in reverence.

Another man passed through the door, his movements more energetic. He took the chair at table's apex. At first Michaels thought him younger than himself, but as he studied the man, he saw the lines around his mouth and eyes and the liberal streaks of gray through the trim light-brown hair. He was a lot older than he appeared, probably due to expensive age-regression treatments. His brown eyes flashed, taking in the room, the visitors, his fellow board members, and his monitor all within seconds. No sooner was he seated than he was ready to get on with the interview so that other, more important items could be taken care of.

"Anthony Michaels," he said in a strong voice that cut through the empty hall. "And Geoff Thatcher. Thank you for coming. My name is Pieter Tabor. We never met formally, Mr. Michaels, but you may remember the name.

"Ten years and eleven months ago, I spoke at length with your former associate, Jon Perry. We discussed the business of the consolidation of this planet, and he was very instrumental in its success. You no doubt recall that our company financed the Tz-en overthrow of the El'aran government. We are once again acting on behalf of the Tz-en in the present situation. We regret Mr. Perry's unfortunate death during the consolidation. His expertise would have been invaluable at present."

"What's the situation?" Michaels asked.

Tabor's hand glided over his keypad. "We've studied your records, Mr. Michaels. Although your career has been mediocre over the past decade, you have had your moments. You are familiar with a variety of environments. Your records show that you have been hired to serve in numerous conflicts and perform certain sensitive assignments throughout the Arm. Some have not ended desirably. You have moderate leadership qualities. You are resourceful. However, you do not seem to have a good sense for the business aspects of your own career. Presently, you have two thousand six hundred twenty-one credits to your name. You are in debt on three worlds for many times that amount to people of questionable backgrounds. There is also the matter of an outstanding warrant on Cetus Four. There is one point in your favor that does counteract all others. Do you know what that is, Mr. Michaels?"

Michaels shook his head as he wondered if he had been complimented or insulted.

"You are a survivor. Someone of your profession has a predictably short life span, no matter how good they are in this particular business. Most of the other professionals who were hired at the time of the consolidation are now dead. Two are invalids, one of whom makes a meager living begging in the streets of Gateway. We prefer to use someone familiar with this planet. You are the last one. You are an enigma. You have survived a long time in your field.

"Before we discuss the situation which has forced us to bring you here, we will make you an offer. If you agree to work for us, you will receive three million credits at the completion of the task."

He paused, apparently waiting for a reply.

Michaels parted his dry lips. Three million? Three bloody million! He could buy a planet with his share. Some little out of the way rock. Retire before he got his head blown off. There had never been any hope for that before. He glanced over at Thatcher and saw the crooked smile ripping across his dark face.

Michaels tried to calm himself as he gazed back at Tabor.

"What's the job?"

"It is actually a simple matter. I won't go into details until we have your agreement legally documented. Suffice it to say that it involves an uprising of a small group of Shir'ka in the western desert. These nomadic tribes have given no trouble to the government since the consolidation. However, unrest has surfaced. Tz-en peacekeeping forces have been unsuccessful in squashing this unrest. They are unfamiliar with desert warfare and the terrorist tactics of the Shir'ka. The government has come to Deltan Technologies for assistance. We determined that the unrest must be stopped immediately to prevent it from escalating. As I have mentioned, you are the last one familiar with this planet from the consolidation. Our generous offer is to ensure a speedy end to the situation."

"What if we're not successful?" After all, he admitted to himself, it had been known to happen. Rare, of course.

"I don't foresee that possibility. However, I will stipulate that a small percentage will be paid in the event you are unsuccessful and the board agrees that you cannot do any more for the situation. Three thousand credits and transportation back to the Deenar system. If you reject our offer now, you will receive one thousand for your consideration and transport back to Deenar Four. And you will be under legal obligation to not communicate a word of this to anyone. Do you need time to consider the offer?"

"We'll do it," he said. He was in no position to turn down the offer.

CHAPTER TWO
KHADEEJ

After completing the legal formalities, they settled into modest hotel rooms in Jhamrahl. Michaels sent Thatcher to the establishment called the *Red Tarnac*, a tavern in the old sector of the city. It was not a place he had previously visited, but he knew it by reputation. Since the consolidation, its clientele were mostly off-worlders. A few tourists, but mostly spacers and the occasional professional.

Vindal brought computer wafers of the information Michaels needed, plus physical maps. Over a late dinner, Michaels read reports on a borrowed company tablet, checked charts and satellite images, and marked the maps with a luminous marker.

As he expected, he noticed a pattern pointing along the Ahraj Mountains, near the desert fringe. Tz-en patrols in the Ahram Pass were attacked, their transports damaged beyond repair, some of their men injured. Two mining facilities had machine failures. And an airway beacon tower wasn't there anymore. No one saw any of the culprits, but Shir'ka were suspected. Michaels was curious that there were no deaths involved, though some serious injuries, and the possibility of death to those who had to walk or be carried back through the Pass when their vehicles were destroyed.

"In the morning, we'll head to Khadeej," he told Vindal.

A groggy Vindal yawned and nodded. "I'll make arrangements. But it's almost morning now."

"There's no need for you to come with us."

"Oh yes there is. I am your liaison. We will need to stop in on the local governor and coordinate any actions with his people."

"Then you'd better run along and grab a couple of hours sleep," Michaels said, folding up his maps.

As Vindal approached the door, it burst open and Thatcher staggered in, looking rumpled and wafting with the odor of alcohol.

Vindal glared at the big man. "You're drunk!"

Thatcher gave a crooked grin. "Not yet, but there's still hope."

He collapsed on the sofa Vindal had just vacated.

Vindal flushed with anger. "Now see here, this is totally unprofessional behavior."

Michaels waved a hand at him. "Don't get excited. I sent Geoff out on an errand. A few drinks is expected, and it takes a lot to get him drunk, believe me."

"Errand? What errand?"

"There's this little place in the old sector of town known for catering to some of our fellow professionals. Geoff went to see if we might get some back-up. Now, Tz-en are good at a few things, and standing out in a crowded room is one of them. We needed some people who wouldn't draw much notice."

Vindal scowled, but his anger evaporated. "Very well, but you should have mentioned it beforehand. We need to keep the situation, and your mission, from public knowledge."

"Don't worry. Our people know how to keep secrets or they wouldn't be in our profession long. How did you do, Geoff?"

"Five, so far. Had to give them an advance, though. Two hundred each. Only know one of them. Ringer. But he vouches for the others. One of them, Grips, says he worked with you on the Henson Colony a few years back."

Michaels shrugged. "Grips? Can't remember the name, but then there were a lot of us on Henson. Did you give them instructions?"

"Yeah. They're on their way to Khadeej."

"A thousand creds in advance," Michaels said, shaking his head. They could have demanded more up front. He certainly would have. But if they were stuck on El'aris, they were far from any other job.

"Oh," Thatcher added, "also ran into Capetti."

"Harry Capetti?"

"Yep. He's got a little freighter now. Planet hops cargo runs. Asked about you. Said he'd be back around soon on another run and he'll catch up with you then."

"He was one good fighter pilot," Michaels said. "Glad he's settled down to a quieter life." Maybe he'd buy a little cargo hauler once they finished this job. Boring career, but the life expectancy was longer.

"And," Thatcher said, "there was this girl from Helbent ... she wanted to jump in, but I didn't like the looks of her. A little wild in the eyes. Some of those Helbenders aren't working on all thrusters. So I told her the locals had a thing about women. She'd be pretty conspicuous."

"Good. Sounds like we have enough anyway," Michaels said. "Maybe they can get some intel from the locals. Hit the rack, we'll be leaving at sunrise."

The mounted head of the krylar hinted to the horizontal black and white stripes running the length of its supple body. The gray face wrinkled in a perpetual snarl, baring two inch canines. Michaels had seen one years ago, prowling through the foothills of the Ahraj Mountains. This was how he preferred to see them, decapitated, hard as a rock and mounted on a wall. It kept company with three other odd species. One had a long snout tapering from a wide head covered in short brown bristles. Its teeth were small and needle sharp. The next was definitely reptilian. Its large, green-scaled head bore rows of flat, herbivorous teeth. The last animal was difficult to recognize as reptile or mammal or bird. Three horns protruded from its bony brow. A hooked beak covered its mouth. Its eyes were small black marbles. Weapons hung on the walls on either side of the trophies. Spears and bows, swords, percussion guns, old blasters. Michaels recognized a couple of El'aran design. Most of the weapons were off-world. Callarie. DelMon. Grenpheire. He had used a few of those weapons in his time and fought against some at other times. Most belonged in museums.

The huge wooden desk, centered in front of the trophy wall, bore a stand with an El'aran dagger engraved with the emblem of the M'ji house, an ornamental weapon from the last El'aran ruler. Maybe this man had taken it when the palace had been sacked.

Michaels studied the Tz-en carefully. Governor Nhung-Chi returned the stare with eyes paler than most of his race. His coarse white hair, tied back with a gold-threaded thong, receded from his brow.

"We are grateful for you assistance, Mr. Michaels." His words, hissing slightly, rang with insincerity. He remained seated behind his desk, long fingers steepled.

Through the wide tinted window to the left of the territorial governor, Michaels caught the view of Khadeej and the Arijon River. A cargo ship drifted on its way to Jhamrahl, carrying gold or silver or some of those precious minerals cut from the formidable Ahraj Mountains. Between the government plaza and the river, a small airfield stretched its tarmac, littered with a range of craft from small fliers to bulky transports. The real Khadeej lay on the other side of the government plaza, out of Michaels' view. The ancient town of low, whitewashed buildings and high arches, steeped in a rich history all its own held its ground against the invading modern universe and off-worldness. The government plaza stood on the edge of Khadeej, casting its plexisteel shadow upon the town, yet never quite penetrating. With the Ahram Pass only a few miles away, Khadeej was one of the largest and most popular markets for Shir'ka clans, receiving fame across the sector for their exotic glass and crafts created by the Shir'ka as well as precious gems mined by El'arans.

Some tourists ventured this far to sample the flavor of the border town. What Khadeej lacked in modern facilities it more than made up with its ancient beauty and its treasures in the market. Occasionally, a caravan entered from the Pass. Then Shir'ka would flood the streets, selling and buying. The local merchants bartered little then. No one argued with Shir'ka. But the merchants would triple their money when selling the desert crafts to off-worlders. Shir'ka glass was all the rage on a dozen worlds. Gold artifacts and jewelry had been abundant before the Tz-en government took control of the mines. Now gold was restricted to the technologies market. He wondered how many spaceships were wired with or had their ports filtered through El'aran gold. El'aris produced more gold than any other planet, and the technological universe swallowed it up.

"You remember me, Mr. Michaels?" Nhung-Chi asked, baring his sharp teeth in a crude approximation of a smile. "Perhaps not. There were many of us then. And few of you. We learned fast, did we not?"

"You were one of the Tz-en warriors that we trained?"

"Of course. I was an officer in the raid upon the palace. It was a great time for my people. A great victory."

"A great massacre."

"Exactly," Nhung-Chi agreed with an emphatic nod. "Magnificent. I am glad you remember it as fondly as I do. But with age comes other duties. I now have the responsibility of the Khadeej territory. Very important, considering that it includes the surrounding mining operations and ore shipping. As well as tourism; which is a nuisance."

Vindal poked his finger into the air. "I wouldn't say that, Governor. Tourism is a major income for the planet, even greater than the gold industries, considering the casino interests."

"Can we get on with this?" Michaels asked.

"Quite right, Mr. Michaels," Nhung-Chi said. "You are alone?"

"My associate is in the town, seeing to other arrangements."

"Even so, my personal aide will attend to you. Commander Jiin is an excellent officer and is familiar with the territory as well as with the situation."

"That's okay. I have my own personnel."

The governor's faded blue eyes expanded. "I'm afraid I must insist. Commander Jiin will accompany you throughout your operation."

"Yeah, that's not happening."

Nhung-Chi shot a glare at Vindal. "Mr. Vindal, this is not agreeable. Mr. Michaels must report to us. Must we contact the First Minister?"

Vindal waved his hands to calm the governor. "Now, Governor, I'm certain Mr. Michaels will not object to having a Tz-en liaison. He is, however, responsible to Deltan Technologies, with the blessings of the First Minister. And I am the intermediary between Mr. Michaels, the company, and the government. This a joint venture. Mr. Michaels, your contract stipulates cooperation with the local government. Shall I recite the exact terms? If you don't fulfill the contract, you must leave El'aris."

Michaels opened his mouth to shoot out some snappy retort. He closed his mouth when none came to mind. "Fine."

Nhung-Chi activated an intercom button on his desk panel. "Commander, please come in."

Jiin stood equally as tall as her male counterparts, better than six feet. Her skin was just as pale. Her hair, tied into a tight braid running the course of her spine, shown like white silk, appearing softer than any male's. Below the sharp window's peak, her eyes were a darker blue and closer set. The teeth beneath full, more feminine lips still held their edge. The canines were just as long. Her leather uniform followed the long, very feminine curves of her body. He found himself staring. She was almost Human, yet utterly inhuman.

She glanced at Michaels with irritation.

Her attention turned on Nhung-Chi. "Governor, there is an urgent matter to discuss." She held up a tablet in one hand, indicating something on the screen.

The governor tilted his head slightly. "Information on the Shir'ka terrorists?"

Her head moved slightly in Michaels' direction, not quite acknowledging his existence. "Yes."

"Then speak," Nhung-Chi said.

"Last night, a disaster occurred at Mining Station Five. Commander Yung drove in from the mountains this morning and reported to his immediate superiors. Yung made a complete report, which just reached us. He states that there was a fire involving the station's reactor, which caused it to explode. Our people were able to get clear, but there was no time to evacuate the workers."

A scowl darkened the governors white features, turning him momentarily bluish gray. "Intolerable. Are there indications that this was sabotage?"

"Undetermined," Jiin said. "If we could access surveillance records, we would be able to determine sabotage, but if the station is destroyed —"

"Destroyed?" Vindal said suddenly. "What do you mean?"

Michaels said, "A nuclear disaster, if I read this right."

Vindal's jaw hung open. "No, no, no. That won't do. We need that station. Do you realize how much that mine produces? And there is no way that we can keep this from the media."

"Ah, but perhaps this can be used to our advantage," Nhung-Chi said, giving a more genuine grin and becoming a disturbing apparition. "If we can gather evidence that Shir'ka were responsible, then we can publicize it. We can pass the details to the media and turn public opinion against the Shir'ka."

"How so?" Michaels asked.

"The deaths. There were at least a hundred El'aran workers in the mines. Perhaps even some Shir'ka. If these terrorists are responsible for the deaths of their own people, then the El'arans themselves will turn against them and stop supporting them."

Michaels wrinkled his brow, confused. "Aren't these mines automated?"

"To some extent," Nhung-Chi said. "Certain robotics, but a large number of unskilled labor is utilized. At least our people were able to evacuate, but that still leaves many El'arans."

"If the station is destroyed," Jiin said, "there will be no evidence of the sabotage."

The governor shrugged. "No matter. The media will accept whatever we say. If we tell them we have proof that will be enough. It is the matter of all those deaths that will sway the people."

"Can we see this facility?" Michaels asked. "Do you have satellite surveillance?"

"Of course," Jiin said. She tapped on her tablet, then held out the device so that everyone could see the image.

"I have altered the satellite imagery to capture the mining station. We may not be able to see the exact incident, but we will be able to see it in real time."

"Don't see any damage," Michaels said, squinting at the image. "You said the reactor exploded?"

Jiin glanced down at the device. "That is what we were told by Yung."

She altered the image, closing in to separate buildings of the facility, scrolling over the structures in a blur. "Indeed, there is no damage. A reactor explosion would have leveled the mountain and left a cloud of radiated debris. Since there appears to be no damage, I will be able to access the facility's surveillance vids."

She set the tablet on the desk and brought up a ghostly three dimensional image of people standing outside of a transparent building.

"That is Yung, in front of the reactor complex," she said, pointing out one of the tiny figures.

White vapor billowed from the doorway of the structure, out of it running another transparent figure, a bearded man in coveralls. He gesticulated at Yung and his small group of Tz-en followers. There then came flashes of white from the building's doorway. The Tz-en ran in the opposite direction.

Curiously, once the Tz-en had left the scene, the bearded man lost all sense of urgency. He walked casually away.

"Can we follow that fellow?" Michaels asked.

Jiin reached her long, thin hand through the image, tapped on the tablet screen, then stood back.

The image bounced around from different angles but followed the man with the beard. He entered a long, low building, then came out a moment later leading a large group of people.

"He is releasing the workers," Jiin said.

"Releasing?" Michaels asked. "As in they were prisoners?"

"Yes," Nhung-Chi replied. "They were convicted criminals. Now they have escaped."

"That doesn't explain why the reactor is still in one piece," Vindal said. "We all saw the explosions. The place should have been leveled."

"Yeah, that's an old trick," Michaels said. "Can you access cameras inside the reactor building right before that smoke appeared?"

Jiin bent over the tablet, made some adjustments, then stood back to allow everyone a view.

The bearded man was inside, removing small bundles from inside his baggy coveralls. He set them on the floor just inside the door. One began billowing smoke. He ran through it to the outside, leaving the door open. After a few minutes, the smoke blotted out the interior of the complex. Bright flashes exploded within the dark fog.

Eventually, the air cleared, showing the undamaged control room of the reactor and a few piles of dust that had been the bundles the man had placed on the floor.

"Smoke bombs and flash bangs," Michaels said. "Homemade, by the looks of it, but very effective." He didn't add that the typical Tz-en didn't have the imagination to believe they were being fooled. They had seen smoke and saw and heard explosions. That was enough to send them running. "So much for your sabotage," he finished, amused by the actions of this terrorist who didn't kill anyone.

Nhung-Chi mumbled something Michaels didn't understand.

"No evidence, either," Michaels continued. "No one dead, no damage to the facility."

As he spoke, he looked at the holo hovering over the desk. The bearded man returned. He went directly to an array of control and began throwing a series of switches. The image dissolved.

"What happened?" Vindal demanded.

"Well," Michaels said, "there's your sabotage. He's done exactly what I would have done. He's shut down the reactor."

"But the system is still active, or we wouldn't have been able to access it," Vindal insisted.

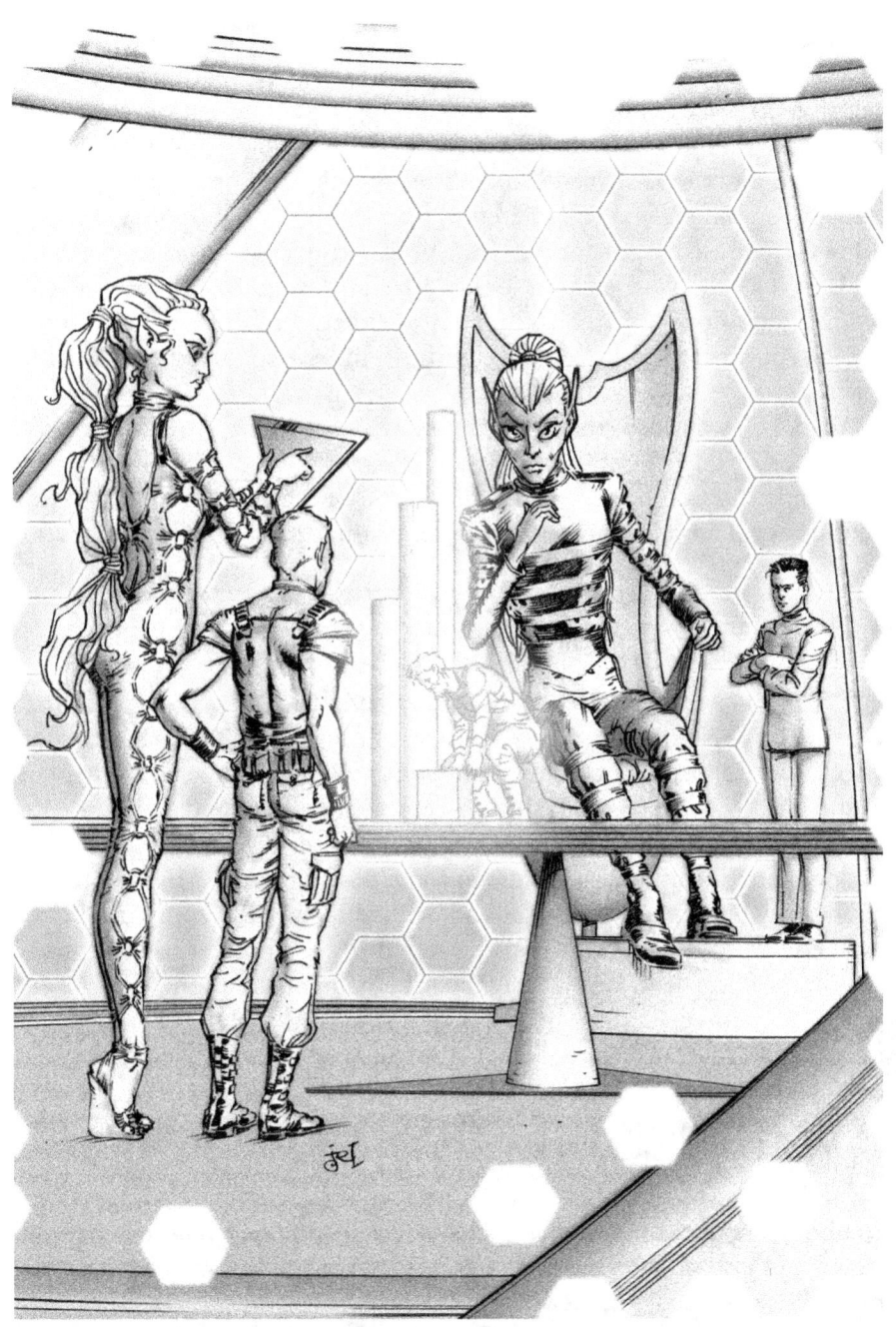

"Jiin bent over the tablet, made some adjustments…"

"Emergency power supply," Michaels said.

Jiin took up the tablet and consulted it. "He is correct. There are no longer any power readings from the station with the exception of a weak emergency supply."

"My guess is that there is something missing in your reactor, some piece of equipment that will prevent it from coming back on-line without going through some great use of time or expense. That's what I would do, anyway. It's what your suspect looked like he was up to. The reactor will be intact but inoperable for a while. This saboteur knows what he's doing."

"You sound as though you admire him," Jiin said, glaring at him with cold eyes.

"Yeah. In a way. He's smart. He knows what he's doing. And he operates like me."

"Then it should not be difficult for you to find him," Nhung-Chi said. "Before he and his accomplices cause more damage and begin taking lives."

CHAPTER THREE
THE SHIR'KA IN THE CAFE

From his corner table, Michaels watched the other patrons of the cafe. This establishment was one of the largest in Khadeej, catering to locals as well as the occasional off-world tourist. At the end of the day, it filled with an odd assortment: El'aran merchants and laborers, Tz-en warriors and government workers, off-worlder business types, some obvious tourists, and even a couple of the desert nomads. He had taken inventory when he and Thatcher had arrived for their evening meal and watched idly as each new customer entered. He paid particular attention to a Shir'ka man and woman on the other side of the room, dressed in their rust-colored clothes and headwraps, sitting with an El'aran and acting quite innocent. They seemed more interested in their meal than in any type of conspiracy.

The man's brown face was surrounded by the headwrap and his trim beard. Michaels could see only half of him, at this angle. The woman he saw well, and was grateful for that. Her own headwrap lay back, draping her shoulders, exposing the long tousled black hair. Her magnificent face, brown and smooth, lit from her green eyes to her full lips with humor and joy as she conversed with her companions.

The El'aran companion seemed nondescript. Simple clothes of a local, neither rich nor poor. Michaels found it difficult to class him into any particular profession. They spoke openly, with occasional laughter.

His attention moved on to analyze other customers.

"Ringer and the others didn't find out much," Thatcher mumbled past another mouthful. Michaels almost missed his words over a sudden burst of noise from a distant table. "Seems the locals don't like off-worlders much, and they can spot them pretty easily. And they like the Tz-en even less."

"Can't say I blame them," Michaels admitted.

He glanced at the far table where four Tz-en warriors made angry remarks about the service, the food, and the general establishment. They made demands of their server, punctuated with crude insults and threats. On any other planet, they would have thrown them out, but here the El'arans were timid and kept their distance and avoided eye contact.

Geoff took another oversized bite and continued as he chewed. Not a pretty sight. "The El'arans are pretty fed up with the Tz-en. Things are ripe for a little revolution."

"El'arans aren't fighters," Michaels told him. The cafe workers and patrons were prime examples. "They lived for centuries in peace. How else would a minority race be able to take control and hold it. Any other planet would have kicked the Tz-en back onto their glacier. But not the El'arans. Maybe the Shir'ka would, they're pretty tough. And that's what worries our Tz-en friends. If the Shir'ka stir things up too much, your little revolution might come true. And that would be bad for business."

Thatcher nodded behind his mug, spilling some beer over his chin. He wiped it clean with a length of his sleeve. "So what do we do? Infiltrate the Shir'ka?"

"Not likely."

One of the Tz-en shouted in disgust. "El'aran scum cannot prepare a simple dish! How many times must we warn you brainless creatures that we Tz-en do not care for your spices? They are intolerable."

The server bowed her trembling head and apologized in a timid voice Michaels couldn't hear.

The offended Tz-en back-handed her across her face.

Michaels stood up, his hand on the blaster under his El'aran coat. Then he stopped and sank back into his chair.

The Shir'ka, who had been sitting with the woman and the El'aran man, now stood behind the Tz-en, appearing like a red-shrouded ghost. Michaels never noticed him crossing the cafe. He said something too low for Michaels to hear. Whatever it was, the Tz-en became enraged. He drew a knife and swung it toward the Shir'ka. The man simply caught the knife-hand in his.

The other three Tz-en stood and faced the Shir'ka.

The Shir'ka held the knife-welding Tz-en effortlessly immobile. In the sudden stillness of the cafe came the sound of crunching bone. The Tz-en's face turned from rage to agony. The Shir'ka released his hold. The knife clattered to the floor. The Tz-en stumbled back, staring at limp, twisted fingers.

Two other warriors drew their blasters.

The Shir'ka kicked an empty chair, sending it flying into one of the Tz-en. The other warrior raised his weapon, but the Shir'ka stepped into him in a swirl of red robes. The weapon flew in one direction, the Tz-en in the other.

Untangling himself from the chair, the other Tz-en tried to take aim, but the Shir'ka was so swift that the soldier lay unconscious before he could shoot.

The last Tz-en reached for the blaster holstered at his side, but froze as the Shir'ka turned to him. Perhaps he could penetrate the shadows of the headwrap and see the man's eyes, or perhaps the Shir'ka said something. In any case, the Tz-en never drew his weapon.

The Shir'ka disappeared through the crowd of patrons who had all stood to watch the altercation.

Michaels expected the man to return to his table, but he was gone. So were his two companions.

He stared at the empty table and said to Thatcher, "I think that Shir'ka was the same man at the mining station. The terrorist."

The crisp morning breeze fluttered through the Market Street which wound its way among the red sandstone and brick buildings of old Khadeej toward the docks and warehouses that bristled the bank of the Arijon. The shops, stalls, and canopied stands had not changed through generations of El'arans. In Jhamrahl, the markets were modernized, civilized, and commercialized for the sake of tourism and commerce. Here, it was a way of life. No cheap off-world products sold by off-world merchants to off-world visitors. These locals scratched out a living under the watchful eye of the Tz-en government. The tourists were noticeable and few, intrepid visitors out to see a slice of history, not the fantasy that had become

Jhamrahl, with its casinos and resorts.

Michaels posed some questions at an old woman selling a delicious treat of crushed ice and fruit. She shrugged in reply and refused any more money than the refreshment was worth. An old cloth merchant grunted and shook his head, ignoring a fist full of credit bills. Finally he found a glass merchant who wouldn't stop talking.

"Shir'ka? Barbarians, they are. Move all over the desert, in their clans. No sense of technology. But let me tell you, *cyte*, they are geniuses in the art of glass. They come to Khadeej now and then, or Rhimj or any other town along the mountains. Do their trading then. My, what a festival! The streets flood with their red robes. They sell their crafts. Like this glass. Or carvings. Or clothes spun from the silk of the Ahram spider. Did you touch some of it while you were at Tobia's shop? No? Incredible material. And durable. And then there's ... well, you should come during one of their caravan stops. The trouble is no one knows when that will be. The Shir'ka don't keep a calendar. They travel at random. I have people watching for them. Sometimes my people will even go through the Pass if there's a clan camping close. The most beautiful glass you would ever see, no matter how many worlds you've been to, *cyte*. Just look at these fluted bottles. Look at the colors in these goblets. And the fine detail. Almost as durable as plexisteel. I challenge any off-world machine to duplicate even the crudest Shir'ka work." He held up a delicate decanter of soft, translucent red. Michaels expected it to crumble in the man's thick fingers.

Michaels nodded and mumbled his thanks.

As he walked on, Thatcher bounded up beside him, shaking the earth under his feet. "Any luck?"

Michaels frowned. "Nope."

"They usually don't like off-worlders."

Michaels gave his partner a quick glance. "You heard something?"

"Ringer's gotten in good with a Belgiran girl who works in a bakery. Ringer lived on Belgira, I think. Even though she's an off-worlder, she's pretty well accepted around here. Got stranded here a couple of years ago. Some hotshot planet-hopping boyfriend dumped her with no money and no way back."

"Can we skip the personal history and go right in for the meat?"

Thatcher shrugged without commitment. "According to Ringer, she says the terrorists are moving in, getting pretty popular among the El'arans. The whole thing could blow at any time, start a full scale revolt. Seems it started with a Shir'ka. He popped up now and then telling some of the more influential El'arans to stand up. The usual speeches. Not too many took him seriously until all these things began happening. Some of the workers that were supposed to have been killed in that fake mining accident are showing up, telling about how this Shir'ka arranged everything. Don't know if it's the same person. The Tz-en will probably come down hard on them if they do try to revolt. Taxes are pretty high now. All land belongs to the government, and so do the businesses. The Tz-en could have everything shut down and starve the people."

Michaels shook his head. "An empty stomach can make anyone pretty mean."

"Let's hope we can stop it before it gets that far. If the Tz-en have to resort to a police action, then we're out of a job."

They passed among fish mongers closer to the docks. Out of the corner of his eye he caught a man seated on a low wall, watching an ore carrier floating down the river. He noticed the rust-red cloak and clothes immediately. Of course, this wasn't the first Shir'ka he'd seen in the market.

He turned to get a better look, but the Shir'ka had already dropped from the wall and was passing through the crowd.

"Come on." He slapped Thatcher's arm.

"What?" Thatcher asked, following.

"I want to follow that Shir'ka. Something familiar about him."

"You think he's the one from last night?"

"Maybe."

The Shir'ka passed among the stalls, glancing at the items in each. He stopped at a produce stand, chose a green and yellow striped fruit, dropped a coin in the vender's palm, then continued on his way while he ate. He turned down a side street that headed toward a small cove on the river. A dozen small craft tugged at their moorings along docks that stretched out into the water. Most were small fishing boats, but a couple were definitely designed for pleasure. Only three or four masts pointed into the air. The rest were various types of motored craft. Maybe two modern, the rest antiquated.

Michaels threw his arm out to stop Thatcher, then tugged the bigger man into the shadows of a shack near the edge of the marina. He watched the Shir'ka stroll along the pier. The man pulled off his cloak, folded it neatly, and tucked it under his arm.

Further out, an El'aran woman leaned against a pile. The man walked up to her, handed her his folded robe, then curled his arm around her waist.

"That's the girl we saw in the cafe," Michaels said.

"So?"

"So ... she's dressed in local clothes. Last night she was dressed like a Shir'ka. She *is* a Shir'ka. Notice her skin? Darker then an El'aran's. She's a Shir'ka all right. And now, look over there. There's someone else I recognize."

He pointed along the row of sheds that bordered the marina. An El'aran set down a tool he had been using to weave a repair in a torn fishing net. He very meticulously folded the net and set it aside, then walked onto the pier, toward the Shir'ka leaning on the pile. As he approached, the woman walked away.

The El'aran met the Shir'ka and both climbed onto a fifteen foot pleasure boat. The Shir'ka tossed the lines free while the El'aran started the engines. The boat purred as the bow turned to open water. There was more to these two men than a simple boat ride. The El'aran's appearance did not suggest the affluence necessary for owning such a boat. He didn't even look like he could own one of the small fishing boats.

Michaels pulled on Thatcher. "Let's grab a boat."

He needed something fast, but not conspicuous. A fishing boat would be too slow; a speed boat would be too noticeable. He didn't want the Shir'ka and his friend to know they were being followed, but he didn't want to lose them. Unfortunately, there were few choices. He ran up and down the pier. Which one? The twelve foot pleasure boat. Its hull showed some dents, its deck some stains, the engine some rust. It was far from new, but it might be fast enough. From the scattered clothing and food containers, he guessed its owner just had it out. The craft probably belonged to one of the groups he had seen along the marina.

He could explain it to them later. Matter of planetary security. That always worked.

He jumped into the boat. Thatcher shook his head, then tossed off the lines. Michaels stood before the instrument board, gathering it all in. Key! It took a blasted key.

The boat rocked as Geoff climbed on board. It began to drift from its slot, with its moorings gone.

Michaels ran his finger over the board, down the housing. He found the access plate and popped it open. He heard a shout from shore. Maybe the boat's owner. The voice sounded angry enough, though he couldn't understand what it said. He had to hurry.

"Keep an eye on that boat, Geoff. We can't lose them."

He pulled out a handful of wires and began tracing them. A simple mechanism. He could do this with his eyes closed if he wasn't in such a hurry. Pull the wires free from the key slot, twist them together.

Michaels hit the starter. The engine sputtered, then caught and he guided the boat away from the dock, its wake bouncing other boats against their moorings.

"Geoff!"

Thatcher grunted acknowledgment from behind.

"Get up here. I told you to keep an eye on that boat. Now where is it?" He squinted at the river. All he could see was the reflected sunlight and the dark shape of an ore carrier headed downstream.

Thatcher's meaty hand shot past him, one finger pointed to the left of their course. "There."

"I don't see it." He squinted his eyes tighter. It was hard to see without his shades, but they were dressed as locals and locals didn't wear shades. The ore ship took on definition. Between them and it, a wake bubbled up. Their quarry topped a small wave, becoming visible.

He opened the throttle to try to close the distance a little between them and the Shir'ka. Just enough space to keep them visible. The ore carrier grew as they approached. Michaels wondered why the Shir'ka would bring his boat so close to the ship. The wake would make it hard to maneuver. Maybe it was an attempt to lose any tail. Maybe they needed to get around it to the further shore. Or maybe they intended to rendezvous with the ship. Michaels felt confident that they hadn't been spotted. He took a course parallel to that of the ore carrier and edged a little more speed from the throttle.

"Found these," Thatcher said, shoving something at Michaels.

He took hold of a pair of binoculars. "Take the wheel. And keep us on course."

He stepped aside and adjusted the binoculars. The screen lit up with the bouncing image of the ore ship. He activated the jitter compensator, calmed the image, then zoomed magnification. With light adjustments, he located the two men on the little boat. He pressed the record button. Later he could find out who the boat belonged to, maybe track them down.

"What the ..."

Whoever piloted the boat cut it sharply toward the ship and kicked open the throttle. It streaked over the water. He watched as two figures dove over the side into the churning river.

"They bailed out," he said. "But the boat's still going. Right for that ship."

He barely got the last word out when the boat struck the hull of the ore ship at the waterline. An explosion flashed, then thundered across the river.

He shook his head and laughed. "What are they trying to do, sink it? Those ships have so many compartments, half the hull could be gone and it'll still stay afloat." He watched through the binoculars as the smoke cleared to reveal the great hole gaping in the hull. The water boiled white as it rushed in.

"Let's keep our distance and follow those two to shore." He scanned the water with the binoculars, catching the two swimmers in the distance.

"Hey, Mick."

"What?" He turned to follow Thatcher's finger pointing at the scarred ore ship.

"Looks like those two knew what they were doing after all."

The ship lurched, listing to port. Sirens on board blared. Dozens of figures scrambled over the deck, along the railing. Lifeboats swung out on cranes and were lowered to the water. The hole in the hull all but vanished beneath the surface. The ship filled quickly with water.

Michaels scowled. "Time to pick those two up." He pulled out his blaster and nodded toward the two swimmers.

Thatcher opened the throttle, spun the wheel, and headed the boat toward the fugitives.

An energy bolt shot past their starboard, sizzling into the water a meter off their bow.

"What the –"

Michaels turned, raising his blaster.

Then he lowered it. The boat that approached from behind held a crew of Tz-en warriors, all wearing tinted goggles. Three laser rifles took aim on their little stolen boat, while a gunner on the bow swiveled a mini particle canon. An officer on the bow next to the gunner motioned for them to cut their engines.

"It's okay!" he called. "We're working for —"

"Place your weapons on the deck and prepare to be boarded," the officer shouted back.

Two men secured lines to their boat.

Michaels lost his smile as he slowly set his blaster on the deck. Thatcher did the same.

The officer motioned to three warriors, who boarded the boat. One removed two pairs of wrist binders from a pouch on his belt, while the other two held their rifles steady.

"You are under arrest," the officer said. "For stealing this boat. And for carrying weapons. And also for the attack on that ship." His goggled eyes took in the ore carrier, which lost most of its profile to the river.

Michaels tried to stay calm. He held out his hands. "Now wait a minute. We're working for your government. I'm Michaels. This is Thatcher. We were following two men, who ended up blowing a hole in the side of that ship. They're getting away while we stand here chatting."

The Tz-en placed the binders to his right wrist and activated the restraining field. Michaels' hands flew together as though drawn by a magnet. Both his hands tingled inside the field.

"Now hold on!"

"You will be taken to interrogation immediately," the officer said in his unconcerned voice. "If you resist, you will be shot."

And not by a stunner, Michaels realized.

CHAPTER FOUR
A FEW COINS

Stev Vindal paced erratically at the head of the conference table. His face flushed with indignation. "This is outrageous! Do any of you realize how much has been lost by this incident? Hundreds of millions of credits. The problem with the mining station was a big enough problem. Together with this, it's intolerable. To have an ore ship sunk right out of its dock! And to have our two operatives witness the entire affair. At least *that* hasn't gotten into the media. What an embarrassment! Do you know what Mr. Tabor told me? The executive board is outraged. They haven't begun to calculate the loss in time and credits. This is a total fiasco."

Michaels sat back in the chair at the far end, resting his boots on the edge of the polished table, hoping the heels scuffed the finish. "If that patrol boat hadn't stopped us, we could have caught those two."

Vindal threw up his arms. "You stole a boat!"

Michaels dropped his feet hard onto the floor. "So did they! If we had a little cooperation from the locals, but nooo! We had to be shot at and cuffed. They didn't know a thing about us. Didn't have the vaguest idea what we were doing. Don't you people have any kind of communications network?" he demanded, turning on Jiin.

Her eyes burned through him. "That is why I have been assigned to accompany you. If you had not been on your own, none of this would have happened."

"And we would have never gotten close enough to see what they were up to."

Governor Nhung-Chi, at the head of the table, asked Jiin, "Is there more information on the boat they used?"

She tapped on her tablet. "It was indeed stolen. The owner was Fez J'reehl, an El'aran merchant influential in the shipping lines. He is a representative of Khadeej Transports, the company that owns the *Ab'urda*, which was the ship sunk. He was a lower level executive in the company when it was under El'aran control. He rose to a trusted level after Tz-en takeover. He has been interrogated, since suspicions surfaced when we discovered that someone had opened all the lower level hatches in order for the hull to successfully fill when the boat exploded. However, we suspect one or more of the crew. They are being sought, though not all have been accounted for. Since no bodies have been located, we assume they disappeared in Khadeej or moved elsewhere to avoid interrogation. As far as J'reehl is concerned, he appears loyal enough, although he tends to enjoy pleasurable entertainment to excess. Security reports claim that he is unpopular with the major El'aran population because of his Tz-en sympathy. It is my guess that his boat was chosen on purpose."

"Now there's a revelation," Michaels declared under his breath.

It wasn't lost on Jiin. He met her chill glare with his own heated scowl.

She went on, undisturbed. "I believe the terrorists chose that particular boat as an example. Apparently the Shir'ka woman located it and observed it, learning that it was unattended during the necessary times. "

Nhung-Chi said, "We have descriptions of the three suspects involved. Our search has started. Soon we will have one if not all three. A simple interrogation will reveal the nest of these Shir'ka malcontents."

"Whoa!" Michaels shook his head, chuckling. "You're not going to find them. These guys are good. And the town people will hide them. One of them is an El'aran, so the El'arans are already involved along with the Shir'ka. We don't have any idea how deep this cooperation goes. You start sending troops through the town, and we may never learn a thing until it's too late to act."

Vindal laid his hands on the table, leaning over and beaming at him. "You have a plan, don't you? I knew you would devise something. I knew Mr. Tabor wasn't mistaken in hiring you."

Jiin scoffed. "He has no plan. He is lying."

Michaels leaned back in the chair, throwing his feet back onto the edge of the table and folding his arms over his chest in satisfaction. "Of course

I have a plan. I'm just not going to disclose it until all the pieces fall into place."

After he thought one up.

This might not be such a good plan.

The place stunk. Light-years beyond rank. And that was just the hallway. The odor rose up like a force field. Not just recent smells, but unrecognizable things that lingered from a dim, dank past. They bludgeoned his senses, making his eyes water and his sinuses sting. Breathing through his mouth only added a bad taste to the suffering. At least he hadn't eaten lunch. How embarrassing to lose it in front of this dull-witted Tz-en escorting him.

The prison of Khadeej dated back before the M'ji dynasties, built shortly after the colonization and isolation, dug into the rocks beneath the young mining town. The builders utilized the natural system of caves, smoothing them and cutting chambers into their walls, digging out any valuable resources. The chambers became cells. Over the decades, a ventilation system had been added by someone with an extensive knowledge in a field other than ventilation. Enough air came down to keep prisoners alive. The early M'ji had attempted a reconstruction. Later ones gave up and sealed off the tunnels. The Tz-en thought the prison convenient and reopened it, first for prisoners of war and later for political prisoners and criminals.

According to Jiin, many laborers in the mines were prisoners working off their sentences. If Michaels had been given the choice, he'd leap at the chance for mining rather than spend an hour in these cells. The mining tunnels had to be five star hotels in comparison.

Something moved past his foot.

"Don't you ever clean this place?" he asked.

Something crunched under his boot, sending a shiver up his back.

The stocky guard eased out a slow, hissing breath. He looked down at Michaels. The bulb hovering over them cast long shadows over his face, which thickened the crescent scar curving over the guard's cheek and lengthened his pointed canines, one of which was chipped at the tip. By Tz-en standards, he was ugly. Which said a lot.

He finished his lengthy sigh, then shrugged. "They are only El'arans."

As if Michaels should have known that.

"Oh."

They stopped before one door. The guard peered through the grid in the panel, then checked his data tablet for the prisoner's ID.

"There's no Tz-en prisoners?" Michaels asked.

The guard humphed, his version of a laugh. "Of course not."

The guard tapped on his tablet. "This one is old."

"What's he in for?"

"Taxes."

"How long's he been here?" Michaels moved up and peered through door grate. A single bulb gave off a feeble glow that deepened shadows in the small chamber. A raised stone on the far side served as a bed, a table, and a chair. It was the only thing that passed for furniture and must have been carved from the stone of the walls and floor. On it sat a small, crooked figure in filthy rags.

"He's been here since I've been assigned."

"What's his release date?"

The guard had already moved on, looking through the grate of the next door.

"This one's already gone. Transferred to the mines."

At the cell opposite, he paused and tapped on his tablet. He looked through the grate, then shook his head. "This one ... I think is sick. Hasn't eaten in a few days. Hasn't moved."

"Maybe he's dead," Michaels suggested, keeping his distance.

The guard sniffed the air. "We'll wait a day or so, just to make certain." He moved on.

"How can you tell?" Michaels mumbled.

They passed to the opposite side of the corridor. "This one came in last week. Young. But he's too small for the mines. He's nothing but bones wrapped in skin. Maybe he will fatten up a little, then we can transfer him to one of the mines."

Michaels peered through the grill in the door. A small figure huddled on the stone platform, faintly visible in the glow from the single ceiling bulb. Tattered cloth hung from his bony limbs. Every centimeter of his skin was covered with grime. Large eyes glared suspiciously out from a tangled mass of filthy hair.

"What did he do?" Michaels asked the guard.

The guard consulted his tablet. "Theft."

Michaels stuck his face to the grill, trying not to suck in any of the stagnant air. "Hey, kid! What are you in for?"

The boy's face reflected annoyance under its grungy layers. He ignored

Michaels' questions.

"He's probably an idiot," the guard said.

Michaels frowned at the guard and raised his voice. "What did you do, kid? Why were you arrested?"

"I stole!" the boy spat.

"Yeah. What?"

"Food."

"Is that it?"

The boy shrugged. "Money to buy food. What else is there?"

Michaels grinned. "Ever kill anyone, kid?"

"No." His tone lost the bitterness. He could tell Michaels wasn't Tz-en. He gazed down at the dark floor between him and the door, then looked back up at Michaels. "How much for it?"

Michaels grinned. He crooked his finger to the guard and stepped back.

The guard scowled as he stepped forward with his keycard. "Him? What good can he be?"

"More than what anyone might think," Michaels assured him. "That's the beauty of it."

He had to repeat himself half an hour later when Jiin demanded the same question. The boy had been scrubbed, disinfected, and groomed ... under protest from all concerned. Clean clothes had been provided, though three sizes too large. He was brought to a room in the upper levels of the prison where food had been laid out. As the boy gorged himself, Michaels stood by, balancing happily on the balls of his feet. Jiin scowled at the waste of time and expense. She refused to go any nearer than the doorway, insisting that the scrubbing had not rid the boy of the odor from his cell or the streets, a stench which also lingered on Michaels.

She bared her canines as her nose wrinkled in disgust. "You expect to use him –"

"Shh!" he warned her, placing a finger to his lips. "Just keep quiet and watch an expert."

He moved to the table, flashing his most amiable, most charming smile. "Is everything all right, J'sef?" The boy gulped sauced meat and mumbled as he nodded. "Good. Now, J'sef, I suppose you've been wondering why I brought you here."

He opened a mouth full of masticated food. "Yes. You're an off-worlder."

"Yep. I was hired to do a certain job. But it's getting a little difficult. I need some help." He bent nearer, cast Jiin a suspicious glance, then lowered his voice in confidence. "I can't trust the Tz-en. And the El'arans don't trust me. You look like a smart kid. That's why I asked for you to help me."

"Me, help you?" He paused to shove a wad of sauce-dipped bread into his mouth. His gaunt cheeks threatened to burst.

"Where's your home, J'sef?"

"Khadeej."

"No, I mean, where do you live? A house. Apartment. Whatever."

He shrugged. "Have none."

"Where do you sleep?"

The boy's shoulders bounced. "Wherever it's warm. Usually in the alley behind Baker's Tavern. Sometimes on one of the boats tied up at the docks."

"He's an urchin," Jiin explained impatiently. "Homeless. If you had taken the time to read his arrest re–"

Michaels frantically waved his hand to silence her. He poured more fruit nectar for J'sef. "How would you like a place of your own, kid?"

The boy's eyes narrowed over the brim of his cup as he made loud gulping sounds. He wiped his mouth with a single swipe of his sleeve. "Who wouldn't?"

"And clothes? Food whenever you want it? A ticket for anywhere in the galaxy?"

His eyes brightened. "Anywhere? Off El'aris?"

Michaels had caught him. He found the kid's one great desire, beyond just surviving. He threw out his arms. "Anywhere! In style. Nothing but the best."

The boy snorted. The light in his eyes died quickly with stinging reality. "Sure!" He spilled nectar over his littered plate before slamming the cup down.

"Honest, kid. If you help me get this job done, you'll get a big share. All you need to do is help me find some people. Criminals."

"You're working for the Tz-en," J'sef said acidly, with a vicious glance at Jiin.

"No, I'm not. I'm working for a private company whose profits are being hurt by these people. And the whole planet's economy will suffer, too. You help me and you'll be helping your own people."

The boy shrugged. "It doesn't matter. I haven't anyone here. Where can I go? Planet, I mean. I don't know any. I've just heard stories. I haven't even been to Jhamrahl."

Michaels waved a dismissive hand. "You'll love it, kid. And as far as the planets, I've been to most and know the rest."

"Remember reading about a place called Tapestry. Can I go there?"

"Sure." Michaels never heard of such a place. The kid probably read about it in a tenth credit novel. Pure fantasy. It didn't matter, though. Once he paid the kid off, J'sef would settle for anyplace remotely civilized. "No problem. We'll take care of you. Here," he pulled out a handful of the local currency. "Here's a down payment."

The coins clinked onto the table, some rolling against the plate. The boy's eyes widened as he stared at the coins. "What do you want me to do?"

Michaels whistled loudly as he burst through the door to the rooms he shared with Thatcher. Even the disgusted look on Geoff's face couldn't discourage him.

"Pew! What's that smell? You been rolling around in a dung pile, Mick?"

Heading for the fresher, Michaels peeled off his shirt. "That, Geoff old buddy, is the scent of a flower among the thorns." He fell to whistling a tune from Epsilon Cestus Three. As he recalled, the words were unrepeatable in mixed company. He even flushed as he thought of the second verse.

Thatcher's broad face wrinkled. "Huh?"

"Our spy. I set him loose. I'll explain after my bath."

"Before you get yourself in a lather, I've heard from Ringer."

Michaels froze with his hand on the shower knob. He wrapped a towel around himself and padded out toward Thatcher.

"What?"

Thatcher grinned and rubbed his paws together. "There may be a hit in Khadeej. A small government building in town. Tax and records office. From what Ringer heard, they're planning on making the hit and erasing all the records. Middle of the night, when nobody's there."

"When?"

"Tonight."

"Get me the location. I'll get Jiin to help secure the place. Get Ringer. I want to talk to him. It won't hurt for him to be with us. We'll see if he's earning his pay. Right now, I need a bath."

"You sure do," Thatcher said as he turned to leave.

The tax office sat in the central district of Khadeej, surrounded by small businesses. Like its neighbors on Bridle Street, it was a two story brick building of unknown age. Its large bricks had been constructed with the red desert sands. Newer buildings would hold that color for a time. Here, the red had faded under the constant assault of rain and wind and sunlight over many generations. At night, there was little color to make a difference. To the left of the office stood a cobbler shop at the corner intersecting Caravan Street. On the right was a restaurant whose clients were more local and less off-worlder or traveler. A narrow alley ran behind the buildings, running the length of Bridle between Caravan and Ahjan. The opposite side of the alley was a small leather goods manufacturer, with two heavy service doors about fifty meters down the alley toward Ahjan Street. Michaels had examined the area carefully, as unobtrusively as possible. The leather manufacturer closed at dusk. The workers deserted the building. Michaels passed along it, wrapped in an El'aran cloak, casually checking the big doors opening into the alley. They were secure.

He stepped out of the alley, rounded the corner in time to see the El'aran brothers locking up their cobbler shop. They hurried toward the Desert Winds restaurant, just past the tax office. Following at a slower pace, Michaels paused to test the knob on the shop door. Locked tight.

He glanced through the window at the tax office as he walked by. The El'aran staff readied themselves to leave for the night. Three women and one man, who took care of computer records. The Tz-en supervisor was probably still in his upstairs office, having a long chat with Jiin. Those four workers would look more glum soon enough, when Tz-en warriors intercepted them on their individual ways home. Detention and interrogation, Jiin had phrased it. That they were probably innocent meant nothing. They were El'arans.

Michaels stepped into the subdued hum of the Desert Winds. He passed the table with the four Tz-en, without giving them the slightest notice. Those warriors looked ridiculous in casual clothes. They sat stiff, their blaster obvious under coats, their expectant attitude even more obvious. He rolled his eyes helplessly as he approached Thatcher and Ringer's table.

"Let's see if we can do this without tripping over those Tz-en," he said as he leaned on the table.

Thatcher gave a grunt and got up.

"Don't worry," Ringer said. "I'll keep an eye on them. Just give me a holler when you need me." He tapped the com unit hidden under his shirt.

Outside, Michaels and Thatcher passed two older women from the tax office. Jiin's people would pick them up as soon as they turned down Ahjan Street. The other two, he knew, went by way of Caravan and were probably already in custody and on their way to the government plaza.

The office lights went out, the front door opening wide to let out the Tz-en manager. As he left, Michaels and Thatcher slipped in. The manager closed the door behind them and activated the lock.

Jiin stepped out of the darkness of the hall leading to the rear of the building.

"The alley door is secure," she said.

"Yeah, I saw that lock when I strolled down the alley," Michaels said. "I could have picked that when I was twelve."

"What if they want to just blow up the building?" Thatcher asked. He pulled his blaster from under his coat and checked the charge.

Michaels hadn't thought of that possibility. "Ah, that isn't their style."

"Exactly what did your informant say they are after?" Jiin asked.

"Operative," Michaels corrected. "Ringer's contact said they want to wipe clean the computer records. I guess they don't realize that something like tax records are backed up in other systems. Aren't they?"

He felt Jiin's eyes boring into him through the darkness. "That is not among my responsibilities. You might be under the false impression that our government has finances for a highly technological bureaucracy. We have been attempting to computerize all the information formerly recorded exclusively on hard copy. In some situations, there may not be sufficient duplications of records to compensate. The district offices have been satisfactorily handling the records. The divisional offices rely on them."

Michaels rubbed his eyes, wishing his headache would leave. "In other words, you don't know, and there probably aren't backups."

"Yes."

He dropped his hands at his sides. "I have a feeling we should have brought more backup."

He saw her hand moving to the com unit on her wrist. "I shall call –"

"No. We can handle it. They probably won't send too many in for this job. They only used two to sink an entire ore freighter. Three, if you count that woman. Tonight, they just want to dump some computer files. We'll get into our hiding places and sit tight. They only have two ways in, front or back door. My bet's on the back. You two settle in, I'm going upstairs to have a look around. That office in the back has a nice view of the alley."

He climbed the stairs. The short hall contained two doors facing one

"The alley door is secure," she said.

another and a third at the end, opening to a lavatory. He slid open the door on his left, peered into the small storage room with its windows looking out to the main street. The street lamps gave enough glow to illuminate the room with its shelves of boxes and office supplies. Satisfied, he turned to the opposite door and entered the supervisor's office. This rear room was larger than the front one, letting Michaels understand why the supervisor chose an alley view rather than a street view. He stood in the doorway for a moment, orienting himself in the dark, locating and recognizing furnishings. He walked to the windows behind the desk, sat in the chair and leaned forward, low enough not to be visible from below. The alley lay gloomy and dead. Empty.

This could be a long night.

Every half hour, he sent and received a round of checks through the com unit. Four checks came and went, and he still stared out the window at the alley that still remained empty.

He shifted uneasily in the chair. The office seemed smaller to him, the darkness deeper. His heart gave a few resounding thumps in his chest. Blood pulsed in his ears through the stillness. He felt ... movement.

He wasn't alone.

A glance over his shoulder told him the door still stood open, as he had left it.

Geoff could never move that quietly. Jiin? The Tz-en were generally clumsy, but she was an exception.

He remained still, slowly sliding his right hand toward his blaster. His left went toward the com in his pocket. Very slowly. His ears strained in search of sounds. Silence. No breathing but his own. No movement except his hands.

"Don't," was all the voice said

He froze.

The man stood behind him, about three meters off his right shoulder. No anger or hatred came through that word. No threat. No bravado. A simple warning, which he heeded. He knew that single word was backed by very real consequences.

In brief seconds, the word ran through his mind. Not enough to place an accent. Definitely not a Tz-en, though. No breathlessness to the voice. The voice was strong, commanding. Probably not an El'aran. Probably a Shir'ka. And probably with a blaster aimed at the soft spot between his shoulders.

"Mind if I turn around?" he asked casually. After all, he was just enjoying the view in the dark.

"Raise your hands first."

Michaels did so. He didn't care for the position, no matter how many times he performed it. But it was better than the alternative – being very dead. Slowly, he rotated the chair to bring himself face to face with the intruder. He still couldn't place the accent. It hinted at El'aran, but there was something distant in it. Probably Shir'ka, since he couldn't remember ever hearing a Shir'ka speak.

"Stand up. Slowly."

The man was a mass of shadows, gliding closer, circling the desk in an easy stride. From what light ventured through the window, Michaels could see the metallic sheen of the blaster's thin muzzle. Its aim never wavered. Michaels stood up, feeling vulnerable. He still had all his weapons, but he dared not even flinch a muscle. Better to wait.

The man hooked his foot on the leg of the chair and rolled it out of the way. He moved behind Michaels, and Michaels felt the cold circle of the blaster touch the base of his neck. His own blaster left its holster and dropped onto the desk. The needle gun in his boot slid free and joined the blaster. The man's hand moved quickly over Michaels, pulling the throwing knives from his sleeves, the stars from under his lapel, and even the ring needle from his finger. It was not so much a search as a seizure. All his little trinkets were snatched and dropped on the desk. How did he know where to look for each one?

The cold pressure left the base of his skull.

The man walked around the desk. Michaels discerned the bearded face in the gloom. He was the Shir'ka he'd seen before.

"You're a creature of habit, Tony," the man said.

A chill ran through Michaels. His heart paused, then beat so thunderously that it shoved itself into his throat.

The man switched on the little desk lamp. Michaels blinked. He squinted first at the blaster aimed at him, then at the bearded face. A crescent scar curved over the right eye, white against the brown skin. The unruly hair was dark, flecked with gray. The beard showed streaks of gray he hadn't perceived on earlier encounters.

"Better?" the man asked.

Michaels couldn't breath.

"I arranged for this little meeting. Ringer's a good man, but he shouldn't be so gullible. We leaked the information to him. I needed to talk to you. This seemed the best way. You don't look well, Tony. Are you okay? Maybe you should sit down?"

Michaels shook his head. The room spun around him. The face in the center of the whirlpool gazed at him. Brown eyes aged with pain. Eyes that brought back other days, other lives.

"Perry?"

The man nodded. "It's been a while, hasn't it? That's why we needed to meet under these circumstances. I just couldn't go walking up to you in the middle of the market place, or even in that cafe the other night."

Michaels' fingers touched the desk for support. He caught Perry's eyes flicker downward, gauging the distance between his fingers and his discarded weapons.

"How –"

A crooked smile cut through the beard. "No, I didn't die. I had one nasty fall. I would have died, though. But I had some help."

"I tried to find you ..."

"I know. Don't worry, I don't blame you. You did what you could."

"All these years ... What happened? Where have you been?"

"It's a long story. And I don't think we have enough time for it here, with your friends downstairs and hanging around the neighborhood."

"I don't understand. What are you doing? Why are you disguised as a Shir'ka? Whose paying you?"

His smile vanished, his eyes growing hard. His voice cut like steel. "I *am* a Shir'ka. Like I said, it's a long story. For another time."

Michaels stared. What had happened to him? Where had he been for all these years? Why had he never made contact?

"Come with me," he said. "We can go someplace quiet, talk. I need to know. All this time ... I thought you were dead. The others ... Once they understand who you are, they won't bother us. We can talk. Just put that gun down."

Perry shook his head. The blaster stayed steady. "Once they know who I am, I'm dead."

"I don't understand. Who are you working for?"

He moved toward the door, backing out of the room. "Later, Tony. I knew I wouldn't have much time, but I had to see you, warn you." A smile softened his face. "Not that you'd listen. Just for the record, though, get out while you can. This is bigger than you think. I don't want to see anything happen to you."

"Perry ..."

Perry backed out the doorway. "It's good to see you again, Tony."

"Dammit, Perry!" he shouted at the closing door.

He jumped around the desk, then spun back to snatch up his blaster and com link. He thumbed on the link as he shouldered the door open.

"He's coming down. Don't shoot! Repeat, don't shoot."

He nearly fell down the steps. Thatcher met him, crouched, blaster ready. He pulled up as he recognized Michaels.

"Did he come down? Did you see him?"

Thatcher stared through the darkness. "Who? Nobody's come down but you, Mick."

Jiin appeared at Thatcher's right as Michaels hit the last step. "You are making enough noise to be heard across the town. I suppose our element of surprise has just vanished."

"It's too late for that. Now shut up and listen. If you didn't see him come down, then maybe he hid upstairs in the storage room. Come on. Don't shoot, whatever you do. But watch out, 'cause he's armed. I think he's alone, but I can't be sure. Just let me handle it. Stay behind me, and don't make any threatening moves."

At the top of the stairs, he burst into the store room, throwing on the lights. Nothing but boxes and shelves.

Michaels snapped his fingers. "He must have made it downstairs without you seeing him. After all, you were concentrating on the entrances, not the stairs. Come on."

He led them in a dash downstairs and to the rear of the building. Out the back door, he gazed up and down the alley. He waved his blaster to the left. "Geoff, go that way. And remember, don't shoot. Just call me on the com. We'll go this way and circle to the front."

Jiin jogged beside him, a scowl pasted on her pale face.

They stopped where the alley broke onto Caravan Street. He strained to hear, but nothing came to him except the distant sounds from the Desert Winds. He could no longer hear Thatcher's footfalls. Perry had moved so silently in that office, Michaels hadn't heard his movements in a still room. How could he find him here? He looked up and down deserted Caravan. No one. No moving shadows. No patrolling Tz-en constable. He circled the cobbler and looked up Bridle Street. Nothing. Then ... someone stood outside the tavern, leaning against the wall.

Michaels passed the cobbler, then the tax office.

A figure moved from the wall into a circle of light from a street lamp. A weather-beaten face with a pug nose and a few battle scars. Casual local dress. Ringer.

"What's all the commotion, boss?"

Michaels stopped short and let out a frustrated breath. "How long have you been out here? See anyone dressed like a Shir'ka?"

Ringer shoved his hands in his pockets. "Ain't seen no one, boss. Been out here near an hour. What's up?"

Another shape approached out of the night, coming from the corner of Ahjan Street. Michaels could not mistake the shape and gait. Thatcher pounded his way toward them. He cast a glance into the entrance of the Winds and moistened his lips.

"Nothin'," he said.

"Thanks for your enthusiasm," Michaels said. "Look, all this was a set-up. He fed you the information, Ringer, so he could corner me for a quick talk. He's an old friend of mine. But I don't know who he's working for. He wouldn't tell me."

"Friend?" Ringer asked.

"Jon Perry."

"Ah," Jiin said with a nod. "Your deceased associate."

"He's not dead."

"Apparently."

"Listen ... Oh, never mind. I got a few ideas. Let's just get back inside and lock the place up. We've got some work to do. This thing's obviously bigger than anyone thought."

The door to the office stood fully open.

"Thought we had that shut," Thatcher said.

"Yeah." Michaels lifted his blaster and stepped cautiously through the threshold. His free hand sought the light switch. The lights came on, flooding the room.

All appeared as they had left it.

"What's that?" Ringer asked, pointing to a computer monitor at one desk.

Michaels shrugged. "Just a wild a guess, but I'd say it's a computer."

"Yeah, right. I was referring to what's on it. It don't look right."

Michaels drew closer, his eyes darting to each corner of the room, every shadow. The consoles at the other work stations were also on. They had been switched off when the staff had left. Ringer was right. What appeared on the screens was unusual. They scrolled names and various numbers faster than he could read.

Ringer eased past him, looked the screens over, then glanced back. "It's the database. It's being dumped."

"Huh? Where?"

"No, you don't understand. It ain't going anywhere. It's being erased." His hands danced over the keypad.

Michaels hung over his shoulder. He couldn't tell what Ringer was doing. It certainly didn't stop the scrolling screen. Names, numbers. Database. All the information in the tax office files. "Well ... stop it."

"I can't. I'm trying, but I can't. Some kind of virus in the system. It's tricked the system into thinking it's backing up all data, but the data ain't going nowhere. Everything's being trashed."

"Everything?" Jiin asked from behind Michaels. She went to the another station and pounded on the keypad. She bared her canines and gave a throaty growl.

The screens suddenly went blank.

Michaels sighed. "Good. What did you do?"

"Nothing," Ringer said, watching the monitor. He tapped on the pad, then he shook his head. "It's just done. The virus program. It's finished. Everything's gone but the basic programs. The office's whole system is clean."

Michaels shoved his blaster into its holster. He subdued the compulsion to send a few bolts into the offensive monitors, knowing that wouldn't solve anything. He had expected something more unsophisticated like a bomb or a simple blaster raid. He didn't expect a virus. That was ... that was just like Perry. Use your head, he used to say. Use your head before your blaster, and it might save your neck.

"Your so-called friend did this," Jiin said with more hiss to her words than normal. "I want every bit of information on this man that we can get. We must stop him before he wrecks havoc within the government complex itself. If he had access to the main databases ..."

"Perry was always good with computers," Michaels said. He tugged on Ringer's arm, pulling him from the blank monitor. "Listen. You think you could do a search on what Perry's been up to the past eleven years? With the government net?"

"They ain't too sophisticated. They might not have the links we need for off-world intel."

"Then maybe Deltan Technologies has what we need. We'll hit Vindal with the idea. It's about time he did something for us. We've got to find Perry. I've got to talk with him, find out what's going on."

CHAPTER FIVE
A RIDE BY THE RIVER

In a small office in the Khadeej government complex, Michaels hovered over Ringer's shoulder, vaguely aware that he was swaying. The computer screen blurred.

Ringer rubbed his eyes and tapped on the keypad again, bringing up a new window of names and dates. He started the search, bringing up faces with each name. They flashed from one to the next, giving them barely enough time to notice that each one looked nothing like Jon Perry.

"Do you realize how long this will take, boss?" Ringer asked, stifling a yawn. "Even with this facial recognition software. We've been at this for hours already. We've scanned records for only two years after the war and came up with nothing. Just wait till we get to when the town was done over and the casinos opened. Millions of people have come here each year. Ain't no way we're going to scan those files. The software can't handle it. If he's as good as you say he is, he could slip in the port without customs check or any other scan. I've done stuff like that myself. So have you. It ain't hard, even at a place as high tech as this port. We just ain't going to find him, boss."

Michaels couldn't accept that. There had to be some record of Perry leaving El'aris after the war. Maybe something of his return. And there certainly had to be something of his life off-world. Where had he gone? Back home? Why hadn't he tried to contact Michaels? After the war, Michaels had wandered around, planet to planet, job to job. It might have been difficult, but if he had wanted to get in touch, Perry would have found a way.

He felt betrayed that he was left to believe that Perry was dead for all this time.

"Even if we find when he came or went," Ringer continued, "that still ain't going to tell us why he's here now. You think he's working for someone?"

"Sure. What else? There's got to be some rival company paying him to sabotage things here. After all, the terrorists have hit things like mining and shipping. That equals profit. El'aris deals with companies like Deltan for off-world business. Maybe someone wants to cut Deltan out and move in. This is a very profitable planet."

"Yeah. Just with the casinos. But a lot of companies got their fingers on El'aris. Not just Deltan."

"Maybe one of them wants a bigger piece of the action."

"You want I should check out some of them?"

"Not yet. I want to find Perry and back-track him. I want to find out what he's been up to all these years. He's changed." He remembered the coldness in the eyes. Pain.

"Happens to the best of us, boss. I'll set the software to scan another batch, then I'm taking a rest. Fire me if you want, but I can't keep my eyes open."

"Me too." Michaels patted Ringer on the shoulder and left him to his work.

The last person he wanted to see was the first person he met as he left the little office. She glared at him. A chill ran through his spine. Sometimes the Tz-en just reminded him of walking dead. And he'd seen enough dead to not want to see any walking.

"You are being ridiculous," she said.

"Yeah? The hell I am. I suppose you ran to your boss to push to get me fired."

"I made a report, but that was not my intentions. I merely stated the facts, though they do not appear to favor your position. However, since I was in secondary command, I was reprimanded for my inefficiency. I suspect a report has passed on to Stev Vindal and other channels within Deltan Technologies. They would not appreciate your irrationality last night."

"I wasn't being irrational. Just ... cautious. Perry's my friend. Or was. But he's also a top professional. If he's been hired by someone, then there's more here than just a band of terrorists stirring up a little trouble. This could mean political or corporate conspiracy. He was trying to warn me about something. He said it was bigger than I thought. Chances are he's right."

"That the man was Jon Perry has not been verified. He has been listed as deceased for eleven years."

"His body was never found. It could have happened just as he said. Besides, I know Perry. It was him."

"You didn't recognize him before, and you saw him twice.'

"Yeah. Like I said, he's changed."

"We have only your word as confirmation that it is him. My government will expect more, as will Deltan's executives. I understand Vindal was very vocal on the subject."

Michaels mumbled under his breath what he thought Vindal could do.

They came to the outer door to the government building, under the eyes of visual scanners and Tz-en guards. He wandered if Jiin had other business, or if she was specifically assigned to annoy him. He was relieved to see her stop at the exit.

"Michaels ... if he was indeed your friend, there are other concerns."

He spun on her. His anger faded abruptly as he gazed into her eyes. The blue had lost the icy edge.

"If this is Jon Perry," she said, "then you may be in jeopardy of a conflict of interest. Can you fulfill your agreement with Deltan Technologies?"

"Of course."

"Even if that means a conflict with your former partner?"

"Of course." After all, there was a lot of money involved.

"These are questions that are passing through the minds of everyone above our level, you understand."

"I don't care what they think. I can work this out. Perry will contact me again, or I'll find him. Either way, we'll work it out. No matter who he's working for, he'll come around. Just wait. I can handle it."

"I hope so."

Before he stormed out, he glanced back at her. She meant that. It shocked him. He watched her walk back across the lobby. He studied her movements and wished she was more Human.

"Oh well," he said, "nobody's perfect."

At the edge of the plaza, a battered ground car with a faded taxi sign magnetically attached to the roof sat waiting for patrons. An El'aran sat behind the wheel, a cap drawn down over his eyes as he dozed. Michaels banged on the door, startling the driver awake. He gave the name of his hotel, then sank into the back seat.

As the car pulled out, he dropped his head back and swirled through the tornado of thoughts. The fact that Perry was alive still shocked him. He lost eleven years, feeling like they had just left each other. He forced himself to remember those cold years between, the losses that he had lived through, the deaths he had seen and escaped. A lot of death. A lot of jobs. Some successful, some not. Each one was to be the last. He hadn't the hunger for them like when he and Perry fought side by side. It wasn't the same.

The late day sun eclipsed suddenly. The putter of the car's engine echoed.

Michaels' head shot up. His hand fell onto his blaster.

The car had entered a vast empty building. Sunlight sliced through cracks in the walls and roof, through broken windows. Through an atmosphere of dust motes, he saw the dark interior of an old warehouse. He hadn't been paying attention. Fatal mistake number one. The driver stopped the car near the center of the building and shut down the engine. In the ensuing silence, Michaels heard the footfalls on the cement and debris.

He pressed the barrel of his blaster to the back of the driver's head.

"You'll be the first to go, buster. Tell them to back off."

"My apologies, *cyte*," the El'aran said. "I am ready to die. Are you?"

"Depends. Why are you so ready to die?"

"Freedom is a strong motivator, *cyte*."

"Who are you? Who are they, out there?"

"The ones you seek."

"You've gone to elaborate means to get rid of me."

The man laughed. "If we had wanted you dead, you would not be here. There is one who would speak with you. You will not be harmed. You will be released presently and permitted to return. Otherwise, shoot me now and end your own life."

Out of the corner of his eyes he saw figures converging on the vehicle from the shadows.

Stalemate. He could shoot the driver and be killed. He could drop his blaster and be killed. He could try to fight his way out, though he had no idea of the odds against him. He could surrender and perhaps learn something useful, and gain a better chance to fight his way out.

He lowered the blaster from the driver's head, though he kept it ready.

The passenger door opened. He stepped out.

Ten men stood in a wide circle around the taxi. Six were bearded, dressed in the rusty sand-colored clothes and cloaks of Shir'ka. Four were clean-shaven, wearing typical local clothing, though threadbare and faded. They ranged from a tall, lanky youth with sparse whiskers on his brown face to a stocky old man with a gray beard and peppered hair. Michaels counted seven blasters. Two Shir'ka carried bulky projectile guns whose stock were ornately carved and inlaid with gold. Another Shir'ka carried a laser rifle of the design used by the Tz-en. Each Shir'ka also wore a curved knife in an elaborate scabbard. All ten were hard-featured, even the youth. Scars marked their faces and hands. Their deep-set eyes watched his every movement, alternating from his own eyes to the blaster in his hand. He heard slight movement among the deeper shadows on high scaffolding across the warehouse. Snipers were no doubt in position.

Michaels took in all the details of the ten in a glance. Then he turned toward the man who held open the car door.

Perry still wore the clothes of a Shir'ka, looking every bit the part as the others encircling them. Perhaps his skin wasn't as dark, but there were variations among the desert clans. At that moment, Michaels recognized less of his old friend in those eyes than he might have imagined the night before.

"Holster your gun," Perry told him.

Michaels slid the blaster into its holster. The act was completed before he realized it. He wondered at the ease Perry had commanded him. Why was he permitted to keep the weapon?

"What's this about?" he asked, trying to sound stern. "Are these the terrorists who've been attacking and sabotaging?"

Perry waved his hand to encompass the dispersed group. "These are the people of El'aris. Patriots. Freedom fighters. El'sadar. Different names, but the same purpose."

"One man's freedom fighter is another man's terrorist."

"Don't call us terrorists," Perry said, his anger surprising Michaels. "Terrorists kill innocent people, civilians, children. We do not. Their weapon is fear. Ours is knowledge."

"Why'd you bring me here?"

"To continue our talk." He calmed instantly, his tone friendly.

"With armed men as insurance?"

"To insure you don't do something stupid."

Michaels raised his hands expectantly. "I'm here. Let's talk. Or would you prefer someplace more private?"

"This will do. I told you last night that I would explain some things. Now is the time. We won't be interrupted, though I don't want to keep you long. You'll be taken back to your hotel shortly, so that no one's suspicions will be raised."

"Okay. So talk. Where have you been for eleven years?"

"Here. On El'aris. We had gone on patrol in the mountains that day. Hunting down resistant groups of the M'ji supporters, remnants of palace guards or military leaders. Remember? We led a Tz-en patrol and came upon a camp of about thirty refugees, mostly sick and exhausted men and women running for their lives, but they fought valiantly to the last. I would have preferred prisoners, but it never entered the minds of the Tz-en. The El'arans knew that. Three or four at a time, they would attack one Tz-en, shooting or hacking while blaster bolts cut them down. You were on the left flank, I on the right. Four came at me, pushing me back. Only one had a pistol, an old style projectile shooter. I dropped two, but the remaining two closed in with sword and club. My blaster was knocked loose. My head was clubbed. My side was cut open. Then I fell off the edge.

"I don't remember the fall. I don't remember being found. Weeks passed before I was conscious enough to make sense of things. If the crevasse had been on the eastern side of the mountains, my bones would still be there. But I fell on the western side. Near the Arijon Desert. A group of gatherers from the clan of B'sheer had climbed the rocks the next morning in search of spider silk. A young woman named Mar'a found me. She took on the responsibility of bringing me back to health. She had the others help build a litter to drag me out. None of the others thought I would live another minute, but she had faith. She had their healer set my broken bones and seal my wounds. She fed me their herbal medicines and antibiotics. The other members of the clan developed a sort of awe toward me, since I survived incredible odds. Some were certain I'd stay a crippled invalid and be a burden on the clan. It took time, but eventually I could not only walk again, but I could ride *sildars* with the best of them."

Michaels found himself caught up with the story. He remembered vividly the scene in the mountain camp, when they stumbled upon the El'arans settling down for the evening. The battle had been short but fierce. The El'arans made their last stand, and they knew it. He had barely escaped injury. His blaster had overheated in the fight. He had seen Perry attacked by a group, though wasn't sure if it was three or five. Some had gone down while others fell on Perry. He remembered Perry plunging over the edge, down into the deep, wide crevasse.

He had tried searching the next day, but never found any trace of Perry. The terrain was too treacherous and the Tz-en refused to help no matter how much he swore at them. He was on the verge of using violence, but thought better of it. He was now alone with six remaining Tz-en warriors, who didn't much like him to begin with. He could very easily disappear and no one would care to question the warriors.

Perry's recovery might have happened the way he had said. Michaels never had reason to doubt Perry. Yet, something in Perry's eyes told him this wasn't the same man he had known.

"Why didn't you get back and send out a message?" he asked.

Perry gave a short, haunted laugh. "Maybe you don't understand the vastness of the desert. The Shir'ka clans travel with their herds. They may not return to a certain spot for years. I stayed with the B'sheer clan for two years before trying to get back to one of the towns. Occasionally, clans pass each other. They'll camp together and have a festival. Young men of each clan will court women of the other for marriage. Auctions are held for their animals, to strengthen the herds' gene pools. Knowledge is also exchanged. You'd never witness such a thing, no matter how many worlds you visit.

"At one of these festivals, I learned that the other clan would pass near the Ahram Mountains in three months. I convinced my friends I needed to learn what had happened with the war. I needed to contact you as well, to find out if you were alive or not, and to let you know I was still alive."

"So, you made it back?"

"I came first to Rhimj, which is a town in the north. The Shir'ka sell to the merchants there, as in Khadeej. Khadeej is better, because of the river connecting it to the east. In Rhimj, I learned about the planet's transformation. The M'ji government was gone. The Tz-en government ruled. A garrison had been placed in the town, and martial law was the standard. I traveled to Khadeej, where I thought I could get to Jhamrahl. Once in Khadeej, I sought out transportation east and a way to communicate off planet. However, the Tz-en didn't like my activities. They control the movements of El'arans, especially then, when their government was new and fragile. They took me as a Shir'ka and arrested me. I was imprisoned without a trial, and then sent to the mines."

"How long were you sentenced to the mines?"

"I'd still be there if I hadn't escaped. Years passed. I remember only a fog of pain and exhaustion. Darkness. Sickness. When I escaped, I found I had lost four years."

"Escaped? How?"

"A bout of sickness. I couldn't eat. I found my head began to clear. The fog I had lived in began to lift. The Tz-en use a drug to make their prisoners complacent. It's a common procedure on a number of worlds. Once I was able to think again, I was able to escape. I went back to Khadeej, though not openly. I made some friends, then headed back through the Ahram pass in search of my clan. That took the better part of another year. But on the way, I spread the word of what had happened to El'aris, from what I had seen and what I had learned from others. The problem was that few El'arans were willing to stand against the Tz-en, since they were immediately imprisoned. The Shir'ka weren't interested, since the Tz-en hadn't bothered with the desert. There isn't much out there that would turn a profit."

"But you came back here. Why?"

"I'm trying to undo what we did eleven years ago, Tony. I'll tell you more later. This is enough for now. Digest it. We'll talk again."

Perry turned away.

"Wait!"

Ten weapons snapped up. Michaels held out his hands, fingers splayed. "Hold on, hold on. Take it easy. Perry, what are you planning?"

Perry stopped and looked over his shoulder. His eyes didn't connect with Michaels. "I'm helping them take back their world."

"Fine! But the planet belongs to the Tz-en, too. Maybe you haven't seen all that's been done. Jhamrahl's a resort now. It's making a fortune. El'aris is a rich planet. Before the Tz-en took control, it was wasting away."

Perry turned and glared at him. "No. El'aris was rich before the Tz-en. Now it's poor. Look into the profits, and you'll see what we know. Follow the money, Tony."

He walked into the shadows, followed by his ten men.

Michaels wrestled with the thought of chasing after him. Was all that true about the mines? About living with the Shir'ka tribes? He held back, placing a hand on the door of the ground car. Perry wasn't the same. Something had happened to him, changed him. Perry wouldn't lie to him, but ... Perry wouldn't treat him this way, either, holding him at gunpoint. Not the Perry he knew years ago, that he grew up with, the man who was more of a brother than his own brothers.

"I've told you everything he told me," Michaels said. "Now I want to know a few things."

They sat around the conference table, Vindal at the end with the blank screen on the wall behind him. The corporate representative listened patiently with folded arms, a half-cocked grin pasted on his lips. Jiin sat next to Michaels at the other end, her posture stiff, hands folded on the table in front of her.

"I resent the implications that our justice system is ... is barbaric," Jiin snapped. The hiss in her speech became more pronounced.

Vindal, still grinning, waved a calming hand. "Now, now, Commander. I'm certain Mr. Michaels had no such intentions. And Mr. Michaels, before you jump into something you might regret, I think we should have a look into a few things. You said your associate, Mr. Ringer, is running checks through the government's network. That does have limitations. We have, however, access to Deltan's corporate network, which stretches far beyond

El'aris. Had you asked, we could have worked together and saved some time. Be that as it may, I went ahead on my own initiative to conduct a search. You'll find the results fascinating.

"First, I started with the known backgrounds of you and your former partner." Vindal tapped his tablet. In response, the screen behind him came to life. A much younger image of Michaels appeared, with a few bits of biographical information. He stared at the face. A kid's face. The screen split, and Perry's image came up at the side. He recognized the haunted look behind the cocky expression. Clean-shaven, with a crooked grin. They were two kids taking on the universe.

"Now," Vindal continued, "I designed variations on physical descriptions. I was able to trace you, since you didn't alter your name. Except for that time three and a half years ago when you wanted to leave Hyperion in a hurry. Something about deeds to a gas mine? No matter. You see, you're an open book. Mr. Perry wasn't, until I knew what to look for. Then everything opened up."

He tapped a key, and an image appeared that resembled Perry, but not quite. The man's dark hair was cut short, as was his beard. A scar cut over his eye. His expression was hard, unsmiling.

"This man, Jeremiah Farber, left El'aris ten years ago on a privately owned freighter, *Maria Si*. The freighter made scheduled stops among this sector's inner systems. Any trace of Jeremiah Farber vanishes after the ship stops at Delbia IV. Here, Grant Kessling pops into existence with the same general description, minus the beard. He reportedly spent almost two years among the Delbians during their war with their sister planet. Kessling was reportedly killed six days before the planet was extinguished. Two days after that reported death, a person of identical appearance, Sam Williams, signed on as a mechanic on the *G'Reernaq*, a Hhorffalphian freighter. The curious fact is that no other record of Sam Williams exists on Delbia IV. The problem is that most records were destroyed with all life on the planet, but we haven't found any other records of the man existing anywhere else. Once he leaves the service of the Hhorffalphians six months later, he vanishes and William Greggorovich pops up. Actually, there were two William Greggoroviches at the same time on Feilding's Colony. It posed some confusion until one disappeared. At that time, Jrej Nurian, a Gorriean mystic, suddenly makes himself know, allegedly having lived in the wilderness for ten years, and leaves Feilding's Colony for Alberici. He also has the same general description.

"This activity continues for some time with some dozen aliases. Different professional jobs took him to all corners of the galaxy. The most recent name was Thomas Riley. He left Perrolius Prime a year ago and arrived on Jhamrahl with a sizable increase in his personal credit account. He stayed at the El'arisa Inn. There are a few miscellaneous documents of his visit. Even to Khadeej no less than three times. There are gaps, as if he dropped out of existence periodically. There is, however, no record of his leaving. I checked the documentation, and cross-checked it with El'aris's network records of Riley. He appears to be Jon Perry. But I want you to check this out yourself. Don't take my word for it."

"I won't," Michaels assured him.

"The documentation speaks for itself. Now, my theory is that he was hired to disrupt commerce on El'aris. He has been partially successful in that aspect. Since Deltan Technologies is the major supporter for the Tz-en government, it has hurt the company's financial concerns. This may ultimately damage the relationship between the government and Deltan. Should another company enter and offer to take up the loss, for a sizable percentage of the concern, they would stand to gain a great deal, financially. Our only problem is that we have too many rivals. We cannot pinpoint one particular company that would stoop to this strategy. Perhaps you and you particular resources can. Offer Mr. Perry more than our competition. Buying him out might prove better than the alternatives. One is that we capture him and interrogate him. The second is that he is killed, eliminating the problem altogether. Although if that is the case, we will be unable to determine who hired him and prevent this from occurring again with some other operative."

Michaels watched the wall screen. Data scrolled across it. Photos flashed in and out, each depicting the same man in various stages of hair and beard growth and color. Even skin color changed, which wasn't difficult considering the variety of pharmaceuticals on the market. Always that same crescent scar over the eye. Always the same cold eyes and serious set of the jaw. He had no doubt it was Perry.

"I want my people to check this out," he said.

"I thought as much." Vindal slid the tablet across the table, into Michaels' hands. "Access codes into certain sections of Deltan Technologies' network are available. You'll understand why you can't have full access. But that will get your man to the appropriate levels where he may access the data you desire."

He took the tablet and went to the office where Ringer worked feverishly at the keypad.

"See if you can find a hole in this data," he told Ringer, after highlighting what Vindal had told him.

"I want my people to check this out."

Ringer ran through the files. "This is good. Real good. But it'll take some time to verify it all, boss."

Michaels left him to it. He had been lied to. He would prefer if it had been by Vindal, but he doubted it. The evidence was mountainous that Perry had lied and betrayed their friendship. Still, he did not want to kill Perry. Capture, yes. He did not believe Perry could be bought out of his contract with whoever hired him, but then Perry apparently was not as loyal as he used to be. Once captured, he could be given the option. Cooperate or be interrogated by the Tz-en. It wouldn't be up to Michaels.

An hour later, he sat with Thatcher in a dark alley off Peddler's Street. The shops at his back had closed long ago. Something scurried along the broken crates and metal dumpsters. The meager lighting did little to chase the night away. Still, he felt that anyone might come along, see them in the alley. Or someone might overhear. This wasn't the best place for a meeting, but then J'sef knew Khadeej better than he did.

The boy turned into the alley. He walked casually toward them, hands shoved deep in the pockets of his grimy clothes. He only bothered to glance around once.

Michaels listened hard, but he couldn't hear signs of anyone following the kid.

"This place isn't secure," he said.

J'sef shrugged. "No one around."

"What do you have?"

"They have meetings with El'arans in Khadeej. No one knows where they stay, and no one seems to know when or where a meeting will be until the last moment. But they're looking for people to join them. They don't trust everyone, and I got to be careful. A lot of Shir'ka are involved, and nobody messes with Shir'ka."

"Any word about an off-worlder?"

J'sef shook his head. "I only heard about Shir'ka, though haven't seen any yet. I think I can get in one of their meetings."

"Do it. And see what you can learn about any off-worlders involved."

"If there's too many Shir'ka, I'm staying clear. Don't like Shir'ka. They're hard to fool. They don't trust no one."

"Try," Michaels insisted. He pulled a few local coins from his pocket and dropped them into the boy's palm.

Ringer slurped down the strong El'aran coffee. Its aroma stung Michaels' nose, but it worked its miracle on Ringer. His eyes, sunken deep, bore no redness. His hands passed over the keypad as agile as if he had just sat down. He hopped from one screen to another with disturbing quickness.

"I checked it through, boss. I went through every line that Vindal gave you. Sure enough, it matches. Now, I went through Deltan's net, but I also crossed over to the main net on Primus. That took some time for the transmission and download. I took a nap. But what I got was worth the wait. It verifies Vindal's information. Fact is, I found a few details he missed. But I think I dug a bit deeper. Made more cross references. Your ole buddy came here a year ago as Thomas Riley, from Perrolius Prime. He stayed at the El'arisa Inn off and on, but there ain't no record of him leaving the planet. All that other stuff, all those different names and places, they all check out, and more. I got some medical records of him staying on Delbia IV as Jeremiah Farber, after he left the freighter *Maria Si*. Some bones that hadn't healed right. They had to redo them. That might be from that fall he took in the mountains."

"Let me see it."

Ringer brought up the report. Along with an image of Perry. He looked long at the scar over the eyes. How could that be faked? He never had that scar before El'aris. Any previous record would not contain it. Either he gained it in his fall or while on the *Maria Si*.

He glanced over the list of specifics.

"Disappeared before release," Ringer said, pointing to the comment from the clinic.

"Yeah, but why'd he come back here? Who's paying him?"

Ringer grinned and stabbed his finger into the air. "Ah! That's the jewel in the crown, boss. It took some doing, but I finally picked it out. I tracked some of his banking under certain names, and some names were just for the banks, so that made it harder. This guy is damn good at covering his tracks. But I found someone who paid him off recently. A small company called Magellan Terraformers. I ran a check on them. Fact that they'd never terraformed anything larger than an aquarium is interesting. They're owned by DeVore Enterprises. That's a pretty big group, ain't it?"

"Yeah. And they've been in trouble with the Consortium a few times recently. Unethical behavior, or something." Michaels tried to remember, but he never paid much attention to the corporate newscasts.

"Are you sure this stuff is real?"

Ringer moved his finger in a cross over his chest. "Swear it, boss. Real as real. This stuff goes too deep."

Nothing like being betrayed and lied to by someone you believed was your best friend.

"Okay. Download everything on wafers. Then keep going over it for anything you might have missed. Dig into that DeVore company. See if they foot the bill for Perry's mission here. Looks like Perry's the one who's been lying to me and I want to be armed with as much truth as possible."

CHAPTER SIX
TRIAL AND ERROR

He had his ammunition. Data wafers and hard copies, a more elaborate portfolio than he could imagine from Vindal's original revelation. He had the truth about Perry's life since his supposed death eleven years ago. A sour taste filled his mouth every time he looked at the material. Perry lied. Perry had never even contacted him through all those years. Now he lied. What had happened to that friendship they had? His mind strolled through memories of their childhood, two boys racing through thick woods, over fields, flying wooden spaceships, climbing into space stations nailed in trees, fighting off the dreaded alien horde. As adults, they had fought against dozens of enemies. Side by side. Now they were on opposite sides. Now Michaels stared out over the foothills of the Ahraj Mountains, watching the ghostly images through his night visor. Now he set the trap for his closest friend.

He shifted his position uneasily, reaching up to adjust the binocular setting on his helmet's visor. Images zoomed, but he still could not detect any life forms.

He ran a cursory check of his armor and weapons. The gouge in the side of his chest plate that came from that skirmish on Mirniar 12 still worried him. He should have repaired that long before now. His weapons were fully charged. He hoped he wouldn't need the show of force.

He scanned the hills again.

Maybe the boy was wrong. J'sef had shown them where Perry and his group camped beyond the reaches of Khadeej. Their camp moved each night, sometimes high into the mountains. Tonight it was here. But he still could find no trace of them.

His helmet com clicked. Thatcher's voice whispered through the jack in his ear.

"That high altitude drone's got them. About one klick northwest, to your right. Count eight targets. Heavy air ready to move on command."

"Just keep them back until I give the word," he whispered into the mike. Those Tz-en were likely to jump in and wipe out the whole group. Hopefully they learned a little discipline over the years. If he didn't need them now, he wouldn't let them anywhere near the site. At least Jiin was on board. She seemed to have a level head.

He adjusted the visor to magnification zero, then threaded his way among the shrubs and rocks to his right.

He heard nothing but his own breathing, saw nothing but the rough hills.

The helmet com clicked. "They're on the move. They know you're there."

"Where? Which way?"

Click. "Stop. Got one target zeroing in on you."

He dropped down, holding his position to give the high altitude drone a stationary reference. It would be picking up the tracer signal from his helmet as well as his life readings. And the life readings of the terrorists. He waited for Thatcher to relay the coordinates of the approaching terrorist.

"Where the hell is he?" he demanded his voice only loud enough for the mike.

Click. "Gone. Or on top of you."

Ridiculous. How could a person disappear?

He turned slowly to see the ghostly image of a man standing over him, a blaster in each hand aimed at the center of his visor. The short, stocky figure and bearded countenance were plainly discernible. He was one of the Shir'ka who had been with Perry in the old warehouse.

He let his rifle drop and moved his hands out at either side.

"I want to talk to Perry."

"He is waiting."

"Will you take me to him?"

"Remove the helmet."

Michaels unsnapped the helmet and let it drop beside the rifle. Without it, the drone would not be able to tell him from the terrorists. He would also not be able to communicate with Thatcher and give him the command to fulfill his plan. He had to come up with an alternative, fast.

"This way."

The Shir'ka motioned with his left hand blaster. Michaels went ahead of him, his unaided eyes trying to adjust to the darkness. He stumbled over stones, branches, and roots. The Shir'ka followed with silent footfalls.

Perry sat on a rock about two meters high.

"To what do we owe this pleasure, Tony?"

"I want to talk. You never left a forwarding address, so I wasn't sure where to find you."

"You picked the spot pretty well. I guess the bird in the sky has something to do with that." He pointed up to the starlit sky.

Michaels could see nothing but the brilliant field of stars and the colorful brushstroke of the Carino Nebula in the north. The Arm spread out in a wide arc that covered half the sky. Not a cloud marred the view. Then a few stars winked out, while others near them blinked into existence. A small, dark shape passed in front of them, blotting some out, revealing itself by it opaqueness. The drone, drifting high overhead.

Michaels shrugged. "How else was I to find you?" Maybe Perry hadn't guessed about the young informant.

"Okay. You're here now. Talk."

Michaels glanced over at the Shir'ka holding the two blasters. He wouldn't be able to get much out of Perry while that man was here. Maybe if they were alone, Perry might open up with the truth.

Perry nodded to the Shir'ka. "It's all right. Go on with the others."

The man faded into the night without a word or a sound. Like a ghost.

"Perry, you need to come back with me."

"And let your Tz-en friends take care of me? I've been through their so-called justice system. I don't recommend it."

"I'll see to it that doesn't happen. But if you don't come back, they'll end up wiping out you and your friends. They've got too much fire power. If you're trying to organize these locals to fight, it's a battle already lost. They don't have it in them. We saw that eleven years ago. The Tz-en will just crush them. Is it worth it?"

"Yes."

"How much? How much are they paying you?"

"It's my fight now, just as much as theirs."

"Is that what DeVore Enterprises is paying for? For you to join a revolution? DeVore is behind this, right?"

"No one's behind it. This is for the El'arans."

"The planet belongs to the Tz-en, too. Not just the Shir'ka or the El'arans. Right now the Tz-en are in control. The El'arans are in no position to overthrow them, even if they had the heart. Besides, things aren't bad under the Tz-en. I've seen some of this place. No one seems to be starving."

"Then you haven't seen much. The Tz-en took this world wrongly, and we helped. Now I want to help give it back."

"By yourself?"

"Not necessarily."

"What's DeVore paying you? Whatever the price, Deltan Technologies will double it. They'd give us both enough to retire on. We could buy our own planet. We could go home in style, like we always wanted to do."

"This is my home."

"Dammit, Jon! You must've landed on your head when you fell off that cliff."

Perry shook his head slowly. "You don't quite understand. Go back and find out who really controls El'aris. Who gets the profit from Jhamrahl's fancy traps? The El'arans get nothing, and they are taxed into poverty. You saw Jhamrahl. Use your head. Why –"

An explosion flashed in the hills above, showering debris. The ground shook.

Another missile struck, thundering another shock wave.

Dark shapes from the east drove away the stars. Running lights came up, with slow, steady flashing. Six gunships fired their engines and drew closer, sending a series of missiles into the hills.

Michaels stared up at the blaster suddenly in Perry's hand. He saw the coldness in his eyes.

"Hold it, Jon. They've targeted your friends. Now, I'll make a deal with you, unless you think they can get away. Or unless you don't care about them."

"Talk." The coldness had sunk into his voice. The blaster twitched.

"Here's the deal. You come back with me, and I'll call them off. Otherwise, they'll level the mountain. For now, they just want you. I'll keep them back, and we can do a deal with them. But you have to come back with me."

Perry gave a curt nod. "All right."

"I need my helmet."

Perry slid off the rock and landed like a cat in front of Michaels. Perry led the way over the stones, between the shrubs, to where the Shir'ka had caught him. Michaels doubted he would have ever found the way back in daylight, let alone in the darkness interrupted by the flashes of explosions.

Michaels' heart tore at his chest. They had to hurry. Those Tz-en couldn't wait for the signal, which he couldn't give to them anyway. They blundered in as usual, ready to wipe out everything in their path.

Where was that blasted helmet?

Perry stopped suddenly, stooped, then turned to Michaels. He tossed a round object, and Michaels snatched at the helmet, nearly dropping it.

He slapped it on and activated the com. "Abort! Repeat, abort attack! Thatcher, come in. Geoff! Stop the attack. Pull them out. Hurry!"

Click. "No problem, Mick. You okay? Jiin got tired of waiting and decided you needed a little help when you ditched your com."

"Everything's fine. Just make sure they stop firing. Let the targets go. Repeat, let the targets go."

The explosions stopped. The running lights of the gunships hovered high overhead.

Michaels tried to make out Perry's shape in the darkness. He could see the blaster still in his hand. It moved, turning. He realized the grip pointed out toward him instead of the barrel.

"Shall we go?" Perry asked, as though he were suggesting a social visit.

Michaels took his blaster.

"Why did you give up so easy?" Michaels asked. Not that he was complaining.

"Was anyone killed in that attack?" Perry asked.

"None were reported. Why?"

Perry ignored him, his eyes growing distant.

Michaels glanced around the interrogation room. A ten foot cube with lighting only over the chair bolted to the center of the floor. No other furnishing. Surveillance scanners lined the walls. Perry sat straight in the chair. He couldn't blink an eyelash without a monitor registering it. The guards outside would never let him live past one minute if he tried anything. Maybe Michaels was allowed to keep his blaster in hopes that Perry would grab it in an attempt to escape.

One of the heavy doors slid open.

Vindal entered with Jiin. An officer named Quan followed with six warriors, who wormed their way in to take positions along the wall.

"Well, well," Vindal said as he approached, that insufferable grin plastered across his face. "So this is the infamous Jon Perry. Your career seems to have come to a screeching halt."

Perry sat still, ignoring him, looking through him.

"What'll happen to him?" Michaels asked. He didn't like the dark expression on Quan. Jiin seemed agitated. And Vindal was just obnoxious.

"We will interrogate him," Quan said.

"Right." Vindal bounced on his heels. "We must know who he's working for. And how far this insurrection has reached. But let me preface this, Mr. Perry, by stating that we already know most of the facts. We know your history and we have information pointing to your employer. All you need to do is give us the final word."

He watched Perry's silent stare for a moment, then pulled a data tablet from his jacket pocket.

"First of all, we have a list of your aliases. Jeremiah Farber, Grant Freeman, Sam Williams, William Greggorovich, Jrej Nurian, Thomas Riley. Should I go on? You've worked for the Delbians, the Hhorffalphians, and the Xenor, as well as for the Galactic Spice Company, DeVore Enterprises, and Star Trading. I'm certain I'm leaving some out. This is just a cursory inventory. All this is, of course, documented. We believe your present assignment is under the direction of DeVore. Now, all you have to do is confirm this, and you will be released and evicted from the planet. You'll be given safe passage to any star system of your choice."

He paused to take in the silence.

"Please make this as easy for yourself as possible, Mr. Perry. Things can only get difficult. You owe DeVore nothing. They'll disown you, you understand. You're on your own. If you help us, Deltan Technologies can offer you a sizable remuneration. It would be the least we could do. There's no need for you to suffer from your failure to fulfill your commitment to DeVore. Simply help us and you'll be compensated. It's as easy as that. Furthermore, you will be assisting your old friend and comrade, Mr. Michaels."

Michaels looked at Perry, who could have been blind and deaf for all the expression he had. He moved into Perry's line of sight, but failed to get focused.

"C'mon, Jon," he said. "Give us a hand. Then we can both get off this rock. Retire. Both of us."

Perry's eyes caught his suddenly. He shook his head once, slowly. "You don't understand, do you?"

"I understand enough. They'll interrogate you to get what they want. You'll end up in their jail for God knows how long. And this DeVore company won't give a crap. If you help them, we can work together again."

A tight smile cut Perry's beard. He shook his head again, more curtly.

"We will take over now, Mr. Vindal," Quan said. "He is, after all, our responsibility. Michaels has completed his assignment."

"Yes, well, I suppose he has. Congratulations, Mr. Michaels. Mission completed. You may leave."

"What? Leave?" Michaels stared at Vindal, then glanced at Perry. To Perry, the room might well have been empty. "I'm not leaving. What are you planning to do?"

"Interrogation, as we stated," Quan said, the hiss of his accent annoyingly prominent.

Vindal drew close and spoke in more confidential tones, guiding him toward the doorway. "Really, Mr. Michaels. There's not much more you could do. As you see, Mr. Perry is being unreasonable. Your former friendship means nothing to him now. I think we've proved that. However, I will personally guarantee that no harm will befall him. He will be incarcerated until he reveals his employers and accomplices. Beyond that, there is little we can do. At worse, he will be tried for terrorism in the courts of the Consortium, perhaps on Primus. If he cooperates, the Tz-en government will simply deport him and level their charges against DeVore Enterprises, or whomever employed him. Simply put, it is out of your hands. I suggest you and your associates return to Jhamrahl, enjoy some recreation, and await the next transport to the system of your choice."

Michaels felt a tight grip on his arm.

"Come," Jiin said beside him. "There is nothing you can do here, except make matters worse."

She led him past the guards. The heavy door crashed shut behind him.

CHAPTER SEVEN
ESCAPE

Perry's mind whirled through a sea of fog.

He struggled against waves of nausea and an aching head to sit up, swinging one leg at a time over the rough edge of the stone platform. The pungent smell hammered him. He pushed aside the rotting cloth that might have once been a mattress. His fingers touched the cool sliminess of the slab underneath.

"This brings back memories," he said, his voice sounding hollow in the emptiness of the cell.

It may have been the same cell he had been in years ago. He couldn't tell. The single light over the stone slab gave a meager glow over the filthy walls and floor. The rats and roaches had free reign.

He forced himself to his feet, standing unsteadily.

Drugs, he realized. They had drugged him with something. Had he talked about the others? Had he betrayed them?

With shuffling footsteps, he surveyed the cell.

Did they throw him here to break his will? Did they want to make him suffer, then offer him freedom with a price? Or were they done with him and tossed him here to forget about him?

Footsteps echoed down the corridor outside, accompanied by an irritating whine from wheels in need of oiling. Every few step, they would stop. After few assorted shuffling sounds, the footsteps continued. They eventually stopped in front of the door to his cell. Light flooded in from a square in the door, a shadow passing between. Perry made out the head of a Tz-en soldier in the small barred opening.

"So you're the new one, eh?" the soldier said. "Heard about you, off-worlder. You're all over the news programs."

"It's nice to be recognized," Perry said under his breath. "Sorry, no autographs."

Next to the door, a small ledge protruded from the outer wall. A small opening slid up, and the guard pushed a nutrient bar and a flask of water onto the ledge.

"We're honored to have such a celebrity in our prison," he went on. "We don't get many terrorists, off-worlders or locals. Figured you'd be an off-worlder. No El'aran has the guts to stand up to us. They're a weak lot. No spirit."

Perry heard the scratching along the dimly lit walls. The odor of the bar had stirred his little companions. If he was to eat, he had to move fast. The rats were quick.

The guard walked away, mumbling his dissertation on the ineptitude of El'arans and the attributes of the Tz-en. His cart wheels squeaked up to the next cell, where he passed out the next meal.

Perry picked up the bar. It contained all the good things nature intended to keep a body alive, though odor and flavor argued that pronouncement. He took a tentative bite. The bland bits crunched under his teeth. He caught the slight metallic taste and spat the mouthful onto the floor.

Drugged. A nice little present to keep him docile.

He dropped the rest of the bar on the ledge, then took the flask. The water was warm and unfiltered, and its origin was questionable, but at least he couldn't detect any drug. Finishing the water, he placed the flask on the ledge. As he went back to the stone platform, he heard the rats competing for the bar.

He laid back, wondering how long they might keep him here. A few weeks, indefinitely? Or were their plans for an execution more immediate?

He hoped the others would continue now that he was gone. He had started the movement, but it wasn't entirely his fight. Mar'a understood, but would she have the force to keep the others organized. The link between the Shir'ka and the El'arans was so fragile. Could they hold together and grow? Could they finish what he had started?

More than likely they would squabble among themselves and fall prey to pride and fear.

The sound of footsteps and squeaking wheels brought him to realize he had dozed off a number of times. His stomach growled in anticipation of this next meal's nutrient bar. He moved to sit up, but thought better of it. He wasn't about to eat that drug-laced food substitute. When they came for him, he wanted a clear mind. He'd refuse to eat just as long as he was a prisoner. If he happened to starve himself, at least he'd cheat them out of executing him.

The sounds finally stopped in front of his cell. The guard peered through the opening.

"Lunch time, off-worlder," the Tz-en said. The little panel slid open and he dropped the flask and bar on the ledge. "Or is it breakfast. Come to think of it, I believe it's dinner."

Perry lay still, ignoring the guard. He stared up at the old bulb in the ceiling.

"Better hurry before your little friends get it."

Perry didn't move a muscle.

"Fine," the guard said. "You'll miss out on your meal. You'll learn. Just because you're some off-worlder, don't think you'll get privileges. You're scum. You haven't heard what the media reports are saying about you. You've deceived a lot of people, but we will soon put an end to that. And an end to your killing and destruction."

Perry wondered what kind of publicity he was getting. It wasn't very flattering, by the guard's account of it. The government must be stirring the locals up for a public execution.

He wondered if he would get a trial. Probably not. Trials were a waste of time for the Tz-en court system.

He heard the guard making the last of his rounds, then pass the door once more. The guard paused briefly, probably to look in his cell. What would the guard be thinking, provided he had that capacity?

Scratching near the door indicated that the rats were feasting on the drugged nutrient bar. Two squealed and scuffled. The flask tipped over, tapping onto the ledge. Water gurgled out, then trickled and dripped to the floor.

Perry allowed himself to doze off. He needed to forget the writhing of his empty stomach and the torment in his mind.

"Ho!"

A hoarse, croaking whisper brought his mind alert. The sound did not come from the guard. Perry knew that the guard's footsteps would have stirred him long before the Tz-en reached the door of the cell. Furthermore, the sound came from the right hand wall, not the corridor.

He listening hard, hearing the faint scratching of rats.

Of course, it could not have been the rats. Unless he was hallucinating. Maybe they had drugged the water, or this was the last vestiges of the chemicals not yet flushed from his body.

"Ho! Are you there?"

He climbed from the slab and, at the wall, dropped to his hands and knees. He moved his hand over the rough rock wall, jerking back at the touch of something soft and warm. When he touched again, it grabbed hold and held on weakly.

"Thank God!" the voice croaked with a sob. "Who are you? Talk to me, please!" The fingers let Perry loose and withdrew through the hole barely large enough to admit the hand through the wall.

"My name's Perry. Who are you?"

"Jor'm. Thank God, someone to talk with, after all this time. What day is it? Never mind. What year is it? What's happening out there?"

"Easy," Perry said. "How long have you been here?"

"I don't know. I tried counting how often they bring food, but now I can't be sure."

"Why are you here?"

"Taxes! They charged me more than I earned. When I couldn't pay, they took my land. When I spoke out, they threw me down here. I don't even know what happened to my family."

"How did you dig this hole?" he asked.

"A broken bowl. Found it in the dirt on the floor. I've been cutting into the wall for ... well, a long time. It keeps my mind alive. I would have gone insane if I had just sat here all this time, thinking of my wife and ... and my son. I have a good size crater on this side. I knew there was only another cell on the other side, but I only wanted to keep busy, not get myself shot for attempting to escape."

Perry stuck his hand through the hole, feeling the indentation on the other side. "Move aside. I'll kick some of this free." He sat on the filthy ground and braced his hands behind him. He kicked, the heel of his boot striking the weakened rock around the hole. Again and again he struck, while bits of rock broke free. After a moment, the hole was as large as it was going to get and his foot ached.

A grizzled head appeared in the widened opening. The man wiggled through like a worm. Perry reached down and grabbed hold of the thin, bony figure. His mind flashed with memories of the mines under the Ahraj Mountains. How many times had he pulled someone free of fallen debris? Most times they had been cold to the touch. He was relieved to feel the warmth beneath Jor'm's dry skin. He soon stood before Perry: a thin, pale old man with gray hair and beard. Faded rags covered his bones. His gray hair and beard terminated in ragged ends, as though roughly cut by some crude, dull instrument.

"Your room smells worse than mine," he said, wrinkling his grimy nose.

Perry smiled, then shrugged apologetically. "The maid quit."

"No wonder!" Jor'm studied him intently with sharp eyes. "A Shir'ka, eh? Don't recall having run across your kind before. I expect they'll be sending you to the mines soon enough."

"I think they have other plans for me. I'm sort of a political prisoner."

"Aren't we all?" Jor'm laughed with a husky cough that demonstrated his throat was unused to the exercise. He waved his hands to dismiss any explanation and sat down on the edge of the sleeping platform.

"Any family?"

"Yes," answered Perry.

"Ah, I hear the concern in your voice. I, too, miss my wife. My heart aches. Is she still alive, I wonder. What has happened to her after all these years? I was sent here five years after the Tz-en took control. Tell me, how long would that be?"

"Six years."

Jor'm's head sank to his chest. His voice came weakly. "I ... I thought as much. I thought I would go insane. My prayers have kept my mind. Maybe they've preserved my R'behka. I can only hope, and keep praying. The Creator of all will preserve us."

"Tell me about your life, before the Tz-en."

"I was a farmer, to the south of Achari. It wasn't much of a farm, but we survived. It had been in my family for years, and would have gone to K'leb, our son ..." He talked on for hours about his family and his quiet life, accentuating the peacefulness and solitude of their existence. He diverged occasionally, his mind traveling several routes at a single time. He stopped to argue over the silliness of fashions, remarking in detail how some men and women of the upper class fell into certain trends. Another time found him expounding on politics, with references to names Perry could not recognize. He bubbled with the excitement of finally having someone to talk with.

Jor'm was a charming old man, very articulate and educated. The inconsistencies, however, bothered Perry. He refused to think the man was planted by either Michaels or the Tz-en. After all, what information would they gain from tricking him into revealing certain aspects of his recent activities? He couldn't betray others, since they would have vanished into hiding for a while. There had to be another reason for Jor'm's claim to be a simple, isolated farmer when his attitude showed him to be more educated and refined than most farmers Perry had encountered. Perry had grown up on an agrarian world. He had worked on farms throughout his youth, before he and Michaels had joined the militia. After a few subtle questions, Perry decided Jor'm had only a rudimentary knowledge of agriculture. He was no farmer.

Michaels stared out the window of their suite, barely noticing the waves lapping against the white sands of the beach below. He caught movement of tourists on the beach and boats on the water, but they didn't seem real. This whole place wasn't real. Jhamrahl was a resort, so far removed from the little town near the mountains and the prison and ...

"Ease up, Mick," Thatcher told him. "You can't do anything for him. Be thankful it ended as easily as it did."

"Yeah, boss," Ringer said. "Relax."

Michaels watched their reflections in the window. Both sat on opposite sides of the u-shaped couch. Thatcher leaned forward with elbows on knees, punching commands into the remote for the holo projector between them. Ringer leaned back, flip-up computer on his lap, feet crossed and resting on the edge of the projector's table. A chorus of voices, mingled and butchered as Thatcher flipped through frequencies, floated annoyingly through the room. Ringer offered accompaniment with the finger taps on his keypad.

"Here, what's this?" Thatcher said suddenly.

Michaels turned as Geoff increased the volume. The image was distorted. Thatcher swatted Ringer's feet off the table, and the image coalesced into a woman newscaster. Her disembodied head and torso floated above the projector.

" ... And the government of El'aris stated that the off-world mercenary's confession reveals his primary role in numerous incidents that have stricken El'aris recently, including a mining disaster and the sinking of an ore-carrying freighter. Government representatives insist that no visitor to El'aris was under any danger. The terrorist activities were aimed at planetary economics. Thanks to the resourcefulness and effectiveness of the Tz-en constabulary, the terrorist was swiftly apprehended before the threat could spread to more populated areas, such as Jhamrahl. A portion of the confession was publicly released today."

Her imaged shrank to the left, while another figure appeared below her. Perry stood only a foot tall. He wore off-world clothes and no longer appeared like one of the Shir'ka.

"My name is Jon Perry," the holo said. "I was hired to infiltrate the society of El'aris and effect terrorist operations. I enlisted locals for the purpose of sabotage and revolt, to cause an economic crisis and dissension between the El'aran races."

The woman's image expanded, flooding away the smaller holo. "The government of El'aris stated publicly that there is not sufficient evidence for the involvement of others, and Perry may well have been acting alone. They are satisfied that these terrorist acts have ceased and that tourism and trade have not been affected. District Governor Nhung-Chi in Khadeej today credits his staff with a quick end to an otherwise disastrous incident."

"Bloody hell!" Thatcher erupted.

"Shh!" Michaels snapped.

"Shipments of El'aran metals may have been delayed, but there is no danger of unfulfilled orders. The Trade Consortium has made no statement, but official sources state that the Consortium may investigate possible involvement of corporations not presently dealing with El'aris. In another story, on Primus today, David Hughes of Hughes Enterprises has reportedly been hospitalized for –"

Michaels waved his hand. "Okay, shut it off."

Thatcher's big fist pounded on the remote. The image vanished, but he glowered at the air where it had been. "Did you here that? That bloody governor's taking all the credit. Didn't mention us at all."

"The only credit worth getting is one you take to the bank," Michaels said, vaguely aware of the words. They came automatically, dredged up from his memories. He could still hear Perry's voice saying them. The two of them single-handedly stopped a coupe on Riglor, allowing the present ruler to keep his throne. The ruler had taken the credit himself, while paying off Michaels and Perry and getting them quickly off planet before the truth was learned.

Michaels dropped heavily into a chair. He felt old.

They had broken Perry, gotten him to confess. All they said was true. Perry had lied to him. Vindal was right. Their friendship didn't mean anything to Perry any more.

He rubbed his eyes. He was exhausted.

"Odd," Ringer mumbled.

"Huh?"

Ringer scratched his head. "I said, odd. They ain't going to prosecute that DeVore company? I thought they had evidence against them. It sure looked convincing to me when I went through those files. They hired Perry. If I was the government, I'd sue DeVore and get reimbursed for the losses, like that ship and the mining stuff."

Michaels shrugged wearily. "They wanted him to blab who hired him, and he won't. So they're prosecuting him instead. He'd take it, rather than talk. Maybe he hasn't changed all that much. I just didn't expect him to confess, to break so quickly." Or to lie to his old friend.

He climbed to his feet. "Listen. Geoff and me are flying out as soon as we can get transport. I got some debts to settle, then I'm hunting for a place to settle down. You want to come along with us, or do you want to stay longer on this rock?"

"Not if I can help it, boss," Ringer said. "Just give me a minute warning so I can pack my toothbrush."

"Right. May not be anything for a day or two, but I'd settle for an ore freighter. I don't even care where it's headed, just so long as it's outbound."

He watched as Ringer went back to tapping in his keypad.

"Why are you still fooling with that? It's out of our hands, Ringer. If they don't want to use that evidence, it doesn't mean anything to us. We still get paid."

"Sure, boss. I'm just having fun going through the nets with those codes that Vindal character gave us. I can get on other nets, though it takes some time with off-world links. I'm trying to figure out if I can get some stock tips. You know, invest my share. It ain't too early to think of retirement."

"Think hard about it, Ringer."

The sounds of footsteps and squeaky wheels put an end to a long conversation. Exhaustion fell over Perry as he watched Jor'm squeeze through the hole between their cells. His stomach groaned and twisted, but he knew he couldn't eat. He dropped back on the stone slab, feeling the cold bite through his clothes. He wondered how long he might fend off hunger. Would he eventually succumb to it and eat the drugged food? What would it matter if he did? The drug wasn't there for any interrogation purposes. Other chemicals were more effective for that. Did it matter if he became complacent? He was stuck in a tiny cell. What could he do anyway?

The guard paused at his door.

"Hey, off-worlder. Didn't die on us, did you?"

Perry remained still.

The Tz-en hurled a series of curses through the opening in the door. He ran through his own version of Perry's genealogy, then paused for a response. Perry left him disappointed.

The water flask was replaced, along with a new nutrient bar, and the guard moved on.

Perry lay still. He heard the rats starting to move toward the food.

On his return, the guard's footsteps paused outside Perry's cell once more. This time, he made no remark. Only his breathing indicated his presence. The rats, Perry noticed, hesitated in their approach, waiting for the man to move on.

Once the noisy cart was well down the corridor, Perry got up. He stepped to the door, scattering the rats. Three rodents, heading off into separate corners. Picking up the flask, he took a drink. It didn't do much for his hunger. The nutrient bar caught his eye, and he stared at it. Maybe it wasn't laced with a heavy dose of the drug. Maybe he could alternate days, thereby cutting down the expected dosage. Of course, he'd been in situations where he hadn't eaten for days. Once for two weeks. It hadn't been that bad, after the first couple of days. However, it was easier not to eat when food wasn't available. Now he had food delivered each day – or an approximation of day.

He picked up the bar.

It would taste like shoe leather wrapped in dried grass. No one would ever get fat eating them, as Jor'm proved. But they kept a person alive.

Alive ... for how long?

He dropped the bar on the ledge and set the flask next to it.

"Aren't you eating?" Jor'm asked.

Perry remained still.

The old man's head stuck out of the wall close to the floor, looking ludicrous in the dull lighting. He wiggled and squirmed and slid further through.

"No," Perry said.

"Why? You want to feed the rats and the roaches? Believe me, they won't starve."

"The food's drugged."

"Really?" Jor'm sat on the stone slab and held his own nutrient bar up to the light. A third of the bar had already been eaten away. "These things are so terrible, how can you tell?"

"It's the same drug they use on the mine workers, to keep them under control. It numbs the mind."

"I could use some of that, my friend. My mind is too active, hopping back and forth. It would be nice not to think for a while. Is my bar drugged too?"

"Maybe not. I hadn't thought of it. I had figured the Tz-en just wanted to keep all prisoners under control, not just me."

"Ah, you must be a terrible criminal to be so persecuted by the Tz-en. I heard the guard call you an off-worlder. What terrible things have you done to warrant a disguise as a Shir'ka?"

"I've been living among the Shir'ka for a while. I'm trying to help your people fight the Tz-en."

"I did hear the guard say something about you being a terrorist. You're a man after my own heart, sir, though I wish my heart would have been braver years ago. Then perhaps I wouldn't have ... But then there would be ..."

He stared at the floor, his words trailing off.

"Here," he said suddenly. "Take my bar. See if it's tainted."

Perry took it in his fingers and raised it to his nose. He could not detect any unusual odor. He broke of a small piece and tasted it. No metallic aftertaste.

"I don't think so. They must want only me drugged."

"Good. Then we'll switch. You eat mine, and I'll eat yours." He waved his hand against protests. "If the drug gets too much for me, then we'll just have to share one bar. I've been meaning to take off a few excess pounds anyway. I still can't see my third rib."

Perry picked up his bar from the ledge. "Are you–"

Jor'm snatched it from his fingered and took a bite. He shrugged and spoke through a mouthful of chewed fiber. "Not too bad. After years of this, the change in the taste adds variety. Just as long as I don't hallucinate."

"I don't believe that's a side effect."

The rats were unusually skittish. Perhaps they sensed his intentions. But Perry had hunted the illusive sand buck in the desert. He was patient and quick. With a little piece of Jor'm's nutrient bar as bait, he crouched in position and stayed motionless. His ears strained to hear the movements. The rats had the scent, but the Human in close proximity gave them cause to hesitate. Perry waited, eyes following every shadow in the grayness.

One grew bolder. It scurried out, muzzle twitching. Hunger overcame fear and the rat moved toward the remains of the bar.

Perry struck before it reached the food – no sense wasting the bait. His toe hit hard, sending the beast hurtling across the cell. It collided with the wall with a small, dull thud, slid to the floor, and lay still.

Perry probed with his foot until he located it, then bent down to squint through the shadows at the mud-brown body. It stayed lifeless.

From down the corridor came the footsteps of the guard and the squeal of his cart. The footsteps stopped at the first cell.

Perry took from his pocket a length of cloth he had torn from his shirt. He made a loop at one end and circled it around the rat's neck. He pulled it tight, just in case the thing wasn't quite dead. Letting it dangle on the cloth string, he carried it to the door. The other end of the string he tied to a bar in the small window in the door, drawing the rat up so that it hung just beneath the opening.

The guard stopped at Jor'm's cell, sliding in his water and nutrient bar.

Perry could see the guard through the little window. He pulled on the string, making it slide down along the metal bar to dig into the wood at its base. From outside, it should be invisible.

The guard placed Jor'm's empty water flask on his cart and moved on.

Perry took a quick step across his cell and dropped onto his back on the rock platform. He carefully placed himself in the same position as before.

The Tz-en's breathing came through the opening in the door. Perry could feel the man's eyes scrutinizing him. He held his breath. He had learned to do that for extended periods when he was young. No one could stay under water longer than him. It used to irritate Tony.

"It isn't good to play *toobacq*, off-worlder," the guard said. He waited, then said, "I will come in and break a few of your bones. They want you alive, but they didn't say in what condition."

He pulled out the water flask, which Perry had left on its side with a generous amount of turbid liquid remaining. He replaced it with a full flask and a new bar.

"Don't let the rats get it, off-worlder." He chuckled as he moved on.

Perry waited until the guard was walking back down the corridor before he sat up and took the bar for Jor'm.

The old man wormed his way into the cell.

As they traded bars, Jor'm narrowed his eyes toward the cell door.

"What in the name of the Ahraj Hills is that?"

Perry glanced over his shoulder. "Oh. That's a rat. They're pretty much standard on most planets. El'aris's are of a generous size, and what they lack in tail length they make up for in teeth."

Jor'm frowned. "I am well aware of their size and sharpness of their teeth. I have been on close terms with several generations of them. Why is it hanging on your door? Now if it were me, I'd hang it on the outside, just to let the guard know what I thought of him."

"I hadn't thought of that."

Jor'm crunched on the nutrient bar. "So, you either have something in mind you would rather not discuss with me, or you are demonstrating a rather bizarre off-world ritual I would rather not know about."

"Tell me some more about your family. How long had you been farming?"

"Since the Tz-en – oh! All my life. I grew up on that farm. It was quite a life. Lots of work, but quiet and peaceful."

Perry ignored the slip. "And I suppose you had only a rudimentary education, being so isolated."

"Indeed. But I have always been a voracious reader."

Perry let him talk on, let him change the subject to other, unimportant things. He had heard the fear spring out in Jor'm's voice and wondered what frightened the man so much. In a brief slip of words, Perry discovered what he already suspected. Jor'm had not been a farmer for long, if at all. Since the Tz-en ... That could only mean the war eleven years ago. Jor'm took to farming then. What had he been before?

Perry asked Jor'm an occasional question about Jhamrahl, Khadeej, and El'aris in general. He had become acquainted recently with parts of Khadeej, so he asked about certain areas. The cafe where he had first seen Michaels, the market district, the docks. Jor'm seemed to have only a passing acquaintance with the town. Jhamrahl, however, he talked about with confidence. He was more familiar with the capital than he openly admitted.

By his calculations, Perry figured they were fed twice a day, though the times may not follow any kind of schedule. By the time the guard came again, there was a second rat hanging from the string on the door. The first already swelled and exuded the beginnings of putrefaction. When the guard put his face to the opening in the door, he sniffed audibly and gagged. Perry lay on the platform, in the same position as before, holding his breath as long as his ears told him the guard watched.

Once the guard left, Jor'm squirmed through from his cell to trade nutrient bars. Perry noticed the slower movements of the man and the glaze that started to cover his eyes. Perry didn't like inflicting the drug on the old man. No telling what it might do for someone of his age and physical condition. However, it would only be for a short time, if Perry's plan fell into place.

"Where in Jhamrahl did you live?" he asked Jor'm.

Without thinking, the old El'aran answered: "Arborj Park."

"How long?"

Jor'm stared at the half eaten bar in his dark-stained fingers. "I grew up there."

In another situation, Perry might not have taken advantage of the man's weakened resistance. But Jor'm had lied to him. Perry had to know why, whether he was an innocent El'aran or not, or a plant sent by the Tz-en. What was Jor'm hiding? He hadn't ingested quite enough drug to make him totally complacent; but at the moment, his eyes had that distant look Perry had seen many times in the eyes of the mine workers. As long as he kept the questions simple, Jor'm might stay under the influence of the drug.

"Were you poor?"

"Oh, no. We were quite affluent. We had a large home, though certainly not an estate."

"Then you had a good education."

"Yes. The university in Jhaldair is small but the alumni is very select. My degree in economics gained me a position in ... in ..."

Jor'm's eyes tried to focus. His brow furrowed deeply for a moment of intense concentration, then relaxed.

Perry let him sit quietly for a few minutes before risking another question.

"When did you meet your wife?"

Jor'm smiled vaguely. "We had an arranged marriage, but we grew up together. She has always been my friend and companion."

"And you have one son?"

"No. We don't have any children." His faces pursed. He stared down at the rotted shoes covering his feet. "I have ... We couldn't ..."

"How long had you been farming before you were thrown in the prison?"

"Four years."

"Are you very good at it?"

"Not very. We barely made enough to eat, let alone sell for taxes. Later, K'leb helped and we began to see a profit. He was always an intelligent boy. He caught on quickly to the farming, even for someone so young."

"Who did the farm belong to?"

"R'behka's brother. He ... we think he died in the war. We never found him."

"Why did you go to the farm?"

"To escape. To hide."

"Escape? Escape what?"

"Those Tz-en. They had killed the M'ji. We had to get away, hide where they would never expect to find us."

"Did you know the M'ji?"

"Of course. I was his economics adviser."

"Where were you when they attacked?"

Jor'm wrapped his thin arms around himself and shivered. "In the palace. I saw them blow apart the gate and storm the palace. I saw them murder our people and kill M'ji J'siah."

"If you were in the throne room when the M'ji was killed, you would have been dead." Perry remembered vividly the carnage in that room, how the Tz-en flew into a frenzy that took to butchery rather than fighting. He had tried to stop them, but they tore apart the M'ji and his wife before he could force his way through the mass of Tz-en soldiers. It was a wonder they hadn't turned on him. Every El'aran in that room had been killed.

Jor'm sank his head onto his chest. His next words came as barely a whisper. "Don't you think I know that? When the attack came, I hurried to the security section to check the monitors. Chaos reigned. I watched the killings. I stood there and watched them kill J'siah. Never once did I think of joining the fight, standing beside my M'ji. Instead, I ran for the passages beneath the palace. There are some that are hidden and can carry a man many kilometers away underground. On my way, I passed through a corridor already devastated by the invaders. Many soldiers and staff people lay scattered over the floor. The burning stench was terrible. One of those bodies moved. It was old Kar'thor, a captain that had served many decades in the M'ji personal guard. I remember staring at his dead eyes and the burnt hole that had been his chest. He was dead, yet moving. My fear froze me. If it hadn't, I might not have seen the small figure beneath the man's body. Kar'thor had shielded young Dh'vid with his own body. The boy was bruised and burnt, but alive. I took him with me, though in the passages beneath the palace he fought hard to return and avenge his people. He had none of the cowardice I had. "

"Who is Dh'vid?" Perry asked.

"J'siah's son."

"What happened after leaving the palace? You obviously made your escape."

"Yes. I ... Yes, I did. I hurried home. We took what little we could carry, then fled south with hundreds of others."

"And your farm?"

Jor'm stayed quiet for a few moments. He watched his hands in the gloom, turning them over to gaze at the grime-lined palms. When he looked up, his eyes were filled with moisture but they held a steady gaze. "I ... I don't know why I said those things. Pay no attention to me. I'm just an old man."

"You have nothing to fear from me," Perry asked.

"You're an off-worlder. You wouldn't understand."

"I understand more than you know, Jor'm," Perry said. "Go rest. We will talk more later. Have no fear, my friend. Together, we will turn things around."

"From prison?"

"I've been in prisons before."

After Jor'm returned to his own cell, Perry lay on his platform and stared at the ceiling bulb.

The footsteps came again as the guard went down the corridor, stopping at each cell, taking out the empty flask, putting in a full one and a nutrient bar.

At his cell, the guard did the same. He took a long moment, probably watching Perry through the opening in the door. Perry held his breath and remained still, imagining the guard inhaling the stench of rotting rats. Then he heard the guard fussing with something. A beep. The lock to his door unlatched and the door swung slowly on its hinges. Now Perry realized that his game might be discovered prematurely. Could the guard see the two rat carcasses dangling from the bars in the door? If he did, he would probably just shut the door again and move on. But the door didn't close.

The guard moved into the cell, his boots crunching across the debris.

Perry's lungs ached with his captured breath. He strained his ears to hear the least movement of the guard. The step of his feet, the bend of his arms. He conjured a mental image of the man and his position. He readied himself. The guard leaned over him.

He opened his eyes as he shot his hands upward. In a heartbeat he located the hand holding the blaster and the guard's bare throat. He tightened a grip on each.

The Tz-en never fired his weapon. With his free hand, he tore at the fingers wrapped around his throat. No matter how he pulled and scratched, Perry's grip held with a pressure just short of crushing the larynx.

The Tz-en's pale skin flushed to a dark gray. His mouth gaped, hissing for breath. His eyes looked like they might explode from their sockets. He thrashed and beat, but he could not escape Perry's strength. When Perry began to wonder how long the guard could go on without air, the Tz-en went limp. The blaster clattered onto the sleeping platform.

Releasing his hold on the man's neck, Perry turned and laid the Tz-en on the platform. He took up the blaster. The guard's breath gurgled through his bruised throat. He was alive, but unconscious.

Under other circumstances, he would have taken the uniform. However, there was no way his tanned, bearded face and dark hair could pass as resembling a Tz-en. He would have to make his escape dressed as he was.

"What's going on?"

Jor'm's head poked out from the hole to the other cell.

"We're getting out of here," Perry said.

Once in Perry's cell, Jor'm straightened. He jumped back from the sight of the prone guard.

"Is ... is he dead?"

"Not quite. But he'll be on liquids for at least a week. We can't waste time. Let's go."

Jor'm backed away and shook his head. Perry saw what little color there was in his face drain away. "I ... I can't."

"I'll admit, it won't be easy. Would you rather stay here? I don't think so."

Jor'm kept shaking his head. "No. I can't. Besides, I would slow you down. I'm too old. I couldn't run. I'd be shot down in seconds."

Perry had known that, but he wasn't willing to leave Jor'm behind, especially after his help and his own guilt for taking advantage of him with the Tz-en drug. With Jor'm along, he would have nearly no chance of succeeding.

"I won't leave you here," he said.

Jor'm straightened himself and put out his chin in a more dignified manner, pushing away his fears and falling back on logic. "You don't have any choice. You must go without me. Just promise me that you'll contact my wife and let her know I'm still alive. Maybe there's a way she could get a message to me whether she is all right or not. And those things I said earlier—"

"You can trust me. Your secret is safe."

"You're an off-worlder. I shouldn't trust you, but I do. I really have no choice. Now go. Stop wasting time."

Perry tore the keycard from the guard's belt, glanced once at Jor'm, then hurried out the door. He closed and locked the door. Peering through the little window, he saw Jor'm wiggling through to his own cell. Before turning away, Perry stepped back and kicked at the keycard reader. On the third kick, the indicator lights went out.

One end of the corridor led deeper into the rocks, leaving the last of the cells behind. They were old tunnels from the days when these were mines. He doubted escape lay in that direction. The other way led to an old lift that rose to the upper levels of the prison. To escape, he would have to pass among the Tz-en soldiers and staff. He had one blaster with a low power output. Somehow the element of surprise didn't outweigh his shortcomings.

He used the keycard to activate the lift.

The doors opened obediently. Once inside, he glanced over his options. Ground level was two levels up, and three more floors were listed beyond that. Ground level would be the busiest. He would be caught almost immediately. However, one of the upper floors might not be as populated. He could have time to investigate an easier escape route. Even gaining roof access would be preferable.

He punched the button to the top level.

The lift groaned in complaint, then rose in jerking movements.

The doors opened on the third floor above ground. He brought up the blaster and took aim on the single figure in the corridor beyond.

The El'aran stopped, mop handle in hand, frozen in the activity of cleaning the floor. He gaped at Perry, fear draining his face of color.

Perry lowered the blaster and held out his hand, palm outward. "It's okay. Can you tell me where the exit is to the roof?"

The El'aran backed slowly, dropped his mop, then ran down the hall.

Perry followed warily. The man might inadvertently lead him to an exit.

He passed the maintenance closet, its door ajar. Inside were the accoutrements for cleaning the building, including a few coveralls hanging on hooks. Glancing along the corridor, Perry ducked into the room. A sink for filling or emptying buckets provided a place for a quick cleaning. Satisfied, he slipped on one of the coveralls. The blaster dropped into one of the deep hip pockets. He grabbed one of the long-handled static vacuums and stepped out in his new disguise. Now he just needed to find the stairs or another service lift.

As he moved down the hall, he heard quiet voices. They rounded the corner just as he dropped the vacuum to the floor and switched it on. Two Tz-en conversed over misplaced files. One was male, one female, and both were in casual dress rather than military uniform. They passed Perry without giving him a glance.

He found another lift and approached it. As he neared, the doors opened to emit a Tz-en officer. He walked past Perry without looking at him, but then stopped short.

"What is the meaning of this?" the officer demanded. "You are not permitted to use this lift."

Perry gripped the vacuum handle, prepared to swing it as a weapon. He kept his head down, eyes on the floor in a subservient way.

The Tz-en jabbed his finger down the corridor to the right.

"Use the maintenance lift, and if I ever catch any of you lazy El'arans using the main lift, you will be spending time in the cells below."

Perry nodded, bowing low, and headed down the side corridor.

He found the lift used by the maintenance staff, took it to the ground level, and exited the rear of the building. In moments he was in the streets of Khadeej.

CHAPTER EIGHT
DISTRUST

A ba'shal stared with wide eyes at Perry. The old merchant stumbled back, tripping over a wad of dyed silk and nearly tumbling over more choice stock of his little warehouse. Perry grabbed his arm to steady him, then warned him to silence with a finger to his lips. Perry, dressed in El'aran clothes, a slouch hat shadowing his face, had stole in through the rear door.

"Is anyone else here?" he asked.

Aba'shal gave a quick nod. "He'lana, my clerk. She is in the office. But we can trust her."

Perry cut him short. "No. No one must know I'm here."

Aba'shal sat heavily on a pile of silk, running his eyes over Perry. "What has happened to you? I had heard the Tz-en had you."

"I didn't like the accommodations, so I left. I'll need to leave Khadeej before I endanger anyone here. I thought it best to go back with the Shir'ka for a few days and work out our strategy. Where are Mar'a and To'mahs?"

"Gone into the mountains, as far as I know. The night you were taken, the Tz-en bombed the hills. Bar'thazel told me that To'mahs was heading back into the desert. Mar'a wanted to go after you, but her father would have none of that. I think Bar'thazel argued with To'mahs. Those two were always at odds. I only have Bar'thazel's version, but he claims To'mahs was angry and declared he would take his clan back to the desert. Without the Shir'ka, we have no chance against the Tz-en. Bar'thazel was angry too, especially after the news about you."

"About my arrest?"

"No. At first, word spread among us that you were arrested, so we all kept quiet and separate. We believed any of us could be next, or that the streets would fill with Tz-en. Then some of us saw the broadcast on the holos and vid screens. The broadcast of your statement."

"I didn't make any statement."

"I didn't see it myself," Aba'shal said in a softer tone. "Bar'thazel and many others saw it."

"What was it?"

"You made your statement of being an off-worlder, hired by someone to start a revolt in order to disrupt the planet's economy."

"I never made such a statement. However, there are ways to fake such a recording and have it appear real. It's rather child's play with the present technology."

"It convinced Bar'thazel and the others," the merchant said quickly. "I realize we aren't as technologically savvy as other worlds, but it produced the desired effect. It has pushed a wedge of doubt between us."

"What about you?" Perry asked.

"I know you, Perry. We have not known each other for long, but I know your heart."

Perry smiled and nodded. "Thank you."

"What will you do now? I fear we are lost."

"We'll need to gather some of us together," Perry said. "The old warehouse tonight. But only a few. L'dhar, A'brem, Ele'zar. Tell Bar'thazel last, but not that I'll be there. Have you seen E'lias?"

"No. But won't it be dangerous to gather together so soon? The Tz-en will be watching."

"They'll always be watching. We can't wait for them to turn their backs. If we don't move now, they may crush any chance for us to do anything."

Aba'shal nodded. "I will contact them, but I cannot force them if they do not want to come."

In the days before the Tz-en invasion, Aba'shal's family business traded with the Shir'ka for silks and glassware that went to other parts of El'aris and even to off-world markets. Now the products went all over the galaxy, but it was no longer Aba'shal's business. Like most, it belonged to the government. Aba'shal was reduced to a manager of his own warehouse. His great family home, like so many in Khadeej, had been confiscated. He now rented a small apartment nearby.

There were others like Aba'shal. One by one Perry had found them. They weren't fighters, but they had influence among the people. Aba'shal left to make arrangements, calling on a few of these trusted men.

Along the wharves of Khadeej, many warehouses were deserted and falling into disrepair. One had belonged to Aba'shal's family. Later in the day, five of the summoned men gathered in the bare room that had once been an office. Perry was relieved to see E'lias. The young man had been indispensable since Perry had helped him escape from the mines. His skills had proven useful during the sinking of the ore freighter. With him was his brother, Ja'nus, who was his senior by only two years. The other men in the room stood apart. Tall and aloof, Fet Bar'thazel stood with his arms folded and pointed chin in the air, his scowl challenging. His features were angular, his brown hair was streaked with gray. His business in produce and livestock had suffered with the new government regulations and taxation, especially when the Tz-en took over farms only to allow them to fall to ruin. Trading with the Shir'ka was one aspect of his business he cared little for. Any Shir'ka herder wanted only a fair price for *gilka* meat, and Bar'thazel wanted only a good profit. But he had no desire to fall in with the Tz-en, as some merchants had. He was greedy, but he had principals.

With him stood Len A'brem, the banker, and Tor L'dhar, master carpenter. A'brem's short, wide figure tried to find comfort in the shadows of his two companions. When Perry's eyes fell on him, he cast his gaze to the dust laden floor and shuffled his feet. L'dhar folded his heavy arms and returned Perry's look with a cold indifference.

"Where's Ele'zar?" Perry asked.

A smirk passed over Bar'thazel's face. "He refused to come. He'll have nothing to do with you and your conspiracies, and I don't blame him. He had doubts about you from the beginning, and now we see them justified. I would have stayed away, too, but I wanted one last opportunity to speak. We weren't told you would be here, but that's all the better for what I have to say. We'll have nothing to do with you any more."

"But you will listen one last time, Bar'thazel," Perry said, leveling his eyes on the older man.

Bar'thazel raised his brows and opened his mouth to retort, but closed it slowly without having said a word.

"You, L'dhar. What is your complaint?" Perry asked of the big carpenter.

"I will listen to what you have to say, Perry. Whether I will trust it remains to be seen."

When Perry looked to A'brem, the banker shook his head and gazed at his shoes.

"First of all, the Tz-en imprisoned me for a short time," Perry said, "but I was able to escape. You three are leaders among the community. Other El'arans will listen to you. You must keep speaking to them, uniting them. If you aren't bound together, the Tz-en will rip you apart and squash any attempt at a revolt. That's what they attempted with capturing me. They thought I controlled the movement. I'm only a catalyst. We need to bring the Shir'ka leaders back, continue working together. Don't you want El'aris to be free? Don't you want to control your own planet?"

Bar'thazel's features grew more sour. "What is it you want out of this, Perry? We have all seen your confession."

"Yes," L'dhar said with a decisive nod.

"I made no such confession," Perry said. "I have not seen it, but I can assure you that it was faked."

"Why should we believe you?" Bar'thazel demanded.

E'lias balled his hands into fists and took a step toward the older El'aran. "Because he's trying to help us, that's why!"

"Like he helped the Tz-en a decade ago?" Bar'thazel stood his ground.

"He's trying to change what happened then," E'lias said. "Look at what he's done. I'd be working a digger underneath a mountain if he hadn't tricked the Tz-en and helped us escape. Each year the Tz-en take more and more. Soon we will have nothing. We need to stop them now, and Perry is the only one who can help us."

"We don't need off-worlders," Bar'thazel said.

"We need Perry," E'lias insisted.

Perry stepped between the two. "You don't need me, you need each other. You need to work together, trust each other. Bar'thazel, you're right. You don't need off-worlders. You don't need our interference. You don't have to trust me or believe me. Just believe in each other. The Tz-en took your business and forced you to work for them. If you don't stand against the Tz-en, soon you'll have nothing. Same with you, A'brem. And you, L'dhar. You each know that. They are making you into slaves. You have two choices. Accept the Tz-en regime or fight it. To fight it, you must fight it as one."

"We heard this speech before, Perry," Bar'thazel said, unimpressed. "And you've heard us say we can't fight the Tz-en. We've no weapons, no soldiers, no organization, no leader – except you, and we will no longer follow an off-worlder."

"You're an old damn fool!" E'lias snapped.

Perry held his hand toward E'lias. He said to Bar'thazel, "I don't want you to follow me. I want you to lead. Weapons we can get. But you need to be a leader of your people."

"I'm a businessman, not a soldier. I may have ruined a few competitors in the past, but I've never killed. Not even Tz-en," Bar'thazel said.

"I'm not asking you to," Perry said. "I want you to lead others. Each of you. Just unite the people against the Tz-en."

"So we can all die together?" Bar'thazel asked, eyes widening.

"No. With the Shir'ka –"

Bar'thazel laughed. "Shir'ka are completely unreliable. They're hermits and barbarians. The first sign of trouble, and they fled to their precious desert to hide. If I didn't have to do business with them, I would have nothing to do with them. At least they don't want to rob me all at once, like the Tz-en."

"If you want to pull your support, Bar'thazel," Perry said finally, "you're welcome to."

"The others feel the same."

Perry looked to L'dhar, who cast a hesitant glance at Bar'thazel. "Well?" Perry asked.

"Ah, well. I don't really have any dealings with Shir'ka. They don't have much need for a carpenter. None have ever done wrong by me, but ... they are a savage lot."

"Savage?" Perry asked, conjuring a mental image of daily life among the tents of a Shir'ka clan. The foods, the songs and music, the storytellers, the bleating herds of *glelk*. "Compared to you? To other El'arans?"

"Yes."

"Compared to the Tz-en?"

"No. From the stories I've heard, the Tz-en are brutal. Though they've left me alone."

"I haven't dealt with many Shir'ka, either," A'brem said, looking expectantly toward Bar'thazel, as if for some cue. "They don't bank their money very often. They don't trust us. And I've heard stories about them, too. Not that I believe every story I hear, but so few El'arans have been into the desert."

"I have," Perry said. "I've lived among them. The basic difference is that the Shir'ka lead a hard life. They have to struggle to survive, but that's normal for them. They have histories of clan wars, of renegades, of battles. I've seen none of that. Now when the clans meet, they have festivals. Their history and their way of life have made them a strong people. El'arans have had a soft life in comparison. Why do you think the Tz-en could conquer you so easily? They had modern weapons, but they also had the ferocity. You didn't. But the Shir'ka do. You can only defeat the Tz-en with their help."

"They won't help us," Bar'thazel said. "To'mahs refused to talk with me after you were captured. He's an arrogant dogmatist. Everything must be his way, or it is not done. He wouldn't listen to a word I said, and took his people into the hills. They don't care what happens on this side of the Ahraj. In their arrogance they believe the Tz-en will never cross their desert."

"I'll talk to To'mahs," Perry said. "If he commits his clan, will you give your full support?"

L'dhar nodded, but Bar'thazel shook his head emphatically. "I cannot trust you, Perry. You're an off-worlder with your own agenda. Like all other off-worlders, you work for money. Money first brought you to our planet. It was the reason you helped the Tz-en destroy our culture. Now, it must also be the reason you are pushing us to confront the Tz-en regime. I'll have no part of it."

"Neither will I," A'brem said with a sharp nod of his head.

L'dhar gazed down his nose at his companions. He said to Perry, "I will listen if To'mahs wants to talk. I have no argument with him or the clans. But I cannot make any promises. I must be able to see the odds in our favor before I make any commitment."

"Odds? A war isn't a game, L'dhar," Perry said. "We aren't gambling.

We're fighting for freedom."

"Our freedom, not yours," Bar'thazel pointed out. "You can leave this planet any time, and never look back."

"Not any more," Perry said. "Bar'thazel, you and A'brem are refusing to cooperate. Will you at least agree not to interfere?"

Bar'thazel nodded slowly, like some ancient sage imparting his wisdom. "I agree. However, I expect not to be tied in with your plots. I want no involvement."

"Of course. E'lias, can you spread word that Bar'thazel and A'brem are to be avoided?"

E'lias grinned. "Gladly."

"Then I'll go into the mountains and locate To'mahs." Perry prayed that Mar'a was with him.

Security at the airfield was normally adequate for the populace of Khadeej. Since no El'aran or Shir'ka could fly any type of aircraft, security surrounding fliers was left to a minimum. If any El'aran or Shir'ka had any designs on the fliers or airships, it would be for sabotage, and the perimeter scanners would detect any illicit movement. Perry had no difficulty locating a fueled flier, of a design he had flown a hundred times in a variety of circumstances. Dressed in a borrowed Tz-en flight suit and helmet, he walked out onto the tarmac, climbed into the craft, and took off despite heated requests to the contrary from the control tower.

Half an hour later, after easily evading two pursuit craft, he dropped over the western slopes of the Ahraj Mountains.

Like a calm sea, the sands stretched out. Flat, featureless, red. He was too high to see any clumps of vegetation that sprang up to capture any moisture the air held. The *woro* weeds kept the *glelk* and *sildars* alive, which in turn kept the Shir'ka alive. He banked south, paralleling the mountains with a five kilometer distance. He approached the Ahram Pass, which cut a ragged way through the mountains. Nothing showed on the infinite rusty horizon. Eventually, he turned back, increasing his distance from the mountains by another five kilometers until he reached his original mark. Then he continued north.

After ten kilometers, he saw the tiny dots scattered over the flat landscape. Small herds of *glelk*, clustered in their own family units, were almost lost in the colors of the sand. Beyond them, the tents were visible only by the shadows they cast.

He banked the craft, making a wide curve. Then he altered course toward the tents and made a swift descent with the sun behind him. They would have already seen him, but the maneuver might momentarily disorient them and give him a chance to land.

As the herds scattered beneath him, and the tents grew larger, he saw the men swarming toward his landing.

The flier settled in a cloud of sand. Perry quickly popped the canopy, unstrapped his helmet, and leaped out of the cockpit. As the cloud dissipated, he found the craft surrounded by dozens of Shir'ka, both men and women. Most were armed with customary rifle-staffs and daggers, while some carried blasters of various ages and states of repair. Their clothing appeared the same at first glance, all of a similar rusty-red color, but Perry had been among their people for a long time. He knew and recognized family designs, individual characteristics, changes in style, and variations in hue. Where a first time observer saw a group of Shir'ka, he saw individuals.

He tucked his pilot helmet under his arm. He noticed one person out of the crowd and locked his gaze with her green eyes. She stood behind two large men, a blaster in her hand. Her eyes grew wide in astonishment.

"Hi honey, I'm home," Perry said, smiling.

Mar'a shouldered her way between the two men in front of her and leaped into Perry's arms. The helmet flew, banging against the flier's fuselage before settling onto the sand underneath.

"You could have been killed!" she shouted at him, squeezing him tight. She released him and slapped him hard across the chest. "How dare you come in that way! We had men setting up a big laser to shoot you down."

"I'm certainly glad they showed some restraint before I landed."

"You're just lucky they couldn't find all the pieces in time."

Looking at the faces around them, he recognized a variety of emotions. Relief, suspicion, happiness, anger. Evidently news of the Tz-en's broadcast had even reached the desert. He had known these people for years, but even some men he had hunted with and fought beside had doubt scored across their brown faces.

"You escaped the prison in that?" Mar'a asked, nodding toward the flier.

"No. I escaped out the back door. I just needed the flier to get here as quickly as possible. I've got to talk to To'mahs."

"He's in his tent," she said, motioning toward the center of the clan's encampment.

Most were armed with rifle-staffs…

They walked together, a path opening among the slowly dispersing crowd.

As they walked among the sand-colored tents, distinguishable by shape, size and ornamentation, Perry explained how he had escaped, leaving details for later. He took greater pains to describe his visit with Bar'thazel and the others, and their reluctance to keep within the movement.

"To'mahs won't like this," Mar'a said. "He had gone into Khadeej after we avoided the attack, when you were captured."

They came to the tent of To'mahs's family, and Mar'a threw back the main flap without ceremony.

Light strips suspended from lines between support poles lit the main chamber, where To'mahs sat on the colorful rugs. An array of tools surrounded him, and before him lay scattered an assortment of pieces to an old rifle-staff. He turned a power cell over in his hand, leaning toward one of the light strips and making adjustments with a small pliers. The older man paused in his work as they entered, but he did not look up. He continued working on the weapon.

"Father ..." Mar'a said, without getting To'mahs's attention. "Father, Perry is here. He escaped."

"I can see that, Mar'a. Hand me the driver, Perry."

Perry bent down, picked up a needle thin pliers and held it out to To'mahs.

The Shir'ka moved to take it, then stopped as his eyes caught it. He flashed a glare at Perry. "I said the driver."

Perry held the pliers out. "You don't want a driver. Not for that power cell. That isn't a screw holding the plates together, it's a clamp. You have to pinch the edges inward, then pull the plate off. Your rifle-staff carries that old style of cell."

A smile split To'mahs's gray streaked beard. "Good. You remember. It's been a long time since I let you use this old thing." He took the pliers and popped open the cell. He dropped the cell onto its charging cradle, then placed a charged one into the chamber, closing the plate. A metallic click told him the clamp took hold.

"How could I forget," Perry said, sitting down across from the Shir'ka. "You had me strip the staff down and put it back together three times before I could take it out on a hunt."

"You brought down a bull *jerlac* that day." He fitted the shaft pieces together. "I am pleased you escaped from the Tz-en. So that was you making all that fuss outside."

"I talked with Bar'thazel."

To'mahs threw down the half assembles weapon. "That man is *glelk* dung!"

"He's pulled out his support. And A'brem. We might still count on L'dhar and the others, but their confidence was shaken."

"The El'arans are weaklings. Like surface sand against a breeze."

"But others still support us. But nothing will happen if the clans aren't behind us."

"The clans won't join. I won't join."

"Father, you can't mean that," Mar'a said

To'mahs's eyes narrowed into shadowed slits beneath bushy brows. "We will not fight their battle for them. The Shir'ka are not slaves to the El'arans any more than we are to the Tz-en. They want their freedom, but they will not fight for it. They expect us to do that. They consider us barbarians because we don't live in stone buildings and we don't live soft lives. Let them fight for their own freedom."

"It isn't a matter of their freedom from the Tz-en, it's yours too. The Tz-en haven't bothered with the clans because they don't have the numbers to fight across the desert. But they'll soon have the weapons to compensate for their fewer numbers. Their aircraft and satellites can pinpoint any camp. They'll have your movements mapped, and they'll use missiles or orbital lasers to wipe you out, if they want to."

"We will not bother them, so they will never have the need to use those weapons."

"They don't need a reason. This planet now belongs to them. The farms, the oceans, the rivers, the mountains, and the deserts. Your lives mean nothing to them. They'll kill half the population and use the other half in servitude."

"The Shir'ka will not be slaves."

"Easy to say, but once a person is drugged, his control is gone. Whether he's a Shir'ka or an El'aran. Or an off-worlder."

To'mahs breathed a deep sigh that deflated his huge stature. "Perry, you are my son-in-marriage. But I have thought of you as a son before that. You I trust. And our clan would follow you, as many others would because of me. But I cannot trust these El'arans. Too many have fallen to worship the Tz-en in order to save their skins. We tried to put away our differences, but you can see from Bar'thazel what they are like. They are softer than sand worms. They argue for the sake of the argument. They enjoy their little market games of bartering with us. A Shir'ka barters for what is fair to both. The El'arans barter for what is an advantage to them. We will do nothing for them. And when the Tz-en reach the desert, we shall meet them on *sildars*."

"And be slaughtered. The only hope you have is to join forces with the El'arans. Not all are like Bar'thazel. Look at E'lias. He and others like him will sacrifice their lives to fight the Tz-en. There are more like them. But they aren't organized and they need the strength of the Shir'ka behind them."

To'mahs moved to speak, but mulled over his words like a *glelk* chewing its *woro*.

"You are as my son," he said at last. "But this clan depends upon me. I cannot commit them as a sacrifice for the El'arans. If the Tz-en cross the desert, then we shall fight them. All the clans. This is not the old glory days, under the M'ji. The M'ji bound our people together through blood, even though cultures separated us. Those days are passed, with the last M'ji."

"To'mahs, I counted on your help. Without your support –"

"Things will go along as they have for these past few years. Little changes."

Perry stood up suddenly. "No. A great deal will change. The Tz-en are growing stronger. They own El'aris. They will soon own the Shir'ka. The Tz-en will have the resources to control the desert. They've all but crushed the El'arans. You and the clans won't be able to escape their fingers."

A cloud shadowed To'mahs's features as he stood to glare at Perry. "No one has ever been permitted to speak to me in this manner. Perry, I am the voice of the clan. You will speak no more of these things."

"Don't worry, I won't. I'll find help somewhere else. Maybe the other clans will listen to reason."

As he turned to leave, Mar'a fell in at his side.

"Mar'a!" cut To'mahs's stern voice. "I forbid you to leave the clan."

"Perry is my clan. I belong with him." Her words lashed back.

Perry placed his hand over her arm. "Wait," he said in little more than a whisper. "Stay here a little while. I've got an idea, but it might be dangerous for both of us. After all, the Tz-en are still looking for me."

"More the reason I should be with you."

"It won't take long. Then we can start things moving in Khadeej."

"Then take me to Khadeej." She shot her father a look of daggers. "I will not stay here."

Perry wrapped his arm around her. "Maybe some of the El'arans in

Khadeej will listen to you, if not me."

They stopped at the tent they shared only long enough for Mar'a to gather a bundle of belongings, then they returned to the flier. Mar'a climbed into the passenger seat and began strapping herself in with a confidence that surprised Perry. After all, she'd never been in a flier before. He dropped into the pilot seat and began a systems check. In a few minutes, the engines rumbled for a vertical lift.

The craft lifted slowly, rotating toward the mountain range. Perry saw To'mahs, standing stiffly outside his tent, watching their departure. The sight was brief, and he couldn't read the Shir'ka's expression. So much depended on the Shir'ka.

CHAPTER NINE
FUGITIVE

Michaels threw a few more chips on the green velvet table. Cards flipped over, mute faces and a variety of numbers. A few young women sighed as the croupier announced the winner. He grimaced. The winner wasn't him. Not for the past five plays.

Time to move on. He rattled the handful of chips still in his pocket.

Finding a corner table, he sat heavily and motioned for another drink.

The casino pulsed with sounds and scents and movements. The motif sprang from a fairy tale concept of the desert nomads. Women in flimsy costumes, the men in flowing robes, curved plastic daggers thrust into silk sashes. Nothing like the Shir'ka. But then none of these employees were even from El'aris. He noticed a Bellatrene accent from his own waitress. He gave a boyish grin at her now as she brought his drink, bending low to offer him an extravagant view.

Why should he even care what had happened to Perry? Perry had lied to him. Perry had survived, but never contacted him. Then he fed him stories a child wouldn't even believe. The point was that Perry had used him.

And he had betrayed Perry and turned him over to the Tz-en.

So? That's what he got paid for. Their friendship didn't exist any more. They weren't those two naive kids from Delnaar. Their ideals fell victim to their profession. Perry had helped him escape his family problems. He never would have survived on the farm, under the thumb of his father. Perry's friendship had eased the troubles. Then, together they fled Delnaar. He'd escaped his father's clutches. He had found excitement, adventure. Now he was just tired.

"I've been looking all over for you, Mick!" Thatcher's voice fell over him like the shadow that covered the table.

Michaels raised his glass in salute. "Good to see you, too, Geoff."

"Why are you wasting your time in here? They got better places than this on Helbent, mate. C'mon. Let's pack up so we can make that cruiser tomorrow."

"I just needed a change of scene."

"This place is a tourist trap, Mick."

A new voice, with a slight hiss to its words, came from his left. "And how many drinks have you imbibed?"

Jiin moved close, slid out one chair, and sat down. She wasn't in uniform, but the long, black dress she wore might well have been one by her attitude.

"Not nearly enough," he said. "Is this an official visit?"

"In a way, yes. The governor wanted me to see if you were still on El'aris. He wanted you to know that Perry has escaped."

"Good."

He raised his glass in a silent salute to his old friend, then gulped it down. He motioned to the waitress and pulled out his credit chip.

"Another, and bring my friends whatever they want."

Jiin shook her head, but Thatcher was quick to order Granite whiskey.

The waitress was back in only a moment, laying his credit chip on the table, but no drinks.

"I'm sorry sir. We cannot access your account."

"Can't access my account? You just did ten minutes ago. What's the problem?"

"Your account has been closed, sir."

Michaels realized that his mouth was hanging open. How could his account be closed? He and Thatcher had been paid by Deltan. They'd set up a special local account, to be transferred when he left El'aris. How could the account be closed?

"Why those dirty, double-dealing –" He glared at Jiin and stabbed his finger at her. "You! You had something to do with this!"

"I assure you that I did not. I am as perplexed as you, though certainly not as irrational."

"It's Deltan! They double-crossed us. I'm going down to Deltan headquarters and give them a lesson in dealing with me!"

"Wait." Jiin clamped her hand over Michaels' wrist as he started to get up. "You won't be allowed in at this time of night. It's probably only a computer glitch. The best scenario is to communicate with Vindal himself.

There is obviously a simple explanation."

"Yeah, right. Let's get to our room and make a few calls."

Thatcher followed in his wake as they headed from the casino. Jiin kept in step.

"Why are you going along?"

"Let us just say that I will be keeping you out of trouble. Since you're leaving tomorrow, I don't want an interstellar incident tonight. Furthermore, it has been suggested that Perry may try to contact you."

In their hotel room, Ringer sat on the couch, feet up, computer on his lap. His head sagged in sleep. Poor fool fell asleep while playing on his computer. Why he insisted on digging through those files and systems, Michaels didn't know. He'd end up driving himself crazy.

Michaels went directly to the communicator and dialed up the bank. A screen popped up with the bank's logo and a female voice calmly stating business hours, which did not happened to be at this particular moment. He could, however, leave a detailed message.

"Mick?"

Michaels turned from the screen to Thatcher, while trying to remember Vindal's number. If he wasn't in his office, he'd get him out of bed.

Thatcher stood behind the couch, hovering over Ringer. Jiin stood beside him.

"Now don't go waking him up," Michaels said. "Leave the poor guy rest."

"Don't think there's much danger of him waking up," Thatcher said.

Michaels moved around the couch and stared down at Ringer.

A fine line cut across Ringer's throat, under the chin. His eyes were closed, the muscles of his face relaxed. Blood drenched his flowered shirt and trousers and soaked into the couch. It had happened no more than an hour.

On Ringers lap sat his computer, its lid open. A curved knife with a brass hilt impaled the machine's keypad, its blade piercing through the plastic casing and into Ringer's leg. Blood covered the blade.

"A Shir'ka dagger," Jiin said.

"You're suggesting a Shir'ka did this? Why?"

Jiin came around to the front of the couch, looked over Ringer's body, then knelt and studied the weapon sticking out of the computer. "I have seen this style before. And I have seen imitations for the tourists. This is real. Look at the artwork on the hilt. It is much more detailed than the imitations, and the blade is much stronger."

"I'm so glad you're an expert on Shir'ka weapons," Michaels said. "That still doesn't answer the question of why a Shir'ka would kill Ringer. He never did them any harm, and whatever he did here recently was for me."

"Maybe they were trying for you, Mick," Thatcher suggested.

"That would make sense," Jiin said.

"Not funny," Michaels said.

"I am not trying to be humorous. I am suggesting, however, that someone has taken exception to you and your coworkers. Since Perry has recently escaped our prison facility, he is the prime suspect."

"Perry? Don't be ridiculous. He had nothing against Ringer. Me, yeah. I captured him. But he'd never make the mistake of killing Ringer instead of me. Besides, it's not his style."

"I suggest we call the local authorities," Jiin said, walking over toward the wall communicator.

"Good," Michaels said. "Let them deal with it. As long as they don't try to pin this on me. You're my alibi, right?"

As she made the call, Michaels stared at Ringer's face. Was that knife intended for him? *Had* Perry done it?

"They are on their way," Jiin said.

She turned back to the communicator screen as the thing beeped. She answered the call, then flipped the hold switch on.

"It's Vindal. He is calling for you."

"Vindal?" He had wanted to talk to the man, now he couldn't think why. At least he could tell him about Ringer.

He took Jiin's place at the communicator and switched on the screen. Vindal's smiling face flashed into existence, twice its normal size. Michaels considered how fitting.

"Mr. Michaels. I have some rather bad news for you. I'm afraid there wasn't much I could do about the situation. I did speak on your behalf, but to no avail. The company executives have made their decision, and we must deal with it. However, I was able to secure some compensation, which might make the situation a little more bearable."

"Vindal, my associate, Mr. Ringer, has just been killed. We're trying to deal with that situation right now."

The smiled vanished. "Oh dear! I'm so sorry to hear that. How did it happen?"

"Just a guess, but I'd say he was murdered. Someone slit his throat and left their calling card. We found a Shir'ka knife, which appears to be the murder weapon."

"Oh my! That may be connected with the situation I was calling about.

Are you certain the knife is Shir'ka?"

"Jiin's the expert. She says it is. Now what were you babbling about?"

"Jon Perry escaped from the prison."

"Yeah, I know. Jiin told me."

"There's an update. A flier was stolen from the airfield in Khadeej. The thief has tentatively been identified as Perry. We tracked the flier until it went over the Ahraj Mountains, into the desert. By the time we had satellite tracking, he must have landed at a nearby Shir'ka camp. We picked him up a short time later, flying back over the mountains and to the outskirts of Khadeej. Then he took off again. We tracked his course as going toward Jhamrahl. Unfortunately, satellite tracking lost him. He was using the river, flying low. But we feel strongly that he was headed toward Jhamrahl."

"What makes you think it was Perry?"

"I can't think of any Shir'ka or El'aran who can fly an aircraft, let alone fly it in such a way that we can't track it. I doubt even Tz-en pilots could do that."

He was right. The Tz-en weren't known for their imagination. And no one else on the planet would be able to fly. Only an off-worlder.

Michaels glanced over at Ringer. He couldn't see the knife sticking in the computer, but he thought of it. He thought of that razor blade slicing into Ringer's throat. Did Perry leave his calling card? It wasn't his style. But then, this wasn't the Perry he knew.

"So you think he killed Ringer?" he asked.

"Of course," Vindal said. "There are not very many Shir'ka in Jhamrahl. In fact, I might say that there are none. It is the logical conclusion that Perry found out where you were staying and attempted to get even with you. Either he mistook your associate for you, or he has delivered a warning to you. Mr. Perry is not quite stable, but I'm certain you are aware of that."

"Okay, okay. I'll consider the possibility that he's behind it."

Vindal went on, "Which brings us to the main point of the situation. Did you have any difficulty with your credit account?"

"Yeah. I was about to call you about that."

"When it was determined that Perry had escaped and was at large, some company executives decided to freeze your assets in the belief that you have not fulfilled your contract."

"What? It's not my fault he escaped. I delivered him, and the Tz-en took over."

"But your contract stated that you would end the terrorism. Since he is at large and stealing fliers, the terrorism has not been stopped. And if we add on the aspect of Mr. Ringer's murder, we see that he has become very dangerous and unpredictable. You are to find him and stop him permanently. The means are left to your expertise. However, you will not be paid until then. I have been able to secure for you a bonus, for expenses. What you already spent in Jhamrahl while you've been waiting for transport will come under that category. I am looking out for your interests, Mr. Michaels. I believe this situation is deplorable, but we must go with the decisions of the executives."

The screen went black, and Michaels swore at the vanished image.

He joined Jiin and Thatcher at the other end of the room and followed their stares toward Ringer.

"Just ain't right," Thatcher said. "He never got a fighting chance. Ain't right."

Long ago, Perry had turned down assassination jobs. It wasn't his style.

Jiin tilted her head, then walked to the body. She bent down, slipped her hand under the couch, and pulled out a small object. She came back and handed it to Michaels.

"A data wafer?" He studied the little square piece of plastic. "Ringer had a hundred of those all over the place."

Jiin shrugged. "There were no others around. None on the table, or the couch, or on the floor. Of course, he might have some in his pockets, but I would rather have the proper authorities search the body."

Michaels held the wafer between his fingers. One more wafer. So what? He dropped it into his shirt pocket, then buttoned the pocket shut.

The door chimed, and Jiin let in the Tz-en police.

Michaels glanced around the office. He'd seen places like this before. The inner workings of bureaucracy. Cubicles and desks and computers. He found Tz-en at their stations, as well as off-worlders. Curiously, he did not notice any El'arans among the office workers.

"So what is this place?" he asked Jiin.

"Census department. They are attempting to reconstruct the census of the population since the consolidation. Many records were lost, and most were not in any type of computer system."

"So this is like that place in Khadeej." He didn't like remembering his first reunion with Perry.

"On a far larger scale. These main computer databases handle the entire population."

"El'aran, Tz-en, and Shir'ka?"

"The Tz-en population is known," she said. "The Shir'ka population is impossible to trace. The El'arans are of more concern, because of the interactions with Tz-en officials. We want to keep track of everyone."

"For taxation?"

"Partly. Work permits, also. We would like to know each person's background."

"And you think Perry broke into this database?"

"Everything suggests it." She motioned toward one work station. "This terminal was activated last night, while we were talking with the police in your rooms. For some reason, no alarms went off. I believe your friend is familiar with security systems. What they noticed this morning were gaps in the database. Someone, presumably Perry, erased various sections. It will take time to replace them. They seem to have been random, nothing connecting the areas."

"Perry doesn't do random. He might have been covering his tracks. Any way to tell what was in those files?"

"Not until the files are retrieved."

Michaels shook his head. "I'm not talking about replacing the data, just what sort of stuff was in them. This is all people oriented information, right? Was he looking for anyone in particular? Or a particular geographical location? Dead people, living people? A certain profession? He was either looking for someone, or information on someone. Can we find out who?"

"I will ask. That may take just as long, depending on how much detail we need."

"Let's look at the generic information first."

During the day, he made some inquiries, none of which delivered. Thatcher wasn't much use at the moment, so Michaels sent him back to Khadeej to discretely look up their young informant. The boy might still prove useful, even though it appeared Perry was now in Jhamrahl.

He waited until evening began to surge over the city, when the tourists turned out in wild herds toward the casinos, before he went to the Red Tarnac. Any earlier, and the best people wouldn't be there yet. Later, and they might be gone or useless. Despite the place not being frequented by tourists, it was crowded with a rather colorful group. Traders, mostly. Some professionals. And a few just odd. There was a girl from Helbent, with severely short hair and wild eyes. She sat with a thin young man with pale hair that stuck straight up. On the other side of the room, a Belgarian merchant bent low over the table, whispering to old Jan Kemmanski. Now there was someone he hadn't seen in ages. Kemmanski used to run a transport business. Maybe he still had a ship. To the left of the bar stood Grips, who had worked with Ringer and had helped them in Khadeej.

And then there was Harry Capetti.

The long, rangy man appeared out of the crowd and grinned at Michaels. He wore a blue flowered shirt and a cap with a logo of some sports team. Michaels wasn't certain what the sport was, let alone the team or planet of origin.

"Well if it ain't Mick!"

Capetti dropped into the chair opposite him and they reached across the table and clasped hands.

"Long time, Harry! Heard you got a real job."

"Yep. Got a nice little cargo hauler. The occasional passenger once in a while. Just minor stuff, like currier runs. This planet is bottled up tight with all the big galactic companies running transports, but I get to squeeze in now and then. Just dropped off a little shipment and I'll be off again in a few days. So, what have you been up to? I see our old friend Jon Perry has landed himself into a mess of trouble. News broadcasts are peppered with him."

"Long story."

"Aren't they all. You know, you should get out of the business before that story has a very abrupt ending. Best thing I ever did, getting my own ship."

"I plan on a nice retirement after leaving here, Harry."

He reached across the table again. "I got to run, Mick. Meet some people, make some deals. My ship's the *Crazy Eight*. I'll be on planet a few days, we should meet, have a drink."

"I'd like that."

Harry Capetti slipped away, heading for the front of the tavern. Michaels was so preoccupied with watching him go that he barely noticed the woman stopping in front of his table.

"Heard you were looking for someone."

She used the toe of her boot to spin around the chair Harry had used and straddled it. Michaels had known other people from Helbent. They all had that crazy look in their eyes. They were good fighters, but their survival rate was low. Any Helbender he ever knew personally was now dead. He wondered how long this one would last. She had that same look in her stark gray eyes and on her tight, drawn face.

She ran her fingers through her short pale blond hair, tousling it slightly. "Name's Hannah. You're Michaels."

"Right."

"Like I said, I heard you're looking."

"Sorry. I don't need anyone right now."

"That's not what I heard. I want off this rock just as bad as anyone else. Nice place to visit, and all that. But I've been here a month. It gets old real fast, especially when you're broke. Now, what are you looking for?"

"Okay," he said, moving in a little closer, not so much for privacy as to just be heard over the ambient noise. He had made a few inquiries earlier, but nothing had panned out. He didn't expect her to have the expertise he wanted. "I need a computer expert. No fighting. No rough stuff. Just computers. Databases, networks, things like that."

"That's it?"

He felt satisfied. She couldn't possibly have the qualifications.

"Yeah."

She bobbed her head slowly. "Thought so. You had the word out earlier today, but I wanted to make sure. Now, I haven't done any computer stuff for maybe a year, but systems don't change that much any more. It's too hard for everyone to keep up. So, what's the job?"

"You know computers?"

"I don't brag, mister. It's what I did on Helbent. It's how I got *off* Helbent. My parents were a bit better off than most, before they got killed. They got me the training, helped get me into a cushy job. Of course, things don't stay stable on Helbent. You probably heard that. I bummed around, got other jobs, bummed some more. Then I got smart. The last job I had, with the government at the time, I used the network to transfer myself off planet. I was gone before anyone realized it, and I haven't looked back since. I even heard they had a price on me, but then that government's probably long gone. Now, do you want to know my jobs since then? I got a list, if you want it, but if you want someone who knows computers, those jobs don't tell you anything. Just set me in front of a keypad, and I'll make it sing."

He couldn't see any way around the situation. "Okay. I'll give you a chance. How early do you turn in?"

She grinned at him. She was attractive, in a stark way, but her smile still sent a chill through him. "Why, what do you have in mind?"

He tried to keep his composure. "Some data work. Downtown."

"Fine, but let's discuss wages first. I don't mind an agreement on a handshake, until we can get it in writing. But I'd like to know what I'm getting myself in for."

"Three hundred a day," he said. He'd add that onto his expenses, since Vindal was so anxious to set that up for him.

She frowned, chilling him just as much as with her grin. "Pretty cheap, there. How about five hundred."

"Three. You got any better offers?"

"Four."

"Okay." What did it matter? The money wasn't coming out of his pay from Deltan. This was just part of his expenses. He shook her hand. Her grip was hard, tight. Too bad they weren't on their way to a fight. She'd be good.

He still had his doubts about Hannah as they walked the distance to the government office building downtown. On the way, he explained the situation to her. She said nothing, but nodded thoughtfully. He expected some questions, but she had none. Most offices were shut down, but the census office was running around the clock to repair the damaged database. Instead of electronic security, Tz-en guards ran the lobby, scrutinizing everyone who entered. Michaels explained that Hannah would be working on the database; that she was to be given clearance to that section. Reluctantly, and only after calls through superior channels, the guards entered her into their security system and provided a temporary pass.

"They don't like me," Hannah observed as they road the elevator up.

"They don't like me either."

"I noticed."

The office manager was a Tz-en who didn't seem to know one end of a computer from the other. He just controlled the people. His name was Li-ju, and he wasn't very pleased to have Michaels bringing in another outsider.

"This is highly irregular," Li-ju said, his white face tightening into a frightful apparition. "I must contact my superiors and get clearance for this ... this person. I was instructed to give you any information you needed, but I was never told about allowing others access to our database and networks."

"The boys downstairs already made the calls. But, hey, if you want, go ahead. Get Pieter Tabor out of bed, if you want. Or the First Minister. I don't care. They'll all tell you the same thing. They want this job done, and done fast. I brought my own expert in to see to it. Now, do you want to explain how you delayed progress so your ego wouldn't get bruised? I'm sure they'll listen to you. You have such a high position in the government."

Li-ju scowled, exposing his canines. "Very well, I will allow your expert a place to work. I am certain she will not get very far. Our people have only replaced a small percentage of the lost data, and we have ten people working continuously."

Hannah sat down at the terminal Li-ju took them to. Michaels leaned against the desk beside her.

"You really can sweet-talk someone, Michaels," she said. "You had that manager eating out of your hand. Better count your fingers."

"He won't bother us. You just show me how good you are, and we'll wrap this up in no time at all."

Hannah's fingers glided over the keypad. She entered the database network and flipped from one screen to another in a flash.

"Listen, Michaels. This'll take a while. This isn't a simple break-in. I need to learn the database first. Each one's different, and I haven't been in many after Helbent. And Helbent isn't known for its sophisticated networks. Why don't you drop in on one of the casinos, see a show or something. Then bring me back a sandwich in a couple hours"

"I thought you were an expert."

"I'm the best one you got, mate. Now shut up."

She came to a highlighted menu which requested another code. She brought up a directory and then entered a series of sub-directories.

"Your friend deleted a lot," she said. "He covered his tracks real good. Too bad we can't cross-reference these things to your friend. It would make things go quicker. I can get sub-directories of those deleted files, but what difference does it make? Even if we had all the files intact, we still wouldn't know which one he was interested in. Maybe it's a good thing you didn't feel like taking in a show."

"Why?"

"I can't cross-reference with other files, but I can cross-reference with you. Now, why would your friend be interested in El'aran dock workers?"

"I don't know."

"How about El'arans born within the past year. Or El'arans with family names between M'jor and Naf'la living in Jhortahl. I think that's a fishing village in the south. Or farmers in the Achari district. Or El'arans who formerly owned property in Jhamrahl. Or criminals held in Khadeej. Or glass dealers in Jhamrahl. Or factory workers in Basenda. Or women with –"

"Criminals? In Khadeej? What was that?"

"Huh? Oh, there was a file listed as political criminals incarcerated in the prison in Khadeej. Don't they have a prison around here?"

"I don't know. The one in Khadeej is pretty old, though. Perry escaped from there."

"Coincidence?"

Michaels shrugged, lifting up his hands. "Beats me. Why would he be interested in a political prisoner. What constitutes a political prisoner, anyway?"

She backed into another sub-directory. "According to the criteria, it could be anything from terrorism to tax evasion. And from what I've heard, tax evasion could be not being able to pay the high taxes. Think there's a connection?"

"We'll put a priority on those files, then check them against Perry's brief stay in the prison."

She ran down the list of files that had been deleted. He didn't find anything particularly noteworthy. The only thing that sparked his interest was the prison list. He went to Li-ju, who was uninterested.

"How can we get the files that had been deleted that came from the prison?"

"Get them from the prison," Li-ju said. "It is where they came from."

"Make a call or whatever you have to do," Michaels said.

Li-ju glared at him. "We are busy with more critical matters. Most of the staff has left. If our schedule allows, we will submit your request in the morning."

When Michaels returned to Hannah, he said, "Li-ju wasn't much help. He obviously isn't impressed by the massive amount of political power I weld."

"Did he say we can get those missing files through the prison records in Khadeej?"

"Yeah. Why?"

She tapped furiously on the keypad. "Because I'm in their system now."

A list of names appeared on the screen. As she scrolled down, he realized there were thousands of names. Each one had its own file to enter, with more specific data that whatever clerk felt inclined to record. She entered a few files at random. Some had dates of incarceration. Some had offenses listed. Some were specified as transferred, though the destination was not given. Not one file was complete.

"Where would they transfer prisoners?"

"To work in the mines," Michaels said.

"You know what's missing on these files. A release date. Most have sentencing dates, or at least dates when they were put in prison. But I can't find how long the sentence is."

"Probably in court records," he suggested. "Try searching for Perry's name."

"Easy."

She brought up the file, which was a little more complete than others. He was a political prisoner for acts of terrorism. The incarceration date was listed, as well as cell designation. There was no mention of his escape. Of course, once he was gone why would they bother updating his file.

"Now, reference other prisoners there at the same time."

A few hundred names popped up at that request. That certainly narrowed the field. But what common denominator would show what Perry was looking for?

"How about the cells? When I paid the place a visit, it didn't look as though anyone shared a room. But what about the cells on either side, or across the hall, or whatever."

She tapped out the request. "I get two people in the one cell, three in the other. Of course, there are different dates of incarceration. No release dates. One was transferred, but no date given. Here's the two latest prisoners. Political prisoner named Jor'm and a convicted thief by the name of Mor'hahd. Says here that Jor'm was in for tax evasion."

"Jor'm and Mor'hahd," Michaels repeated. "Not much to go on. Probably a dead end, Perry's idea of a joke."

"He doesn't strike me as someone who goes in for practical jokes."

"You'd be surprised. Anyway, we'll check on them. Thatcher's in Khadeej. Maybe I'll have him look in on them, toss them a few questions. In the meantime, let's keep digging through those other files."

"Fine. That's what I'm getting paid for."

CHAPTER TEN
IN BASENDA AND KHADEEJ

The house was little more than a shack on a worn dirt street lined with other shacks of various sizes, shapes, and degrees of decay. Not far south, the lights of Jhamrahl lit the sky with a glow rivaling the Carino Nebula to the north. Here in Basenda, darkness reigned. It filled the streets like a heavy rain cloud of despair. The feeble lights burning in the windows of a few shacks could not dispel the gloom. No one bothered to watch the display in the southern sky. No one in Basenda cared for the glitter that had become Jhamrahl. Once, they may have had pride in that city. Once, before the war that ended life as they knew it. Trapped, they were dead to the pleasures Jhamrahl offered. Those things were for off-worlders, tourists who paid fortunes for entertainment forbidden to El'arans. El'arans needed permits even to walk the streets of Jhamrahl. A precious few who had shown their loyalty to the Tz-en were permitted to live within the city, to run businesses now owned by Tz-en, or even to work at menial jobs. To most El'arans, Jhamrahl was a closed city. Once the glory of the planet, now an icon of off-world temptations.

Basenda had always been a small town, an outreach to the farms and the forests of the north. When El'arans were forced from Jhamrahl, the shanty towns popped up around Basenda. Jhamrahl's factories and docks provided jobs. Basenda provided a place to live.

Perry had searched through the streets in the darkness. The few people he met had refused to help him. He was a stranger. Some recognized him as a Shir'ka dressed as an El'aran. Others, unfamiliar with Shir'ka, considered him an off-worlder. Two had offered to answer his questions, since they knew he was not a Tz-en. He passed money to each, and they scurried off to their own respective shacks. Eventually, he found the house. The computer database had merely given a general area within Basenda's outskirts. It had taken a number of cross-references, but he had located them. Now he stood outside the house of unpainted wood and plastic, a patchwork affair much like the others, with a curl of smoke rising up from the stone chimney, carrying the fragrance of cooking vegetables.

The woman who answered the door surprised him. He had expected someone older. Or perhaps she was, but merely wore her age well. Suspicion fell over smooth features that might well have been beautiful in her youth. Bold brown eyes studied him.

"Yes?"

"R'behka?"

"Yes?" she repeated, more sternly this time.

"I'm a friend of Jor'm."

Her face whitened in the gloom. Her eyes widened, and she clutched her hands close to herself. He was aware that she was no longer breathing.

"Jor'm? Is he ... Where is he? Is he alive?"

"He's alive, but still a prisoner in Khadeej."

"Khadeej," she whispered. She sagged against the door frame. "So long. They never told us. I tried to find out where he was, to get him released. Even after they took the farm from us, they still would not release him.

The woman who answered the door surprised him.

They never let me see him, never let me know where he was. They even threatened to throw me into prison. How is he?"

"As well as can be expected."

She glanced down the dark street, then motioned him inside.

A fire chased away the chill of the evening. A black pot hung on a metal hook over the fire. The stewing vegetables filled the little house with their aroma. The home's interior held no resemblance to a shack. The scant furniture was worn and comfortable. Quaint objects sat about: Shir'ka glass figurines, objects carved from wood, a framed photograph of a younger Jor'm and R'behka in happier times. From what he could see, the plumbing was serviceable in the tiny kitchen. He wondered about the water and sewer service in this shanty town. Obviously it was better than he thought. From the battery-powered lamp on the one stand he assumed they had no electricity.

"Jor'm told me about you and your son," he said as he settled into the chair opposite from her. "And about your farm. The government took it from you, didn't they?"

She nodded, swaying slightly. "They raised our taxes higher than we could afford. They did that to many of us. When we couldn't pay the full amount, they took Jor'm away and confiscated the farm. Even with the property, they still wouldn't let Jor'm go. I don't even think there was a trial."

"I doubt it. It's a rather clumsy tactic to gain control, but it worked. Did they bring someone in to work your farm?"

"No. That was the awful thing. It went to ruin. They did nothing with it. And they did the same with other places, from what I've heard since we came here. They throw our men into prison, steal our property, then try to starve us to death. Many have come here, or to places like it. It disgusts us to work in factories now owned by the Tz-en, but we must eat." She turned to stare into the fire.

"Where's your son?" he asked.

"He should be home soon. He's a dock worker at the space port. It's a better job than working in the factories outside Jhamrahl. Too many people are hurt or killed. The Tz-en don't care about safety. After all, we're only El'arans. But at the port, things are more visible. They want to impress the off-worlders." She stopped and looked steadily at Perry.

"Yes," he said. "I'm an off-worlder."

"I thought you were a Shir'ka at first, but it's been so long since I saw one. I've never seen any dressed in our clothes, either. Of course, times change. Your accent is Shir'ka. And you have the bearing of a Shir'ka. Proud, almost noble."

"I've lived among them. They adopted me."

"You should feel honored."

"Not every El'aran feels the same about the Shir'ka."

"You have been talking to the wrong El'arans. Those who are ignorant may be frightened by them. Those traders who look after their own interests may not trust them, but they do not trust their fellow El'arans, either. Those of us who know have a great respect for the Shir'ka. You have lived in good company."

"You don't seem much like a farmer's wife," he said.

She twisted her long, delicate fingers. "I have been many things in my long years. And it is strange for an outsider, let alone an off-worlder, to live among the Shir'ka as an equal."

"I've been many things, too." He smiled, and she mirrored it.

The door swung open and in came a young man in his early twenties. He was tall, broad-shouldered, and relatively handsome under the waves of light brown hair. The sleeves of his shirt were rolled back, expose thick, muscular arms and callous hands. Lines creased his face, evidence of a hard life. His eyes fell on Perry and he stopped short. He glanced at R'behka as he closed the door behind him.

"This man knows Jor'm," R'behka said quickly.

The young man came closer to stand beside her chair, looking down at their visitor with a protective glare.

"Really?" He was not easily convinced. "How?"

"In the prison at Khadeej," Perry said.

"So you were a prisoner?"

"For a time. With Jor'm's help, I left."

"Escape? I've never heard of anyone escaping from the Khadeej prison."

"It happens now and then," Perry said.

"What do you want?"

"I'm here on urgent business, and I can't waste time. Time is something we don't have in abundance."

The young man's eyes narrowed. He wagged his finger at Perry. "I know you. I've seen you somewhere. On the news broadcast, at the port the other day. You're that off-worlder, the terrorist. I want you out of this house immediately!"

Perry crossed his legs and leaned back in the chair. "My name is Jon Perry. Eleven years ago, I was hired to help the Tz-en take over the planet.

Since then, I've been living with the Shir'ka and learning what the Tz-en have done to El'aris. I've been in your prisons; I've been in the mines. I've felt the rod of the Tz-en just as much as any Shir'ka or El'aran. This planet is my home now, and the fight against the Tz-en is my fight. The so-called terrorism I've been accused of has been against the Tz-en government. And I'll continue it until the Tz-en are driven back to their home."

"Nice speech," K'leb said. "Why didn't you say that on the broadcast? It was your confession, you know."

"And you know the Tz-en create lies. I never made that confession. It was fabricated. It's what the Tz-en wanted others to hear. Now, there are more important matters that need our attention. You must come back to Khadeej with me."

"Khadeej? I have a job here. I have no intentions of running off, especially with the likes of you. My mother depends upon me."

"She'll go too, of course. There are some safe places where she can stay. I'm afraid this place may not be very safe after my visit. I tried to wipe out the computer databases with references to you, but there must be backups they'll be able to access. They'll trace my actions soon and be here to investigate. Although they won't be able to guess why I've come here." Perry knew Michaels didn't have the computer expertise, but he'd find a way to dig. He had no choice but to erase more sections of the database than were necessary. The system would have recorded his log-on for the search of Jor'm's family, and the Tz-en would be on Basenda in no time if he hadn't made things a little more difficult. Still, Michaels would not be far behind. He had tenacity.

"You aren't making sense," K'leb said.

"On the contrary. There is a movement to restore El'aris to the El'arans. However, we don't have a consensus. Our people are divided, and I can't pull them together since I'm an off-worlder. That's where I need you. You can bring the people together, El'aran and Shir'ka, so that we can stand up in force against the Tz-en."

"That's insane! The Tz-en have modern weapons. That's how they took control. You above anyone should know that. What can farmers and merchants and factory workers do against blasters? And what could I possibly do to bring them together? I'm not strategist, or a general, or –"

"No, you're the M'ji," Perry said.

K'leb stared at him. "What?"

"I know the truth. Jor'm and R'behka never had a child, not until after they fled the palace during the war. All of a sudden they had a ten year old son. I found that information in the database, though no one happened to notice the inconsistencies. It might have stayed hidden forever had Jor'm and R'behka changed their names. I'm surprised none of you thought of that."

R'behka shrugged. "It never occurred to us. We were never that important in the government."

"Mother! Don't say any more. This man's an off-worlder."

She took his hand in both of hers. "And he's trying to help. He knows the truth, my dear. And he needs your help."

"I know you're the son of J'siah," Perry said. "You're Dh'vid, the only living heir to the M'ji throne. Of anyone on this planet, you're the only one who can pull the people together to fight the Tz-en. Only the M'ji could lead both the El'arans and the Shir'ka, and if they do not join forces, they can't win."

"They can't win anyway. I'm a dock worker, not a M'ji. I move cargo around. I couldn't lead anyone, let alone a planetary revolt."

"Look at your hands," Perry told him.

Despite himself, he raised his hands up to look at them. Callous, strong.

Perry went on. "Do you remember your father? The only time I saw him was when he died. I tried to stop the killing, but the Tz-en warriors had gone wild. I'll make no excuses for myself, though. I was his enemy then, but I watched as he fought the Tz-en. He was a brave man. His blood runs through those hands. Tell me now that you wouldn't like to feel those fingers around the neck of one of those Tz-en. Tell me you wouldn't like to go back to that time and fight by his side."

K'leb's fingers curled into clenched fists. His knuckles turned white as he squeezed. He spun toward the fire, his back to Perry.

"Every day," he said, his voice strained tight. "Every day I think of that. I should have fought. I should have been at their side. But I was taken away. I went with Jor'm. I ran from the fight."

"No, you didn't run from the fight," Perry said quietly. "You ran toward one yet to come. There was nothing that could be done. Your father knew that. But if they could save you, there was hope for a future. That hope almost failed, except for Jor'm. Now, will you fulfill that hope?"

R'behka got up and went to a cabinet. Bending down and reaching inside, she withdrew something wrapped in an old cloth. Pulling the wrap away, she held an old scanning device. "Jor'm saved this when we fled the palace. He told me it would be important some day. I think this is the day."

K'leb turned and took the device, staring down at the crest emblazoned on the casing.

"It's time," K'leb said, handing the device to Perry. "How I've dreamed, day and night, of wiping the Tz-en off the face of El'aris. The nightmares haven't stopped. Every night, even in the day, I can't escape them. I'm no M'ji, but I'll fight. I'll fight them alone if I have to. But it's time."

"You won't fight alone, don't worry about that. We've got to move quickly. We've got to get to Khadeej, and then into the desert to meet with the Shir'ka. Both of you gather together what you want to take."

K'leb shook his head. "I don't trust you, Perry. In a way you're responsible for this, and I don't know your motives now. I'll see for myself what's going on. If you betray us, I'll kill you. Now let's go."

Thatcher leaned in the corner, arms curled over his big chest, an expression of boredom on his broad face that was still intimidating.

Michaels sat in the old wooden chair, elbows on the pitted, scratched table. He watched the thin old man opposite him. The man stank, so Michaels tried to breathe through his mouth but not be obvious about it. The old man's clothes were rags. His hair and beard were matted and unwashed. He doubted the Tz-en worried about prisoner hygiene. There were no political activist groups to lobby for prison reform on El'aris, and few off-worlders would ever see the inside of this prison. Jor'm had been in prison five years for tax evasion. According to the meager records, he was never officially sentenced. He was merely thrown into prison for not paying his over-inflated taxes. Of course, while in prison he'd never earn money to pay up his delinquent taxes, so he'd just stay in prison.

"How would you like to be released?" Michaels asked him.

Jor'm's grime-stained face turned to stare at Michaels. He remained quiet.

"I'm sure you'd like to get back to your family, after all this time. I could arrange for your release. All you have to do is cooperate with me. Answer a few questions. You could be out of here, on your way home, in an hour."

Jor'm gave a small shake of his head, rustling his coarse hair. "I don't think so."

This one wasn't your typical El'aran. Of course he suspected Michaels' motives. That was expected. But there was something more that Michaels couldn't put his finger on. The man was hiding something. He could feel it.

Michaels flashed his friendliest grin and opened his hands. "All I want to know is about another man who was in the prison a few days ago, in the cell next to yours. I need to find him. You might have heard something to help me locate him."

"If you haven't noticed," Jor'm said, his voice cracking like shattering ice, "we aren't encouraged to socialize with our fellow prisoners."

"That doesn't mean you can't talk in some way. Sitting in a cell, all alone, gets to you after a while. Believe me, I know. The man wasn't there for very long, but you might have talked with him through the openings in the doors, or heard someone else talk to him." Michaels couldn't shake the memory of his own incarceration on Illiniar III. The Gnorlinians were not the most abiding hosts. He'd been in their care for nearly a year before he escaped. He couldn't imagine Jor'm living in these conditions for long. Jor'm had been a farmer, not a soldier. He couldn't possibly be used to such a hard life.

"His name was Perry. He's an off-worlder," Michaels said. "You might have noticed his accent, or you might have thought he was a Shir'ka. He was disguised as a Shir'ka."

Jor'm shrugged. "We don't get many Shir'ka down there. I think the last one who used that cell was from Achari. Or was it Basenda? I just can't remember any more."

Michaels sat back and crossed his legs. "Yeah, right."

How could he get the man to open up? This wasn't as simple as giving him a banquet. That strategy may have worked on J'sef, but Jor'm was a bit too clever. There had to be something that could be used as leverage, something that would break him. After all, he was only a farmer. The records stated he had a wife and son. The farm had been taken when he was put in prison.

"Have you seen your wife and son since you've been in here?" he asked. After all, just because he had a problem with his own family didn't mean everyone else did. Perry had a good family relationship, before he lost both his parents. Michaels was just disowned by his.

Jor'm's eyes turned away.

Michaels flashed his grin as honest and reassuring as he could. "You could be with them again. In a few short hours. Just cooperate. I'll see that the charges are dropped and you're released, free and clear. No strings. What d'you say? After all, you don't owe Perry anything. He's an off-worlder."

"Why are you interested?"

"Because he's a terrorist. I want to stop him before he hurts anyone. But I need help to find him. Will you help me?"

"No."

"If you don't cooperate with me, some other people might take more drastic measures," Michaels said. He glanced at Thatcher, who put on his scowl in preparation for his roll as the bad guy interrogator. Jor'm didn't seem impressed. "The Tz-en want this guy, and they'll stop at nothing to get him. If they think you have any information, they'll pick you apart. They aren't very civilized when it comes to interrogation. I just want to get this done nice and clean. Perry used to be a friend of mine. I want to find him before anyone gets hurt. So, will you help?"

"I don't have anything to say. This man could have been three meters tall with six tentacles and eyestalks, for all that I know. I never saw him or spoke to him. Now, do you consider that cooperation?"

Jor'm said nothing more as the guards came at Thatcher's biding and escorted him away. Michaels leaned forward in the chair, cradling his head in his hands. He heard Thatcher close the door and walk over to drop heavily onto the other chair. The wood creaked in protest.

"Think he's lying? Think he knows something, Mick?"

Michaels lifted his head. "Oh, he's hiding something. I just don't know what. It may be useless to us, but all the universe to him."

"Shall we rough him over?"

"Did you see the shape he's in? He's been here for years. He's half dead now. You try anything rough on him, and he'll die and we get nothing."

"How about the truth drugs? Vindal could get us a supply. Maybe even the Tz-en have something."

"Only as a last resort. That stuff could kill him, too, and a lot quicker. His system is crap. We start pumping drugs into him, everything might shut down. No, I have another idea. It's a little old fashioned, but it might work. First, we'll contact Hannah in Jhamrahl. She should be able to get the information we need by now. That database is almost restored. Then I want a troop of Tz-en. It's about time we use them for some leg-work."

"Sure. What about that kid?"

"J'sef? We'll keep our meeting with him. Maybe he'll have something useful."

Michaels couldn't hide his disappointment. He and Thatcher found J'sef inside the old shop, just as J'sef had said. The shop had been a clothier at one time, but had been boarded up some years ago. Only a few signs still hanging on the faded walls and over the outside storefront proclaimed what it had once been. Every bit of furnishing was gone. Dust, garbage, and a few wooden crates littered the floor. Utilities had long been shut off. The only light came filtering through dust clouds from cracks in the planks over the shuttered windows. It was much like the shop on its right, which was like the one on the left, which was like the one across the street. This section of Khadeej had not done as well as the main market street. Shops that had catered to a higher income level quickly vanished after the Tz-en took control.

J'sef had let them through the back door, which he locked afterward. Michaels noticed the lock was new. The front door was heavily boarded, with the nail heads shinier than in other places. He suspected J'sef had moved in, probably living upstairs. He had secured the place, and might have traps set for any invaders.

J'sef sat on an upturned crate and answered Michaels' questions.

He knew nothing about Perry. No word had come of Perry's location. Perry had been in the desert, stopped briefly in Khadeej, but disappeared.

Michaels scowled. "Well then, what do you have?"

A wry smile tugged at one corner of the boy's mouth. "The people who follow him, they're still on the move. Not as many, but they're still there. Didn't I lead you to them before?"

"Yeah." Michaels felt cautious. He wanted Perry. Maybe one of these others would know where he went. Maybe he was just wasting his time with this kid.

The boy's face gleamed. "I know where they are."

"You mean each one?"

"No. The main ones. There's a house, and some of them are staying there. I know where that house is."

"Who's staying there? Where is it?"

"It's here, in Khadeej, of course." He rattled off a number of El'aran names, which sounded too much alike to Michaels.

"Okay, just take us there."

J'sef pursed his lips. "How much?"

The kid learned fast. Michaels dug into his pockets. This was definitely going on his expenses. If the kid wasn't right about this, he was personally going to throw him back into that prison cell. He pulled out some wrinkled bills and a few coins.

"More if this turns out good," he said. "And I don't have to tell you what'll happen if this is a waste of time. Now, take us there."

J'sef bent his head to look through the cracks in the boards over the storefront. "Sun's going down. No one will notice if you walk far behind me. I'll make sure you don't lose me."

Michaels smirked. "Gee, thanks."

J'sef hopped from the crate and unlocked the back door. He stuck his head out and looked up and down the alley. Then he sunk back into the shadows behind the door as he opened it just wide enough for Thatcher to squeeze through.

"Go right to the end of the alley," he told Michaels. "Then circle the block. I'll go down the left side of the alley and wait for you to come around the corner. Stay back far enough and I'll lead you to the house. It should be dark by the time we get there."

Michaels felt foolish. The kid must be watching spy vids or something. These antics wouldn't deceive an expert. True, most casual observers would see the two off-worlders walking alone. Some might associate them with the youth, thinking he was their prey and not their accomplice. But the kid was so smug, as though he were in control.

They quickly left the abandoned businesses behind and came into streets lined with houses butted up against each other. Beyond these, the homes were in slightly better condition and wider spaced. Residents were settling in for evening meals as the sun set and blanketed Khadeej with a cool darkness.

Ahead of them, J'sef vanished. Michaels squinted through the gloom, but he could see nothing but the deserted street.

As they walked further, they passed a small patch of bushes growing in front of one house. The bushes emitted a sound like escaping steam.

"Psst!"

"Where are you?" Michaels whispered sternly. After a few seconds, he could make out the shape of the kid's body crouched behind the shrubbery.

"It's right across the street. Look."

The house looked like any other. Through one oval front window he saw a young woman with dark hair. Two young men appeared behind her from a rear room. One went to the window and pulled a privacy screen across it.

"She looked familiar," he mumbled.

"Yeah," Thatcher said. "Perry's friend."

"That's Mar'a," J'sef whispered from behind them. "She's staying there for now. She's a Shir'ka and she's Perry's wife."

"Wife?" Michaels stared at the shapes playing over the privacy screens. Had Perry actually married a Shir'ka? When had he fit that into his life? Had he done it to win the confidence of the locals? He wondered just how much this woman might mean to Perry?

"I'd like to talk with her," he said.

"I don't think they'll let you in for a social visit, Mick," Thatcher said.

"Then we'll have to invite ourselves. A few dozen Tz-en will help get the door open. Geoff, go get some troops, fully rigged, and get them back here on the double. I'll stay here and keep an eye on the house."

If he was supposed to cooperate with the Tz-en authorities, they had better do the same and provide the manpower. With enough soldiers to cover the front and back, they could take the house and anyone inside. These people weren't soldiers, but he wasn't going to take any chances.

Soon, Thatcher returned with six Tz-en. Eight had been sent to the alley to cover the rear.

Michaels pulled out his blaster and ran across the street, Thatcher and the others trailing him. He fired into the door, three shots shattering the lock and hinges. Thatcher's shoulder shoved the heavy panel inward, where it crashed to the floor.

The lights winked out inside the house. A shadow hurtled through the air, slamming into Thatcher and sending him sprawling onto the floor. Michaels crouched in the doorway, leading with his blaster. In the darkness, he made out Thatcher's body moving under the remains of a wooden chair that had been used as a projectile. He turned his attention to the room, trying to hear signs of life over Thatcher's rumbling groans. He could feel someone inside, waiting, silent. Behind him, the Tz-en crowded for their chance. He felt inclined to let them charge in first and receive the initial volley of energy bolts that surely must be waiting.

Blaster fire came from the back of the house. Damn! He only wanted the other Tz-en to watch the rear, stop anyone from escaping. It sounded as though they were blasting their way through the back walls.

He shouldn't have sent for the Tz-en. They'd ruin everything. If he didn't act immediately, they'd kill everyone in the house.

He leaped through the doorway and rolled across the floor. Blaster bolts strafed the carpet, trailing him as he scrambled for cover behind an old couch.

Whoever shot at him had wedged a thick chair in a doorway, using the chair for cover and the doorway as a possible escape to the rear of the house. They continued to fire, their bolts burning deep into the couch in front of Michaels, setting the material aflame and preventing him from taking aim to return fire.

Tz-en at the front door distracted the fire momentarily. Two men fell before the others had sense enough to keep back. The Tz-en blasting their way through the back of the house had less sense. Michaels heard them storming into the house, weapons tearing into the walls, floors, and ceiling.

The person hiding behind the chair turned to fire at the advancing rear guard.

Michaels climbed from behind the smoldering couch, ran low across the room, and hurled himself unto the person.

A blaster slammed against the side of his face. A knee struck low, fortunately only numbing his thigh. A fist pelted the other side of his face before he could strike a few blows in return. He knocked his opponent down, and in the beams of torches carried by some of the Tz-en, he saw that it was the Shir'ka woman.

He held out his blaster menacingly, though he didn't intend to shoot. Before he could offer his ultimatum, her foot struck out and sent the blaster flying. One blow struck hard on his chin, backing him into the overturned chair. A foot went deep into his chest.

His own fist went out blindly, catching the woman on the side of the head. She tumbled back, and he hit out a few more times.

"Don't shoot! Don't shoot!" he shouted, wondering if the Tz-en would bother to listen to him. They were likely to shoot him as well as her.

Another hit, and the Shir'ka dropped to the floor. Two Tz-en from the rear guard grabbed hold of her and jerked her roughly up, each man clasping tightly to her arms. A third wormed his way in, grabbed hold of her thick hair to bent back her head, and shoved the hot muzzle of his blaster into her neck.

"Don't shoot, you idiot!" Michaels shouted.

Behind him, the chair was shoved out of the way. Thatcher grunted as he stood just behind Michaels.

"We'll interrogate her," the Tz-en holding her said.

"I'll question her," Michaels said calmly. "You just secure her and check the house. If anyone else is here, I'd prefer them breathing so we can question them, too."

The man jerked his head toward the rear of the house. "One man came out the back. He was not intent on being captured."

"So you blew up half the house?"

"We secured the house and prevented escape."

"I wanted prisoners, not a demolition party. You'd have blasted her if I hadn't gotten to her first. Now go search the house, like I said."

The Tz-en opened his mouth, but evidently thought better of what he was about to say and closed it again. With a curt nod, he released the girl and, motioning to the rest of his men, left. The two still holding her bound her wrists behind her back with a pair of binder cuffs. They followed Michaels into the front room, guiding her by holding onto each arm.

Thatcher found the lights and illuminated the debris scattered over the room.

Michaels wiped the blood from his mouth and from the corner of his right eye. Half his face stung from the blow of the blaster. His body ached. She was a good fighter, and, even bruised and beat, she was still a beautiful woman.

"What's your name?" he asked.

She stared at him with those incredible green eyes. He felt the chill of her glare, as though she were willing him death. What was it that kid had called her?

"Okay, Mar'a," he said, "you don't have to cooperate. I don't need you to cooperate. All I want is to talk to Perry. Now you can help me voluntarily, or you can help me involuntarily. Same objective. What'll it be?"

She stood her ground silently, never taking her eyes off him.

"What does he mean to you, anyway?" he asked. He wiped away the blood from his eye. "Friend? Lover? What? Did he make wild promises? Did he pay you?"

A ghost of a smile tugged at her lips. He couldn't guess which word sparked her humor.

He dropped into a chair, still facing her. It felt good to sit. Maybe he was just getting too old for this work.

"Okay. Let me put it this way. What do you owe Perry? He's an off-worlder. He was using you and your people to do a job. We've got his confession. Some company paid him to ruin this planet's economy and government. I don't know what he told you and your friends, but I doubt it's anywhere near the truth. He's a professional. He's done the same stuff on other planets. I should know. We were both here eleven years ago to help the Tz-en. Did he ever tell you that? He was pretty instrumental in training and leading the Tz-en troops in overthrowing the El'aran government. Now he's working against the Tz-en. You see, in our profession, it doesn't matter what side we're on, just who pays the bills. We used to work together. Now we're on opposite sides. That happens in our business, too." He shrugged, not quite feeling as casual as he tried to sound.

"Now," he went on, since she remained silent, her stare locked on him, "I need to find him. My job is to stop him from doing his job. I don't know what he is to you, but if you care anything about him, you'll help me. If I don't get to him first, the Tz-en will eventually find him. They won't be as considerate, and a lot of people will die before they get hold of Perry. And they won't worry about what condition he's in when they bring him in. Me ... We used to be friends. That still counts for something in my book. I'll do my best to see he gets a square deal. If you help, I have a better chance. If you don't, the Tz-en will end up tearing El'aris apart. So, Mar'a, do you want to help Perry?"

She cocked her head to one side, her hair cascading over her shoulder like a midnight waterfall. "He told me about you. Many times, many things. You were part of his life before coming here. That life is over, but not forgotten. I know you as well as he does. Do you think he would believe your words?"

Michaels scowled, then caught himself.

She smiled openly, though for the briefest moment. She'd caught him.

"I want to help him," he said.

"That, I believe. But you do not know what help he needs. Your views oppose."

He watched her for a few minutes. This was no ordinary woman. She wasn't a simple-minded barbarian. If all Shir'ka had half the brains and spirit this girl had, the Tz-en would lose their position of power once they moved against the clans. By then, he'd be long gone from El'aris. In the meantime, he saw no way of tricking her into helping him.

"Okay. I take it I can't rely on your cooperation. We'll just have to do it the hard way. You'll still help us, and you won't even have to do a thing."

He nodded to the soldiers. They turned her around and led her out the door.

When they were left alone, Thatcher righted the overturned chair and flopped into it.

"What's the plan, Mick?"

Michaels ran his fingers through his hair. The waves were sticky with sweat. He sat back, stretching his feet out. "She's the bait. We'll rely on J'sef to pass the word. It'll reach Perry."

"You don't want to press the girl? Press hard enough, she'll spill what she knows."

Michaels shook his head. "No she won't. Don't be so confident that everyone breaks. She's not the type."

"You got that in just a few minutes? That wasn't much of an interrogation, Mick."

"It wasn't meant to be. And with someone like her, a few minutes is enough to learn a lot. Of course, I couldn't tell a thing until she opened her mouth." He thought about her accent, wondering if all Shir'ka roll their r's the way she did. "She won't betray Perry, no matter what their relationship is. If we let the Tz-en work on her, she'd just be dead. She won't break."

"Everyone's got a breaking point."

"You're thinking from the point of someone getting paid for a job. It's different with her. She'd be dead before she'd ever break."

"You expect Perry to give himself up just because you have her locked up? You don't even know what kind of relationship they've got."

"No, it wouldn't be that simple. Even if they're tight, Perry's too much of a professional to risk everything just because she's in jail. There has to be more at stake to appeal to his emotions and override his professional senses. Her life has to be in the balance. Her life for Perry's freedom."

"So you plan to kill her?"

"As far as the plan ... the Tz-en are going to execute her. I'm the good guy who can stop it if I can trade Perry for her. That's the story, and I think our Tz-en friends will go along with it. Jiin can take care of that. Of course, there won't be any real execution plans. Just the motions to make it seem real enough. In case this backfires, I don't want her actually dead. That's why I'm relying on the Tz-en for that, through Jiin. I don't think Perry would ever believe I'd have her, or anyone else, killed out of hand. He'd know something was up. But he knows the Tz-en would use any excuse to kill anyone. But seeing as I have influence, I'd be able to stop it. That's the story J'sef will pass on. Right?"

"Right. I'll talk to the kid."

CHAPTER ELEVEN
THE FIRE IN THE SMOKE

Perry walked into the room, throwing back the hood of his cloak. The men sitting around the room looked up instantly. Their despondent expressions faded into a mix of surprise and shock. E'lias, his face the darkest of all, brightened as he shot to his feet. Aba'shal leaned forward, hands on his knees, and smiled warmly. A'brem sank his round body deeper into the cushions, his fingers tapping the arm of the chair.

L'dhar folded his arms and gave a nod. Three other men who had been standing drew closer. Another stepped to the heavy drapes hanging over the window and peered out into the dark street.

"Perry!" E'lias said. "So much has happened. Have you heard –"

"As you see," L'dhar said, "we received your message. We have gathered here, but at great personal risk. This revolution of yours is beginning to cost."

Perry caught each set of eyes across the room. "What's happened?"

"Mar'a has been captured," E'lias said. "At my brother's house. Ja'nus was with her at the time. They killed him."

Perry reached out to lay his hand on E'lias's shoulder. "E'lias, I'm so sorry. What happened?"

The young El'aran shook his head. "I was there, but had left. From what we've been able to learn, the off-worlder Michaels led the Tz-en on an attack of the house. Ja'nus was shot down. Mar'a was arrested. Later, the Tz-en released a statement that she will be executed for terrorism. But we got word through some of the local shopkeepers that Michaels will intercede on her behalf if you surrender yourself."

A'brem rolled uneasily in his chair. "You see. Bar'thazel was right. We can't win. Like L'dhar said, this is becoming too expensive. Our lives are in danger for just being here. Not just a threat of prison, but execution."

Perry let out a deep, tired sigh. How long would they stay blind and helpless? "Ja'nus wasn't the first to die in this. Thousands died eleven years ago. Hundreds since, a little at a time. Ja'nus died for your freedom from the Tz-en. Do you think freedom comes cheap? It doesn't. I've been telling you that all along. Any one of you could be killed for questioning the Tz-en government. They can imprison or kill anyone they want, no matter what the reason. A rebellion is only one more excuse. If you'd rather roll over and submit to their domination, then you should never have joined us. Each of you, even Bar'thazel, knew the risk. If you're unwilling to pay that risk, then get out now. Right now!"

He threw his finger toward the door and glared at each one in turn.

"But if you want to put an end to this hell on your planet, not just for yourself, but for your entire people, then stay. Be warned of the cost. It isn't cheap. The Tz-en won't step down just because you ask them nicely. You have to fight. Maybe you won't have to carry a blaster, but you have to show the bravery of those who will. It may take years, but you can never give up. A'brem, are you ready to leave? If you question this action, you have no place here. Neither do you, L'dhar."

The carpenter lowered his thick brow. "I'll not be named a coward. I'll stay and carry my weight."

"I ..." A'brem began. "I don't know. I've helped filter money through the bank. I'm already too deep."

"If you leave now," Perry said, "you won't be involved any more. I'm sure you could invent a scapegoat in the unlikely event the Tz-en should check your bookkeeping. Go on. We can't have your indecision interfering."

A'brem pulled on the arms of the chair to raise himself up.

Aba'shal eyed him darkly. "And we'll remember this, A'brem. All of Khadeej will remember."

The banker dropped back into the chair. "I'll stay, Perry. I ... I think you will need my help, even if I'm no good with a blaster."

"Unless we give you a blaster and send you over to join the Tz-en," L'dhar said.

The others laughed, including A'brem.

"We can definitely use your influence," Perry said. "You'll be a great help, and you won't need to carry a blaster."

He turned toward the back of the house, through the dark hall he had used to enter the room. He motioned Dh'vid to come out of the shadows. The young man walked boldly to his side, his cloak curled over his arm. His clothes were threadbare and faded, his boots worn and scarred. But he carried his strong frame in a way that belied his recent years as a laborer.

As the light bathed him, the others in the room looked him over and a few faces clouded with suspicion.

"Who's this?" L'dhar asked.

Before answering, Perry took a small computer pad from his coat pocket. The device had been modified as an ID scanner. Its metal casing was scratched and tarnished. On the upper surface lay embossed a faded crescent moon crossed by three brilliant stars.

"Recognize this?" he asked A'brem, handing him the pad.

The banker turned the pad over. "Of course. It's an old computer for identification recognition. They aren't that old, but we haven't made new ones since the Tz-en took control. The Tz-en get them off-world, now. I must admit, the technology is better than ours was. But they served their purpose. This one has the royal signet on it, so it must have belonged to some official."

"Turn it on."

A'brem did as he was asked. The tiny screen glowed, casting a light across his round face. His eyes passed over the readout. "It still has its original memory."

Perry motioned Dh'vid closer. "Scan him," he told A'brem.

A'brem raised the device, activated the scan mode, then aimed it at the young man's right eye. The pad buzzed when it had gathered enough information. A'brem read the results on the screen.

"By the Creator!" he breathed. His jaw fell slack, his eyes widened. He glanced from the machine to the man, then back. Finally, he shook his head at Perry. "This can't be. You've programmed this thing yourself."

Perry grinned at him. "Check the menu."

A'brem tapped the keypad, then shook his head as he read through the menu. "No, you couldn't have. This is locked with a pass key. It can only be changed by the person who set the lock, identifiable only by retina and DNA scan. I'm sure some modern computer genius could bypass the lock, but it would probably have compromised the set-up. This has not been tampered with."

L'dhar pulled on A'brem's sleeve, nearly tumbling the smaller man from his chair. "What are you babbling about, Len?"

"This!" He held the screen up for L'dhar and the others to see, though the image and letters were too small to be coherent. The carpenter squinted in frustration. A'brem waved his other hand to the stranger in their midst. "It's him. He is Dh'vid."

"Who?" asked one of the younger men.

L'dhar's creased face formed deeper wrinkles in a frown. "Dh'vid? Son of J'siah?"

A'brem nodded emphatically and shoved the ID pad into his hands. "See for yourself."

L'dhar glanced over the device, then punched on the keypad. "That's ridiculous. The M'ji's son died in the attack on the palace. The entire royal family died. Perry, this is one of your tricks, another lie. We all know how well you can manipulate these machines."

"Not this time," A'brem said. He reached over and tapped the pad with a pudgy finger. "It's keyed to one person. No one else can enter the system. Retina and DNA scan prevents that."

"Well, then, whoever it's keyed to," L'dhar insisted.

"It's locked to J'siah's identification, the last M'ji. It belonged to him."

L'dhar punched into the keypad, entered the menu, then said, "Oh."

E'lias looked Dh'vid over closely. "Then, *he* is the M'ji?"

Nodding slowly, A'brem said, "It would appear so."

One of the young men came forward, staring into Dh'vid's face. He

"By the Creator!" he breathed.

drew close like some skittish animal, ready to retreat under the slightest provocation. He glanced at Perry and his cheeks brightened. He looked quickly away. Perry searched his memory for the man's name. He was little more than a boy, really. J'sef.

"You are the M'ji?" the boy asked.

Dh'vid shook his head, his jaw set firm, his eyes like steel. "No. I am J'siah's son. He was the last M'ji. I'm an El'aran, just like you. I work in the warehouses at the spaceport. We have no M'ji now. Not until we are free from the Tz-en."

L'dhar stood up. "I saw your father once in person, many times on vids. You are very much like him. Together, we shall push these Tz-en into the sea and once more have our M'ji."

A'brem waved his hands as he stood. "Much as I like to join in this sentimental patriotism, I think we need to be pragmatic. We don't have the force to push the Tz-en anywhere. Even with you, Dh'vid, to rally all the El'arans in the name of your father, we will still be slaughtered. We have a good supply of more up-to-date weapons, smuggled in by that freighter pilot and stolen from the Tz-en. I have to admit that Perry was right all along. We need the Shir'ka. But after Bar'thazel's confrontation with To'mahs, we can't depend upon them. Can we, Perry? And without them, there is no possible hope of success."

"I can't guarantee anything," Perry said. "To'mahs doesn't speak for all the Shir'ka, but he is important. Especially as a clan leader. Furthermore, there are few clans in the area. The Dor'ja clan is camped north. The Raj'han clan further west. But I'm trying to make arrangements with them. I've sent word to To'mahs that I want to meet with him and representatives of those two clans. And others, too, who could arrive in time. I'm taking Dh'vid there now. If any of you want to come, to add your testimony, you'll be welcomed. And we need to spread word to others here in Khadeej."

Tor L'dhar elected to join Perry on the visit to the Shir'ka clan. The others set about their work in Khadeej. Perry chose a less conspicuous way to travel, borrowing a truck from a Shir'ka trader of the Raj'han clan. The oversized tires made navigating the Ahram Pass difficult, but allowed high speeds once they reached the rolling desert seas.

Sentries spotted their dust trail hours in advance. Herds were moved to the north and west of the camp, and young men and women took up weapons to meet the vehicle. The action wasn't necessarily a sign of mistrust or aggression, but rather a sign of respect, underlain with suspicion. The clans had a long history of confrontations, which had fired ancient wars between them. Disagreements and transgressions were now settled with gaming competition during the festivals, but trust is a very difficult entity to breed. Rather than be insulted by being greeted with rifle and lance when approaching a neighboring clan, a Shir'ka visitor now considered it a demonstration of consideration for his or her strength and abilities. Suspicions were ignored, since each clan member felt the same toward members of other clans.

Perry slowed the old truck as they grew closer. Painted on the pitted sides of the truck was the double-headed lance held horizontal over the image of a *dreen* buck – the symbol of the Raj'han clan. He had gained desert clothes from the trader in Khadeej, though L'dhar had decided against the change. Dh'vid, however, wore the loose rust-colored clothes and headwrap like a clansman, though Perry had to show him which way the wrap twisted. Such an oversight might be considered an insult, unforgivable in the case of an outsider wearing the material.

The truck stopped at the edge of the awaiting line of people. Beneath their wraps, dozens of stern eyes cut through the dusty windscreen to examine the passengers.

Perry stepped out, loosened the wrap over the front of his face, and tossed it back to reveal his head. Many of the Shir'ka around him nodded in recognition. Some smiled slightly, while others remained stoic. He saw expressions change as Dh'vid, face wrapped, and L'dhar, in his city clothes, climb out of the vehicle. Whispers circulated.

To'mahs walked out from among the tents. His own headwrap was down, letting the hot breeze wrinkle the peppered curls of his hair and beard. His brow furrowed, narrowing his eyes.

"Why have you come back, Perry? Is it to beg forgiveness?" He glanced over the visitors, then peered into the truck. "Where is my daughter?"

"She was taken by the off-worlder, held until I trade myself for her. As soon as we conclude our business, I will deal with her release. I'll see that she returns to the clan."

To'mahs frowned. The hardness creased around his eyes, softening slightly. "As she should have remained. But she is her own woman. No person, no clan, owns her. But we have no more business to discuss, Perry. It is done."

He turned to leave.

"Wait!" Perry said. "We aren't finished."

"Did you bring this outsider to help plead your case? I know the carpenter as an honest man, for an El'aran. But he has no influence over us. Nothing he can say will change my mind."

L'dhar stepped closer. His voice boomed over the sand nearly as strong as To'mahs's. "I didn't come here to argue with you, To'mahs. I came to let you see that we are serious. We have a chance now, but only if the Shir'ka help. And they won't if you do not agree."

"Exactly. We have no need to get involved. Your troubles don't touch the desert."

"But they will," L'dhar said. "First, you will feel them from Khadeej and in other market towns. What will happen to the Shir'ka when you can't trade? When you can't buy foods or materials you can't get from the desert? Or when you can't get parts to repair your machines? You think you are separate from us, but we are tied together. And eventually, the Tz-en will control the desert. They are already preparing to conquer it by using the air. They cannot afford to allow your people to have what little freedom you enjoy."

"If they cross the desert, we will fight them."

"How? Can your lances and rifles bring down an airship? Can your *sildars* outdistance a flier? Can your sentries see as far as their satellites? I may be only a carpenter, but I have seen some of the technologies the Tz-en use. I've seen some of their big airships, already in Khadeej. They don't even need to set foot on the sand to wipe the desert clean of Shir'ka."

"They will find that the Shir'ka are not as easily defeated as the El'arans," To'mahs said.

"Years ago, they took our land because we had forgotten how to fight," L'dhar said. "We forgot why we fight. Slowly, we are changing. But we need the help of the Shir'ka."

"And then will you turn against the Shir'ka?" To'mahs asked. "Many El'arans have never hidden their hatred for us."

"And many Shir'ka have voiced their opinions about El'arans," L'dhar pointed out. "Life was not perfect before the Tz-en came, it won't be after we are rid of them."

"No. This is not the fight of the Shir'ka."

"Perhaps," said Dh'vid, stepping forward, "*Cyte* To'mahs speaks for himself rather than the clan of B'sheer."

To'mahs ran his eyes over the young man. His brow deepened its furrows. "I will not be criticized by an El'aran pup who dresses up like a Shir'ka. You mock us, child."

Dh'vid pulled aside the length of headwrap over his face. "Can a Shir'ka mock his own people while showing them respect? My mother was of the R'jor Clan."

To'mahs's eyes became less critical. "Then you have the rights of the clan, as well as the responsibilities. You are still El'aran fathered and raised. You do not understand our position."

"I understand enough to know that if the Tz-en follow through with their designs, both El'arans and Shir'ka will be only a memory whispered on the desert breeze. I claim one right as a Shir'ka. You are only you're own voice, not the whole clan. I will be heard by all the elders, as well as representatives from other clans."

To'mahs nodded his head. "I will grant you the desire to be heard by the elders, but to be heard by other clansmen is not a right unless you go to the other clans."

"Yes, but they will come when you send them messages."

"The elders of B'sheer will hear you first. Whose blood runs through your veins that you can make the claim?"

Dh'vid lowered the headwrap. "My mother was Tal'sha."

"There was only one Tal'sha of the R'jor Clan. If she was your mother, then your father –"

"My father was J'siah, the last M'ji."

A murmur circulated throughout the assembled crowd. It grew steadily louder, until To'mahs had to raise his hands for quiet, that he might be heard.

"You must provide proof," he said.

Dh'vid stood in front of him, glaring into his eyes. He drew out a curved Shir'ka dagger from beneath his cloak. The gray metal blade absorbed the brilliance of the sun, looking almost black. He took the edge across the palm of his left hand. A crimson stripe appeared at the crossing of the blade. Drops of blood rolled over the heel of his hand and fell into the sand between their feet, the dark red mixing with the rust.

"This is my proof," Dh'vid said, finalizing the challenge.

Perry suppressed a smile. He had never told the young man about the old custom. He doubted he learned it from Jor'm. Either he had remembered it from his late mother, or he had done his homework in preparation of this day, despite his misgivings. Dh'vid may not be anxious to step into the place of his father, but he was suited for the heritage. Perry noticed surprise hang for an instant in To'mahs's eyes. It quickly changed to admiration.

The old Shir'ka drew his own dagger and made a similar cut across his own rough palm. Drops of his blood fell into the sand, mingling with those of Dh'vid.

"Welcome, son of Tal'sha," To'mahs said. "My tent is yours. We will talk, then you shall meet with the elders. I shall transmit word to the other clans. I suspect that once word spreads, the clans will converge."

The wheels were moving, Perry decided. Now was time for him to leave.

"To'mahs," he said as the crowd moved to absorb To'mahs and Dh'vid. "I need to get back to Khadeej. Mar'a needs me."

To'mahs nodded slowly. "How many men do you need?"

"Only one *sildar*. I think L'dhar should stay, to act as a representative for the El'arans, so he should keep the vehicle. As far as any of your people going with me, I should go alone. We don't want to alert the Tz-en that we have any sort of organized force. If I can't release her myself, at worse I can trade myself for her. I'm all they want. Neither the Tz-en nor my old friend Tony know about our young friend here. It's best you move quickly before the word spreads to them. We don't know how many of the El'arans we can trust. I still feel someone leaked information, especially Mar'a's whereabouts."

To'mahs motioned toward the herd of *sildars*, grazing on *woro* weeds to the south of the camp.

"Tell the herdsman you are to take the swiftest *sildar*. Bring yourself as well as my daughter back."

Perry smiled in reply.

As he tread across the sand toward the herd, he set a pair of goggles over his eyes and wrapped the headwrap over his head and face. Despite the coverings, the herdsman knew him. He immediately pointed out the quickest mount and helped round it up and tie on the saddle pad. As Perry climbed onto the animal's high sloped back, he glanced at the camp. He could hear singing course over the desert. An old song of a warrior's triumph. He remembered Mar'a singing that when he had brought down his first bull *jerlac*.

They didn't need him here, but Mar'a did. He was the catalyst that started the fire. Now he could let it burn and purify El'aris.

He turned the *sildar*'s thick nose eastward and shook the reins. The animal bounded off, its wide padded feet thumping the sand.

The interrogation room in the prison still smelled of the last prisoner to go through, but Michaels wanted to be near Mar'a. He had arranged for a cell above ground for her, with better amenities than the lower prison had to offer. He figured she deserved as much. He had no doubt that Perry would try to rescue her. He wouldn't have, but Perry was more compassionate than he was. Or at least he had been, years ago. Just how much had Perry changed?

Thatcher, following up a lead from Hannah, appeared on the screen of the portable com unit sitting on the scratched table. The scenery behind him blurred, but it appeared to be the inside of a room.

The door behind Michaels swung open. He glanced over his shoulder to see Jiin enter. Silhouetted in the light from the hallway, her moves were sultry. When she sat next to him at the table, with her pale face catching the glow of the screen, he shivered.

He looked away from her quickly, after giving a nod of greeting. "Geoff, where did you say you are?"

The little com speaker crackled. "*Basenda ... I think. It's some shanty town outside the main town, which ain't that big to begin with. We found the house, or shack, but no one's here.*"

"Why is he there?" Jiin asked.

"Hannah found out the address of Jor'm's family," Michaels said, "from the restored database. Wife and son."

"And you think Perry wiped out the database to hide the address of this man's wife?"

"It's beginning to look that way. But why?"

The speaker crackled again. "*If you two are done, I'd like to leave. I don't think the locals around here like us too much.*"

"No sign of anyone, Geoff?" Michaels asked.

"*Doesn't look like anyone's been around for a couple of days. Furniture and some clothes still here. No food except some cans and jars. Can't get any of the neighbors to talk to us. Can't even tell if this is the right place or not. People probably move around without notifying the government. Don't know how you're going to find 'em.*"

"Post someone at the house just in case they come back, or set up a watcher drone, if the Tz-en have any. Go ahead and come back. We're still waiting on Perry."

"*Still think he'll show?*" Thatcher asked.

"Yeah, I do."

Thatcher moved on the screen, then caught himself. "*Oh, by the way.*"

Hannah wants to talk with you. Said it was pretty urgent, but she wouldn't say anything more."

"She'll have to wait her turn. I guess she wants paid."

"I don't think that was it, Mick. You'd better –"

"I'll deal with her after we've taken care of things here. Now get packed and get back here." He hit the terminate button, and the screen went black.

He sat back and rubbed his eyes. Why would Perry wipe the database for the location of Jor'm's family? What does Jor'm or his wife and son know that could be so important? Perry went through a lot of trouble sabotaging the database. Now Jor'm's family was gone. For all he knew, they might be next door to the shack Thatcher was in, or they might be miles away.

The door opened again. Michaels caught a whiff of cologne and groaned.

"No progress, I see," Vindal said as he entered. "This plan of yours does not have merit. I seriously doubt that Mr. Perry will jeopardize his freedom and life for that barbarous girl. He isn't the type. Whatever you remember of him, Mr. Michaels, he is not the same man. He is completely cold and calculating. A machine. There is nothing he will not do to accomplish his objective. He's lied to you. Your former friendship means nothing to him, unless he can use it to his advantage. This woman is only a means to an end for him. Now, she may have valuable information. We need to interrogate her. Of course, simple questioning would never work. We must institute more elaborate techniques, perhaps some chemical assistance."

"No."

"You are being quite unreasonable, Mr. Michaels. Even if you are right and Mr. Perry comes to her rescue – or, more likely, to terminate her because she knows too much – even then we should still interrogate her. She may be a vital link in this conspiracy."

Michaels squeezed his fingers together. "I gave my word. She goes free when we have Perry."

Jiin's large eyes watched him. "Why?" she asked. "He has betrayed your friendship. What is it you owe him?"

"I gave my word. I'll do my best to keep it whether I gave it to him, or you, or even Vindal. Maybe that's something you can't figure out."

Jiin nodded slowly. "I believe I understand."

"What's that infernal noise?" Vindal demanded suddenly.

An alarm blared outside their room. The soundproofing in the walls prevented it from entering, except for the highest pitch. Vindal went to the door and swung it open. The whine blasted in, numbing their hearing.

With it came billows of black smoke. Vindal immediately closed the door and threw his back against it. He bent over in a fit of coughing.

As the smoke curled through the room, both Michaels and Jiin began coughing.

"Fire!" Vindal said needlessly, choking out the word.

Michaels dropped to the floor, tugging Jiin after him. Their faces were inches apart, the black vapors hanging just above.

"What's emergency procedures like in here?" he asked her. "Are there internal systems for extinguishing fires?"

She coughed several times, then said, "I don't know. This is an old building. I am not part of the staff, so I don't know what is expected during such an emergency. I believe we had better leave."

"Good idea," Vindal said through a silk handkerchief held to his face.

"What about the prisoners?" Michaels asked. If the fire spread, the prisoners in the lower levels were as good as dead. The fire may never reach them, but the poisonous fumes would choke them soon enough. And then there was Mar'a. He had to make sure she was all right.

Wait ... Years ago, the rebel faction on Zeller IV had hired him and Perry to rescue a political prisoner from the palace of the Hordencian potentate. They had posed as off-world merchants. When they had located the prisoner, Michaels released him while Perry provided a diversion.

"It's a trick!" he yelled. "It's not a real fire. Perry's here."

He leaped up, pulling out his blaster. He shoved Vindal aside and swung open the door. The smoke fell over him like a wave. It burned his eyes and cut deep into his throat. Covering his mouth and nose did little to stop the irritation, but he pushed on into the hall. Red lights flashed from high along the walls. The alarm whined painfully in his ears. Shadows ran past him, stumbling. Tz-en, in a panic.

The door that led into the cell area stood wide open. He tripped over a bulky object on the floor. As he bent down, his tear-filled eyes discerned the unconscious body of one guard.

He groped his way down the hall to the first cell, which held Mar'a. Two other unconscious bodies lay beneath the billows of black fumes.

Too late. Perry must already be half way to the mountains by now. If only he had been prepared for one of his little ticks!

Two shapes appeared in the open door of the cell, one tall, one smaller. He heard a muffled coughing that could only come from a woman.

Michaels crouched, lifting his blaster to take aim at the wall above the doorway. He rubbed his eyes to clear them of stinging tears. The larger figure resolved into a man wearing rust colored clothes, with a cloth that wrapped over his head and face. Goggles covered his eyes. He held a supporting arm protectively around the woman.

"Perry, stop!"

The words came out hoarsely. He doubted they even reached the ears of the other man.

Michaels squeezed the trigger. A bolt shot out and shattered wood over Perry's head.

Perry's foot lashed out, striking Michaels' hand, numbing his fingers. His blaster tumbled across the floor.

Perry could finish him and be gone before any of the Tz-en gathered enough sense to even realize he was here. Instead, Perry stood still, holding Mar'a.

Michaels became aware of heavy footsteps and assorted coughing. Immediately he was surrounded by Tz-en guards. The air cleared more quickly, making their features visible. Each man's eyes were bright red from the irritants. He imagined his own were rather colorful, though doubted they stood out so starkly as theirs did against white skin.

He coughed to clear his lungs, doubling as the burning passed through him. A hand clamped over his upper arm, pulling him up for support. He turned to meet Jiin's red-rimmed eyes.

"You should have waited for reinforcements," she said.

More Tz-en arrived, surrounding the prisoners.

Perry raised his hands and allowed his weapons to be removed. Besides a blaster and Shir'ka dagger, they found an assortment of homemade explosives and smokers.

Michaels shook his head. "I should have known you'd pull something like this."

Perry unwrapped his face and pulled down the goggles. "I expected you would have. But I had to try anyway. The effects will wear off in a few minutes. The ingredients are local, so the device was a bit crude and more irritating than I had expected."

Guards clamped binders over his wrists and activated the restraining field. Others took hold of Mar'a, who still suffered from the smoke. They locked a set of binders over her wrists.

"No!" Michaels said, waving at them. He forced a swallow down his parched throat. "No, she goes free." He looked at Perry. "That was the bargain."

Perry nodded once. At that moment, Michaels saw the old Perry. Perry from Delnaar. From the Gateway Militia. From before El'aris.

Vindal pushed his way through the crowded hallway, waving his hands to clear away the last vestiges of the smoke. His words mumbled beneath the handkerchief he held over his mouth and nose.

"I'm afraid not, Mr. Michaels."

"I gave my word. She goes free."

Vindal pulled the handkerchief away and used it to wipe at the air. He grinned. Michaels really hated that grin. "Your word, not mine, Mr. Michaels. Nor that of Deltan Technologies, which is paying your fee."

"She goes free, Vindal. What do you need her for? We have Perry now. He's the leader. You said it yourself, she's only a barbarian."

"Ah, yes. But a knowledgeable barbarian. If Mr. Perry was willing to risk his life for her, she must be very valuable to this anarchistic movement. In any case, with her under lock and key, he will be less likely to attempt escape. This decision actually came from Mr. Tabor himself. She will be sent to Jhamrahl and interrogated."

He motioned to the guards holding her. "Arrange transport to Jhamrahl."

Michaels watched as Mar'a stood straight between the Tz-en soldiers and looked up into Perry's eyes. He couldn't make out what she said as they led her away. He saw a boldness in her eyes, with no trace of defeat.

"Perry, I –"

"It's okay, Tony. You couldn't help it." Perry smiled, and Michaels felt an ache tear inside him.

CHAPTER TWELVE
BEST LAID PLANS

Michaels hired a car to drive back to Jhamrahl. He sent a message ahead for Thatcher not to return to Khadeej. They were leaving El'aris. The job was done. Jiin rode with him, officially to escort him. Unofficially, he wasn't quite sure. She was rather subdued during the trip, but then he wasn't exactly the model conversationalist. He seemed to remember a modest amount of grunts dominating his speech.

At the hotel in Jhamrahl, Thatcher was nowhere to be found. He no doubt missed his instructions.

"You don't have to watch over us," he told Jiin as he brought up the spaceport schedule on the com station, seeing if any transports were due to leave.

"I am not here to watch you. Actually, I've decided to take leave for some time. Michaels, you do not look well."

"I'm fine."

"You are blaming yourself for what your friend has gotten himself into. It isn't your fault. You cannot do more than you have. And you could not have done less. You did the job you were hired for. You gave your word for that, too. Correct?"

"Yeah, right."

"Perry has lied to you, betrayed you. Yet you feel obligated to him. Why?"

He waved his hands, trying to grasp words out of the air. "It's like this. Perry and I were as close as brothers. Maybe even closer, considering my relationship with my brothers."

"I understand what bothers you. You have integrity, but you are in conflict. You are trapped by opposing commitments. I too am in conflict. I am bothered by something that we are forbidden to discuss, yet it grates against my nature. I am not the only Tz-en to have these feelings, though we openly cannot say anything concerning it. If you give me your word you will remain silent, I can trust you. Perhaps you can offer some insight. I realize this is a grave responsibility that I place on you, but it has nothing to do with your work and once you leave El'aris, you will have nothing to do with the situation."

He stared at her for a moment, trying to figure out where this might lead.

"It is because of your concern over your friend, and your inability to keep your word to him, that I feel I can speak."

He smiled with a cockeyed grin. "Okay, shoot."

She drew back suddenly.

He chuckled. "No, I mean go ahead. Tell me. I'll keep my mouth shut."

The apartment door banged open.

"There you are!" the intruder exclaimed. "I've been trying to reach you. You are completely impossible, Mick. Thatcher tried to tell you, but you wouldn't listen. Don't you ever listen to anyone else? Now that you're here, you can't get away. You'll have to listen. Just wait till you see what I've found. Oh, who's this?"

Hannah stopped short, took a breath, and stared down Jiin.

Jiin stood up. "I will return later ... Anthony."

"Ah, sure. We can talk later."

Jiin slipped out of the room under the cold glare of Hannah. When the apartment door shut, Hannah swaggered over to Michaels. Her hair seemed to bristle.

"What was she doing here?"

Michaels watched her face as it darkened. "Tying up loose ends," he said.

"Right," Hannah said as she dropped onto the couch. She pulled her computer from her shoulder bag and set it on the table between them. Her expression still held storms, particularly in the eyes, which avoided his. Her lips were a tight line.

"I want to show you something. I picked it up from Ringer's data wafer you gave me. I'll make the connection to the holo projector in the table. Here."

The projector activated, filling the air above it with a three dimensional representation of Perry. He spoke in a low volume, the confession the media had played over the news broadcasts. The image flickered and the recording played again.

"What's the point?" he asked. He really didn't want to sit there and watch this over again. Vindal had all the details about Perry's life after El'aris. There was no need to rehash it. Besides, the job was done.

"The point is this!"

A three dimensional graph appeared next to Perry's image. Valleys rose and peeks sank as his voice changed with each word. Perfect modulation. The graph altered through phases smoothly, without sudden shifts. Each word registered crisp and clear.

He shrugged. "Maybe I'm dense, but I don't see anything unusual."

"Right. Nothing unusual. Nice and smooth. But look at this."

Perry's image faded. A new voice came over the speakers. It was hers, repeating the same words, and the graph continued to change to follow Hannah's recorded voice. The alterations were not as well defined. A number of smaller peeks and valleys appeared. She stabbed her finger through the image.

"You see this? This is background noise. True, most of it could be cleaned up. But not this regular part. Know what that is? It's breathing. Hard to get rid of breathing. Try to hold your breath and talk like Perry did. You can't. I couldn't. Ringer couldn't. He noticed something everyone else missed and he did a little examining."

The holo returned to Perry, still talking in low volume. The graph smoothed out its roughness.

"Ringer," she went on, "noticed that Perry wasn't breathing. It's fake, Mick, for damn sake. They faked the whole confession."

"The Tz-en? Why would they need to? They had him for terrorism."

With a press of a button, the holograph vanished. "That's only part of it," she said. "I doubt the Tz-en have the ability to do something like this. Most of them don't have the expertise. I've seen what their best can do with computers. It's limited. Besides, like you said, they don't have any reason. They had him for crimes against the state. They could just toss him in prison and forget about him. Or simply execute him. They had help from someone more concerned about the public opinion beyond El'aris."

"Deltan?"

She reached over to slap his shoulder. "Correct! You win the prize, Mick. Deltan is in this up to their three-cornered logo."

"Okay, okay. So Deltan wanted to settle a few nervous tourists."

"It wasn't just the tourists, but I'm sure that was a big part of it. Do you know how big the tourist industry is on this planet? Not many planets have water, let alone large oceans, let alone oceans which have few dangerous organisms. Not to mention the nice climate year round. Besides that, El'aris supplies a lot of minerals to other systems. Those shipments were getting disrupted by what Perry was doing. What company likes dealing with a planet in the throws of a revolution? Now, if this revolution was political, the chances are that capturing one leader would not put an end to it. But if the revolution was triggered by outside sources, then it can be stopped by cutting the bonds to the outside and revealing the true source. And by casting a shadow over a rival company with some vague accusations, they can kill two *glibs* with one arrow. That way, none of the contracts to other systems will be broken."

"So the bottom line is, Perry never made that confession."

"Now you're catching on. But that ain't all, Mick. Ringer must have decided to do some more checking when he figured that confession was a phony. His data wafer contained the files on Perry's background. There are also reports from a couple of systems he must have checked on personally. From what I can tell, all those files match up."

"So what Vindal told me about Perry was true, about the last eleven years."

"That's what I thought. But then I noticed something unusual about the reports from those other systems. Here, take a look."

She turned her computer toward him. He squinted at the screen, but there was just too much information scattered over it for him to make any sense of it.

He shrugged. "What?"

She jabbed at the screen. "There, and there. And here. Can't you see it? Damn, you must be blind. Each of those files were modified within a day of each other, last week."

She paused to let it sink in. He was quicker once he didn't have to hunt through a computer monitor.

"Vindal made the whole thing up," he said.

"Brilliant. You finally got it. He or someone else probably took existing files and modified them, even changing the visuals so that they now resemble Perry. Maybe some other changes. Doesn't matter, since we aren't about to go to court any time too soon."

"He lied, not Perry."

"Right, Mick old buddy."

"Then Perry has been here all the time. Just like he said. And all the rest he said is probably true."

He jumped up and paced across the room, then back. He swore. He slapped his hand against the side of his head. He swore some more. Nothing helped get rid of the feeling of idiocy. He had believed a stranger rather than his friend. *He* had betrayed their friendship, not Perry.

"How could I have been so stupid?"

"It's probably something you've practiced at. Not many can do that well by accident," Hannah said. "Unless it's genetic."

"What can I do now? He's in prison because of me. I could have helped him, but I thought he was crazy." He stopped suddenly and stared at her. "Do you think he's crazy?"

She shrugged. "How should I know? Thing is, you had a job. He's just on the wrong side. Mick, our business doesn't consider friendship. You know that. You've been in it long enough."

"Maybe I could have talked to him, got him to change his mind."

"He chose to fight with the El'arans. That's why he's in prison. It just comes down to the fact that the planet really belongs to the Tz-en, whether we like it or not."

"I made a promise I couldn't keep. Maybe ... maybe you can help me with a little job, before we leave here."

"We? You mean you want to take me away from all this?"

"Ah, I mean we all better book passage out of here as soon as possible. If somebody happens to find out what we're planning, I don't think we should be around. Besides, we've overlooked one important item."

She looked at him. "What?"

He pointed to her computer. "You found out this from Ringer's data

wafer. He had to have found out first. Maybe he was killed because of it."
"Oh."

Michaels made arrangements with Harry Capetti. The pilot was preparing to leave El'aris again but was willing to delay for a couple of unauthorized passengers.

Hannah's skills came in useful in gaining them entry into the Deltan estate. Yes, it had once been the palace of the planetary leader, though on a planet that had seen little in the way of conflicts. And it was now a regional corporate headquarters for a major corporation. Security was probably tighter now than it had been under the M'ji, but it was still only offices and residential suites. Hannah gained access to the estate's staff roll, and now she and Michaels were the proud members of the maintenance team. Thatcher was instrumental in appropriating maintenance crew coveralls, then he retired to Capetti's ship to await extraction.

The rear entrance to the estate was vastly different from the main gates Michaels had previously used. Everything was automated and accessible by means of pass cards Hannah had created to approximate those used by staff personnel. No one paid attention to menials, especially after business hours. Not even other employees, who were only interested in getting their work done and going home. There were enough on staff to allow two new faces anonymity, and any supervisors were only available during daylight hours. Hannah and Michaels blended in with a crew that consisted of off-worlders who probably came to El'aris for reasons other than to clean rooms and offices.

They parked a stolen car in the staff parking lot and joined a dozen others shuffling in to begin their shift. Inside, a screen registered each employee's name and assignment. They, of course, were not listed. Michaels, wearing a cheap wig and a fake mustache, his eyes shaded by a billed cape, gave the screen a cursory glance. Hannah, who somehow managed to find a better quality wig and looking quite nice with wavy blond hair, nudged him and nodded toward an array of cleaning machines in charging stations. He grabbed a floor vacuum, while Hannah took a smaller device used for walls and furniture. Then they headed down one hallway, away from other workers.

In an empty conference room, Hannah took her computer out of her shoulder pack.

"Let me just break into their system," she said.

"You sure you can do this?"

"No worries. Done this a hundred times. Ooh, look. This Tabor person is not very careful. I'm logged in as him, and he's got a bunch of crap in his system."

"Why did you use him?" Michaels asked.

"Because he's the guy who's pulling the shots. He's the one telling them where to stick prisoners. If you haven't noticed, this is a big mansion."

"Yeah, and there are guards here, too."

"Take a look at these files. Those are casino names. Here's a list of companies that own them. And look at this. Here are some of the shipping businesses. Why would he have these files on his system?"

"Just focus."

"I'm getting there. I have to find the right menu. Hey, these look a little funny."

"Did you find it?"

"No. These business listings."

"Forget about those."

"Okay, here's Security. Relax Mick. You're making me nervous."

"I'm making *you* nervous?"

"Shh! No, she's not listed anywhere. But they do have an occupied guest suite. I'd say that's where they have her."

"You sure?"

"No, I'm not sure, but it's the only place I can find. Just let me copy this information down."

"Copy what? Just get the room's location and let's go."

"Force of habit, Mick. When I see something wonky, I like to study it. Downloading the files, I'll look into them later, when we're safely away on your friend's ship."

According to her information, the room was on the end of the third floor, which consisted of apartments for resident executives and visiting VIPs.

They moved quickly through the corridors, as though they had a purpose and a definite destination. They passed an occasional maintenance worker using a scrubber or ion-vac. No one paid them attention.

Exiting the third floor maintenance lift, they passed a man dressed in a business suit.

Michaels became alert the moment the man appeared. His suit was not an expensive variety, certainly not tailored. It fit crudely over his muscles and was not cut to hide the weapon nestled under the jacket, in the hollow of his armpit.

Michaels gauged how long it would take for him to pull his stunner from the deep pocket of his coveralls. Fortunately, the security man's footsteps receded down the corridor.

Another guard, a clone of the first, stood in front of the door of the room they wanted.

Michaels set the vac operating and roughly shoved it along the floor. Hannah took a small device from her pouch and activated it. The scrambler interrupted vid transmissions from any scanner in the hallway. While he ran the ion vacuum in a crude imitation of a typical cleaning pattern, Hannah followed along with the smaller vac to pass it over wall fixtures and the framed artwork that hung between the widely spaced apartment doors.

As they neared the guard, Michaels slid the stunner from his pocket and fired. The guard slumped against the door and slid to the floor.

Deactivating the lock took seconds.

They dragged the guard inside, shoved the door shut, and activated the lights.

Michaels had stayed in expensive, high-class hotels once or twice in his career, sometimes after a particularly fruitful job, sometimes because of the job. This room rivaled any grand hotel suite. The furniture style matched across the room, very tastefully decorated and arranged. The room was empty of occupants, though two other doors probably led to bedrooms.

He turned his attention to the guard, giving him a cursory examination. Besides a blaster, he had a com unit in his left ear. Michaels pulled the receiver from the man's ear and placed it into his own.

Leading with his stunner, he tried the one door, hoping the guest staying here wasn't some visiting VIP. He ducked in time to avoid being brained by a swinging chair. Fabric and wood fragments rained down on him as the furniture smashed into the door frame.

Mar'a stood defiantly with the remnants of the chair in her hands. Her face was overshadowed with a deep scowl.

"Come closer, and I will kill you!" she warned.

"Need help?" Hannah asked.

He motioned her back. "No, I can handle this."

"I was talking to her."

Michaels slipped his stunner back into his pocket. "Now look, Mar'a. We're here to get you out, get you back to your people."

"Just get the room's location and let's go."

"I don't trust you," she said.

"I don't blame you," Hannah said.

"You're not helping," Michaels snapped.

Hannah stepped between them. She pulled a bundle of cloth from her pack and handed it to Mar'a.

"Now look, honey," she said to Mar'a, "we got no time to work this out. We sneaked in here and now we're going to sneak out with you. Put that on, tie your hair back."

Mar'a grunted, glared at Michaels, but took the coveralls. In a moment, she was dressed as a maintenance worker, but Hannah shook her head in disapproval.

"Not quite right. Try this." She snatched the hat off Michaels' head and positioned it on Mar'a, tilting the brim down. "Just keep your head down. You look too pretty, in even baggy coveralls."

Hannah handed her the small ion-vac while Michaels cracked open the door and checked the corridor.

They were in the parking lot when the com unit buzzed with activity. By the time they reached their stolen vehicle, the alarm was set up. Michaels told Hannah to take Mar'a, while he stole a different car to lead any pursuers in a different direction.

"Meet me at the *Crazy Eight* by sunrise," he said.

She never showed.

Waiting in the common room of the little freighter, Michaels sat for a few minutes, paced, and continued to stare out the port.

The sun peeked over the landing field.

He heard the heavy deck pounding and tuned to see Thatcher climbing through the hatchway.

"Still no sign of her," he said.

"We can't leave her," Michaels said.

"Sure we can. She knew the risks. She's smart; she'll figure another way off this rock."

Michaels shook his head. "Not if they caught her. She'll be stuck in that prison if they don't kill her outright."

"Look, Mick. I've been thinking. Don't take this personal, but this is my last job. I'm taking some time off and find some place to settle, run a bar on some out-of-the-way place."

"Sounds good. Maybe I'll get me one of these little freighters and do some planet hopping myself," Michaels said. If Hannah ever arrived and they could make good their escape.

Harry climbed through the hatch.

"Looks like we might have a problem, Mick," he said. "Check out this local news report."

He activated the screen on the bulkhead, bringing up the image of a woman newscaster.

"*The authorities are searching for a woman who is wanted for gaining illegal access to Deltan Technologies' corporate offices last night. She has been identified as Hannah O'Brien of the Helbent Colony. Considering the reputation of those colonists, she is to be considered dangerous. If she is spotted, please notify authorities immediately. Once again, she is to be considered dangerous and is probably armed. Notify authorities immediately.*"

The newscaster faded, replaced by an image of Hannah taken from an old file. The reporter's voice continued with a physical description of the fugitive.

"Don't know what you guys were up to," Harry said, "but I think she might be lying low. We can wait, but that makes it worse for you. Assuming, of course, you were all together last night."

"We'll wait," Michaels said.

"We may not have much choice," Thatcher said as he bent down and looked out the port window. "We've got company."

He joined Geoff at the port that overlooked the landing pad.

On the tarmac, Jiin stood looking up at the old freighter. Her features were tighter than usual, her eyes hidden behind a pair of dark shades. Her uniform looked crisp and official. Thankfully, she was alone.

Michaels stepped out onto the tarmac. If she came to arrest him, why did she come alone?

"You must come with me," she said without preamble.

"Why?"

"It is important. It is related to Perry." Her eyes flashed across the landing field.

"Did he escape again?"

"No, but there is one more item of importance. You must come with me. I will return you in time for your departure."

Perhaps this was unrelated to his exploits of the previous night.

"What's this all about?" He tried to sound casual as she led him to a car with a Tz-en driver.

As they settled into the back seat, she shook her head. "Not now. When we reach our destination."

He leaned back and watched the road ahead, all sorts of scenarios tumbling through his mind. Arrest. Interrogation. Torture. Execution.

Just as Jhamrahl's skyline appeared, the car veered right and followed the south edge of the river.

The car neared the small town of Achari. Before the town, off to the left, tents and temporary buildings lay clustered together, reminding him of a nomadic camp, only this camp sat at the base of a long mound at the edge of a wheat field. He noticed small groups of people milling about, but the highway was too far and they traveled too fast for him to see details.

Achari was smaller than Khadeej. It catered more to the farm community than the river industry. They passed among the old buildings and pulled to a stop in front of a two-story affair with a more modern facade. The sign outside read "Constabulary."

They climbed out of the car. She bent to the window to speak to the driver. "You may return. We will find other transportation later. This business may take some time."

The driver nodded and drove away.

He stood beside her as they faced the police station and wondered why they had come all this way just for her to arrest him.

"Now, will you tell me what this is about?" he asked.

She glanced around. "I did not want others to know until you had finished with this. Come inside. You will soon understand."

As they walked up the steps toward the arched doorway, she whispered, "Did you know about the search for your friend, O'Brien?"

"I saw the news. Is there an equivalent to a warrant for her arrest?"

"Arrest? They don't want her arrested. They want her dead."

He stopped in mid step.

Jiin opened the door. When he stood staring at her, she grabbed his arm and pulled him inside. Her eyes narrowed and her lips tightened. She was warning him not to speak any more.

At the main desk just inside the building, a uniformed woman looked up from her terminal and sat erect at the sight of Jiin's rank pips.

"Commander?" she said. "Can I help you?"

"I am Jiin. I had the El'aran brought here for holding. What room is he in."

"Second floor, room three, Commander."

"Good. When we are through, I want him escorted back to Khadeej and released wherever he requests. And he is not to be abused."

"Yes, Commander."

Michaels followed Jiin up the flight of steps, then down the corridor to the second door on the right.

Inside the small room was a table surrounded by four chairs. A chair also sat near the door. A Tz-en constable sat in this seat, his arms folded over his chest. He stood as Jiin entered. The other occupant of the room sat at the table, staring out the window at the river. The scene was hypnotic, and it took the youth several seconds to register that the door had opened to let visitors in. He turned toward them, his face vague.

"J'sef?" Michaels said. "What are you doing here?"

The boy glanced at Jiin and the other Tz-en. "I tried to contact you. They brought me here."

Jiin motioned to the constable, who slipped out the door. She stepped through the doorway and said, "Speak with him. See if there is anything useful." She closed the door behind her, leaving him alone with the boy.

Michaels went to the table and sat opposite J'sef.

"What's this all about, kid?"

"There's been some things developing. I thought you might want to know."

"Sorry, kid. I'm through with this job. I was about to leave El'aris. Thanks for all your help. Commander Jiin will take care of you; get you a ticket off this planet, if that's what you want."

"You don't understand," the boy said, leaning over the table. "This is important news. Very important. It has to do with the terrorists."

"Save it, kid. I'm not interested."

"But you got to listen. They're moving. They've built up an army, and they're about to make their move."

"It's none of my business now, kid."

"But you have to listen. They're going to attack, first in Khadeej, then Achari. They're going to move east, hoping to pick up more followers until they can attack Jhamrahl. There's about three hundred now. Maybe more. They're getting ready to make their move next week. They've got some weapons, and they hope to get more when they take over Khadeej."

Michaels tried to visualize the plan. Three hundred or more El'arans storming the government buildings in Khadeej. They could easily take the Tz-en by surprise. Maybe they could even win and spark a whole revolution, just the way Perry had hoped. Then again, they may get massacred. If the Tz-en knew in advance, they could wipe out the El'aran revolutionaries immediately.

"Okay, kid. I'll pass the word on. You take off. Maybe head south for a while, until this blows over. Don't say a word to anyone else, El'aran or Tz-en. Not a word. I'll take care of everything. And we'll get you off just as soon as we can. Remember, contact Commander Jiin. No one else."

J'sef nodded vigorously.

Opening the door, he motioned for the constable standing at the stairwell with Jiin. "Take the boy anywhere he wants to go."

The man glanced at Jiin, who nodded. He motioned the boy down the stairs, then followed.

"What did he want?" Jiin asked him. "Was it important?"

He shook his head. "He thought it was. Ended up, it was nothing. He had some news that Mar'a, Perry's wife, escaped from Jhamrahl. I sincerely doubt his sources. He admitted he got this second hand. But I told him I'd look into it. I just wish he'd had told you, instead of wasting my time."

"He made it sound extremely important. I thought it prudent to bring you together immediately. I apologize, Anthony."

"Don't mention it. Now, how do I get back to the port?"

"I will borrow a vehicle. In the meantime, I think we should eat. And I believe you should see the excavation."

"The what?"

CHAPTER THIRTEEN
BURIED TRUTH

"It is the excavation," Jiin said as she pulled a borrowed utility vehicle off the road just outside of Achari, where Michaels had earlier seen tents clustered together, "of the first ship that brought the Humans here. Near it is the settlement that is believed to be Tz-en in origin."

"I'd better get back to my friends."

"You have time."

Other transports from Jhamrahl sat parked outside the camp. Visitors included Humans and non-Humans from a number of systems. He spotted at least two tour groups led by Human guides who recited rhetoric about the buried ship and the village. The mound he had seen from the roadway was actually the remains of the ancient spacecraft, a bullet shaped monstrosity of tarnished and rusted metal. It came from the age of star travel when Humans expanded their colonies. The ships hadn't been designed aesthetically, and some hadn't even been designed for the purpose of far travel. But, surprisingly, many more worlds were colonized than can be remembered. El'aris was only one example of a society isolated over hundred years.

The tents were roped off from visitors, labeled with warning signs. They covered pits in which archeologist painstakingly unearthed remnants of a lost age. He recognized stone foundations in squares and rectangles, denoting the position of huts or houses long crumbled.

As they walked through, he overheard one guide as he pointed out a particularly deep excavation to his gawking off-world followers.

"And here, only weeks ago, archeologist found the skeletal remains of one of the early inhabitants of the village. This was obviously a burial mound at one time, and the former occupant, who has been placed in the Jhamrahl Museum, was positively identified as a Tz-en. This was just one piece of evidence to prove that the Tz-en were here before Humans. Over here, in an upper strata, was located a primitive projectile weapon that was typical to early Human colonists. We are fortunate to have this on display here at the visitors' center." He motioned toward the long, low temporary building near the parked transports. "Now, this way we can see ..."

Michaels followed Jiin toward the mound, then up a set of steps built into a framework that lead to a high platform. The platform overlooked the prow of the old ship. At the top, he leaned on the railing and looked through the rusted hole of the hull and into what remained of the flight deck. The frames of swivel chairs still sat in their joints. The consoles still had their buttons and dials, though discolored with age and deterioration. The deck had been cleared of the dirt that had kept the ship buried, and a sheet of plexi had been placed in the jagged opening to keep out the weather and unwanted guests. He imagined artifacts from the ship were on display in the visitors' center, along with souvenirs for the kiddies.

Jiin stared out over the wheat fields.

"I do not want to go back," she said, her whisper almost unintelligible.

"Back? Back to Jhamrahl? But I have to go back. Harry and Geoff are waiting for me. We'd better get going. Much as I like playing tourist."

"No, I mean where my people are from. Tz-en. It is a harsh, primitive place. I was young when we left, but I can still remember."

"I know, Jiin, I was there. Remember? I helped train your people. I saw the type of environment you had to live in. I wouldn't want to go back there, either. But there isn't any chance of that." Or was there? If the El'arans succeeded, would they force the Tz-en back onto the arctic continent?

"Anthony, things are not as they seem. You see these excavations. But you see only what you are permitted to see."

"Stop talking in riddles. It doesn't matter any more. I'll be leaving soon. You know, you'd do pretty good in my profession. Too bad I'm retiring, or I'd take you on as a partner."

She smiled. With her eyes crinkling behind the shades, exposing her canines was not as disturbing. "I would like that, impractical as it is. Anthony, remember the digs beneath those tents?"

"The old Tz-en village. Yeah."

"They are not Tz-en. The Tz-en were not here when the Human colonists landed. As far as I understand, the Humans were the only sentient beings to live on El'aris."

"What are you talking about?"

She slipped off the shades, her large eyes squinting against the sun. "Look at me, Anthony. Do I, or any of my people, look like we belong in a world with such a sun? Our home had a dim sun. It was cold, and life was hard. Plant life was rare and animal life predatory. When the chance came to leave, nearly everyone took it. Even though we suffer from skin diseases and vision trouble because of the sunlight, none of us want to go back."

"You're not from El'aris?"

"No. We were brought here."

"Why?"

"To –" She stopped short as she looked over his shoulder and down the scaffolding.

Michaels heard the footsteps on the metal steps. He expected to see a squad of Tz-en, but he did not expect to see the grinning face of Stev Vindal climbing up to the platform. Behind him came six Tz-en soldiers. Craning his neck, he could see a seventh Tz-en standing at the bottom of the stairs, turning visitors away from the steps.

"You are a very difficult man to keep track of, Mr. Michaels," Vindal said as he drew close. He stepped next to Michaels and gazed out over the half-buried ship, placing his hands on the platform railing.

"I didn't know you were so anxious to see me, Vindal."

Michaels carefully gauged the positions of each of the Tz-en as they casually moved to different corners of the platform.

"Did you learn anything from that young El'aran?" Vindal asked.

"Nothing important," he replied, wondering how much Vindal already knew.

Vindal turned to fix him with a stare. The grin had vanished without a trace. "Now that's not entirely true. Didn't he mention something about an imminent raid on Khadeej?"

"You believed that?" he asked with a little laugh. "No one would take that seriously. He was feeding us false information."

"You should have passed that information on to us no matter what. But don't worry. We take it seriously enough. We're seeing to it that any rebellious force will be met with an overwhelming counter force and be immediately extinguished. If we are wrong for listening to the ravings of an El'aran urchin, we have lost nothing. If, however, you overreacted in your lethargy, then we will have prevented a tragedy. Don't you agree?"

"If you want to waste the time and money, go right ahead. I've got more important things to worry about."

"Which brings us to another issue. Your associate, Ms O'Brien. Where is she?"

Michaels shrugged. "Sorry. Lost track of her. She promised to write, but you know how that is."

"Speaking of promises, Mr. Michaels, I believe you fulfilled yours to your friend, Mr. Perry. The Shir'ka woman is gone from the Deltan estate. We haven't been able to locate her, but it hasn't been very long since we started the search. The same with Ms O'Brien. We know you and she entered the estate and affected the Shir'ka's escape. We have all the evidence we need. You could spend a very long time on this planet, if we choose to prosecute. I've spoken with Mr. Tabor, however. Considering your recent work for us, we are willing to overlook certain improprieties and drop any pending charges, as long as you cooperate. Actually, we're grateful to you for demonstrating several weaknesses in our security system."

"You're welcome."

"Tell us where we can find Ms O'Brien."

Michaels grinned. "You didn't say please."

Vindal grinned in return. "Please."

"No."

Vindal's smile disappeared, replaced by a scowl that made him look years older. "I can easily hand you over to the Tz-en, and they can get the information from you."

"I very much doubt that. You put too much stock in their methods of torture. I'll let you know, they're pretty weak compared to some other races I've known on more intimate levels. Besides, if, by some bizarre quirk of fate, they were able to break me, they wouldn't learn much. I don't know where Hannah is. Does that save you a lot of bother? Unless you want to make an offer to buy my services in helping to track her down."

Vindal brightened. "Very well, Mr. Michaels, we shall pay for your services. Name your fee."

Michaels shook his head. "Sorry. I've decided I won't work for slime any more."

Vindal's scowl returned. He stepped back and motioned to the Tz-en. They drew their blasters.

Michaels watched the two nearest closing in on him. Out of the corner of his eye he saw Jiin move, no doubt joining in on the arrest. But then he saw a blur of her black uniform crashing into the two approaching soldiers. They toppled over, shoving into Vindal and knocking him into the railing.

Instantly, Michaels crouched. His blaster flew into his hand and three bolts shot across the platform. One Tz-en at the far end cried out as his chest burned open. His staggered backward and fell over the rail. His cry receded to end with a thud upon impact with the ground. A second Tz-en grabbed his head as a bolt took away half his face. He dropped to the platform, dead before he started to fall. The third bolt went wild.

The other two Tz-en returned fire, forcing Michaels to leap across the platform. He caught a glance of Jiin striking down the other two she had tackled. One fell unconscious. The second tried to bring up his blaster.

Michaels shot back at the other two. Bolts flashed around him, exploding shards of plastic from the platform. Their heat burned across his face.

One Tz-en intercepted a shot that took away his arm. Michaels realized the shot did not come from him. He fired at the other man, one of his bolts finally finding a target and bringing the soldier down.

Michaels turned toward the fight in which Jiin had been involved. Both soldiers now lay motionless at her feet, and she had her blaster trained on the man missing a hand.

"Go!" she shouted to him.

He hesitated, confused. What was she doing?

Vindal gained his feet behind Jiin. He snatched up a fallen Tz-en's blaster and fired. As Michaels cried out a warning, the bolt shot through Jiin's back. He saw the flash burn through the front of her uniform, below her left shoulder.

He fired three shots at Vindal. One caught him in the chest. He toppled back, falling over the rail. His left hand clutched at the rail and caught hold, cutting short his fall.

Michaels ran to Jiin, ignoring Vindal as he dangled from the platform.

He caught her as she fell forward. The sharp stench of burnt flesh stung his nostrils. Her face grew snowy white in its paleness. Her hand felt icy in his.

"Hang on, Jiin. We'll get you help."

The last Tz-en soldier, who had guarded the stairs, topped the platform, his blaster drawn. He took aim on Michaels.

Jiin reached out with one hand toward him. "Hold," she said in a weak voice. "He is to go free."

The man looked over the carnage on the platform. Michaels felt a silent communication between him and the woman. Some understanding. The man nodded and slipped his blaster into its holster.

"Get help," Michaels told him. "See if there's a medic here. Quick."

The man hurried away.

"No!" came a rasping cry from behind him. "Stop!"

The soldier was beyond the reach of Vindal's voice.

Jiin gripped Michaels' hand and sat up, leaning her back against the railing.

"Now go, Anthony. I will do what I can for you, but I have no guarantee that you are not already wanted for arrest. Go while you can."

"Why did you help me?"

"There was nothing else to do. None of us want to go back to our homeworld, but some of us are tired of the injustices. We are tired of being puppets. It hurts our sense of honor. You resurrected that in me, Anthony."

"Michaels! Help me!" choked Vindal.

Michaels was amazed that the man held onto the rail as long as he had. He left Jiin and stepped to the railing, looking down at Vindal's dangling body. His right shoulder was useless, a large burn hole nearly severing his right arm away. The blood had drained from his face. His eyes threatened to pop out as he looked up, pleading.

"Help me, please. I promise, I'll help you get away ... I'll see all charges are dropped ... I'll talk Tabor into giving you another million credits. Just pull me up!"

Michaels felt Jiin at his side. She clung to the rail. He circled his arm around her for support and she clung to him. Her eyes narrowed as she glared down at Vindal.

"Your time is through, Human," she said, the words hissing with hoarseness.

"No!" Vindal's face filled with horror, whitening to the hue of a Tz-en.

Jiin's boot came down on Vindal's fingers. Bone and metal crunched. The bar of the rail gave way at the same time his crushed fingers slipped free. He screamed as he fell, until he crashed onto the plexi covering the flight deck of the ancient starship. His body sprawled across the glass, then slid over the curve of the hull and rolled down the mound. Below, a woman screamed.

"I wish you hadn't done that," Michaels told Jiin.

She leaned heavily on him. "Why? Did you want to question him?"

"No. *I* wanted to do it."

"Oh."

Below, the sounds of a crowd grew near. The soldier may have gone for medical help, but the sounds of blasters and falling bodies would certainly bring more Tz-en and unwanted authorities. He doubted Jiin could talk him out of his troubles now.

"I will be fine, Anthony. Please go while you can. I have no way of knowing what information Vindal has passed on about you. You cannot go back to the spaceport. They will be waiting. Try to contact me in Khadeej. I will ..."

She coughed, doubling over.

"Just take it easy. Help's on its way."

"And they will take you if you don't leave. Now go."

She pushed him away and leaned against the railing. "Go," she said.

He looked at her as he walked toward the steps. A group of the curious crept up the stairs, peering cautiously up. He saw no Tz-en among them, just some tour guides, a scattering of archeologists, and a liberal amount of some of the braver or more curious tourists. He climbed down past them, feeling their wondering stares. He tried to convince himself Jiin would be all right. The other Tz-en was a friend of sorts; that much he could gather from the expression he had worn. He would get help to her. Still, something gnawed at him. He hated to leave her.

At the bottom of the platform, among the crowd that had gathered, he hesitated. He could mingle, wait. Even if it meant risking capture. Then he saw the soldier running toward the platform. A Human with a medical kit tried to keep pace.

Michaels turned toward the area where the transports were parked.

⬢

Wearing local clothes, Michaels did not feel inconspicuous as he walked through the market street of Khadeej. He still didn't fool the locals, but they ignored him. He wasn't concerned about the El'arans recognizing him. The Tz-en were on his mind, but they seemed oblivious to him, which was the effect he wanted. On a public broadcast of a news update, Hannah hadn't been located, but now he was added. The off-worlder Anthony Michaels was wanted for multiple murders at the Achari archaeological site. He was considered dangerous. No doubt the Tz-en constabulary were given instruction to shoot to kill, if they could distinguish him from other Humans walking the streets.

He found J'sef's abandoned shop empty. The boy might still return, unless he took Michaels' advice and headed south. He had hoped to reach J'sef, since the boy was his only link to the revolutionaries.

How could he communicate with them? Every El'aran knew who he was. Not only could they pick him out, even dressed like them, but his face was plastered over every holo unit on the planet.

He wished he could contact Geoff and get some of their equipment. But he couldn't hope of breaking into the prison and getting out again with Perry.

He stopped at the stall displaying Shir'ka glass and fingered a rainbow bottle whose colors flowed like sand as he moved it.

"*Cyte*," the stall merchant said.

Michaels looked up at the man.

"You have the face of the lost," the merchant said. "This is the third time you have been by, but you do not have the look of a buyer. I believe I know what you want."

"Oh really."

"Yes, *Cyte* Michaels. I suggest you visit the tailor shop over there."

The man turned away to help a customer by the time it sank into Michaels' numb brain that the merchant had used his name.

He walked into the tailor shop, glancing over the displays of clothing and cloth. These samples were richer than the typical El'aran clothes, probably reserved for the upper class or the occasional tourist who wanted some authentic native costume to take back to their homeworld. He noticed the little round man behind the counter and the young woman in the doorway to a back room.

The girl glanced around the shop, then out the window to the street. Then she motioned to him.

"In here, quickly."

The little tailor also turned his attention to the street, watching.

Michaels rounded the counter and stepped through the doorway and the girl slid the door shut between them.

The room beyond held rolls of material, bright colors like most El'aran fabrics and more somber, rusty colors popular with Shir'ka. Two machines sat at work stations on either side of the room. Another doorway stood ajar opposite.

"Mick!"

Hannah threw the door open and rushed into the room.

"Are you okay?" he asked.

"Yeah. You?"

"Fine. How's it feel to be sharing El'aris's Most Wanted?"

"I had all the fame and glory to myself, then you had to horn in on it. Can't you let a girl have some fun? What happened after I left?"

"I was about to ask you that. You know, if you had come back with Geoff like you were suppose to, we'd be off this rock by now."

"Sorry, Mick. I wanted to get Mar'a south of Jhamrahl. I couldn't just dump her on the streets. I gave her some of my clothes, but she's never been east of Khadeej. On the way, I caught the news on the car receiver. Nice to hear your own name, isn't it? I wondered why they never mentioned you. Thought maybe you pulled a fast one, until I heard the latest installment. What were you up to? Murder in Achari?"

Michaels quickly told her about Jiin taking him to meet J'sef, then about their visit to the archeology site so she could be free to talk. Then about Vindal showing up, and the subsequent encounter.

"So he's dead? Good. And Jiin helped you out? Against her own people? She must have a thing for you."

He gave a shiver. "Don't be ridiculous."

"No, I think she does, in a way. Can't say I blame her none."

"She saved my life," he said. "She wasn't able to stop them from adding me to the public enemy list. How did you end up here?"

"Mar'a brought me here when we heard I was wanted dead or dead. I've been staying upstairs for the time being. Funny, from the start they want me dead but not you?"

"I'm pretty sure that's changed now."

In a room no larger than a closet on the third level above the tailor's shop, Michaels tried to pace. The room's limits refused to yield to his frustrations. He mumbled, but whatever curses he brought forth did not do justice to the situation. The afternoon sun beating down made the attic room unbearable. His shirt clung to him, which made matters worse. Come darkness, he and Hannah had to move on, so they would no longer endanger the tailor and his family.

Hannah sat on the blankets that covered the plank floor under the curve of the roof. Dressed in trousers, boots, and a white tee shirt, she didn't seem to be perspiring as much as him. The stifling heat wasn't bothering her. And she had a pleasant citrus smell, which he found distracting. On her lap rested her computer. She hunched over the screen, her fingers flying over the keypad, pausing, then zipping again.

"Where are you from, Michaels?" she asked, her eyes not leaving the monitor.

"Huh? Oh, Delnaar. Backwater planet."

"Don't they like girls there?"

"Huh?"

"Or is it just you? You don't like girls. Human type girls."

"What are you talking about?"

"Just wondering." She glanced up and flashed him a smile. "I mean, here we are, all alone, in this little room. You've already got me in bed." She slapped the hard wood floor under the blanket.

"Ah, no, you've got it wrong."

Her smile vanished and her eyes stabbed at him. "Oh, so it isn't Humans you like. You prefer the company of that Tz-en. I've seen how close you've become."

He waved his hands at her. "No! No way am I attracted to Jiin. Maybe as friends, but no way it would ever go any further. That would be, that would be … just wrong. On so many levels."

"Yeah, well, I heard the Tz-en women bite out the throats of their men after they make love."

He rolled his eyes. "You just made that up."

She grinned. "Yeah, I did. So, you don't like girls, then. I mean, I'm not promiscuous, but by now I'd be hit on a few times. Your partner hit on me that first night in the tavern. Turned him down twice before he'd let me alone."

"Of course I like girls. Wait, Thatcher hit on you?"

"I'm not saying I'd say yes, but why haven't you? You know, a boy and a girl, alone in a room, imminent danger all around. Wanted criminals and all."

He dropped down on the floor beside her. "I like to keep things professional. You work for me."

"That's just bull. Or is it something about me? I know I'm not the most attractive person on the planet. Next to Mar'a I'm definitely lacking ..."

"No, you are very attractive."

"Then why —"

He leaned into her. "You talk too much." He kissed her, sliding her computer from her lap.

"Remember those files I copied when we were sneaking around the palace? They caught my eye then. Looked odd. I've had time to look them over, and things don't look good at all. See?"

Michaels sat up slowly, rubbing his eyes. The lists on the small screen were too fuzzy. "So?"

She tapped the keypad, then jabbed at the screen.

"See this? El'aran Gold Corporation owns the mines and is primarily controlled by the Tz-en government. The First Minister, Tung-Cho, is among the board members. Of course, no El'aran name appears on the list. Only Tz-en. That's pretty much to be expected. They sell the gold to Deltan, Tri-sector of Aminiar, Argurian Technologies, and a number of other companies. Deltan is the only major company on the list, the rest are small. Which might be expected, since Deltan has an exclusive contract with the Tz-en. Trouble is, Aminiar is on Helbent. There's no such company as Tri-sector. Remember, I worked in the computer systems there."

"Could be another Aminiar."

"Wrong. I did a search. According to records, Tri-sector of Aminiar is on Helbent. Records state its location, which happens to be in the middle of a ghetto, if anyone happened to pay a visit to that address. It's a shadow company."

"A what?"

"It doesn't exist, except in data files. So I checked the others. Argurian Technologies is another one supposedly on a remote planet. The others are too. The systems are less advanced and more remote, so details can't be checked easily. But if you look through any network, there they are, big as life. I'm pretty certain they're all shadow companies."

"So? What's the point of them existing?"

"So Deltan doesn't have a strict monopoly on the El'aran gold," she said. "My guess is that it does."

"What difference does it make if the Tz-en sell their gold to one company or a dozen? It's their gold."

"Yeah, right. But look a little further. Like the casinos and hotels around Jhamrahl. The Bank of Khadeej owns the Crystal Palace and the Red Sands Casinos, as well as the El'aran Hotel, the Arijon Inn, and the Tadamij Hotel. The Bank of Khadeej has the First Minister on its board, as well as Nhung-Chi and four other Tz-en. The bank is owned by the Jhamrahl Fishers Company. The Fishers Company is a joint venture between the Khadeej Mining Fellowship and Arijon Shipping. This goes in circles. All sorts of Tz-en names appear on the list of board members, and many repeat, like Tung-Cho. I've done random checks, and I can't locate at least six out of nine names."

"What do you mean, you can't locate them?" Michaels asked.

"The names only exist in the company records. Not in any census records. Now I can't prove anything with what I've got so far, but I'd say they were e-people."

"E-people?"

She tapped the keypad. "They only exist here. Electronic people. Like the shadow companies."

"They don't –" He broke off and stared, wide awake now. Despite the oppressive heat, ice ran the course of his spine. Silence buzzed in his ears while his mind dredged up a sudden realization. "How did you search for these names?" he asked, hoping she would not give the answer he knew she would.

"I tapped into the local network."

He sank back, his head rolling back and his eyes staring at the ceiling. How else could she have done the search? Just as Ringer had done it. And they found Ringer quick, because they knew where to look. Finding Hannah would take a little more time, but not long if they were waiting for her. He climbed to his feet and stepped to the small, half-moon shaped window. Below lay the market street. The Tz-en patrol stood out among the scatter of brown skin and colorful cloth. El'arans moved aside, avoiding the soldiers, making them even more conspicuous. One soldier held up a small device.

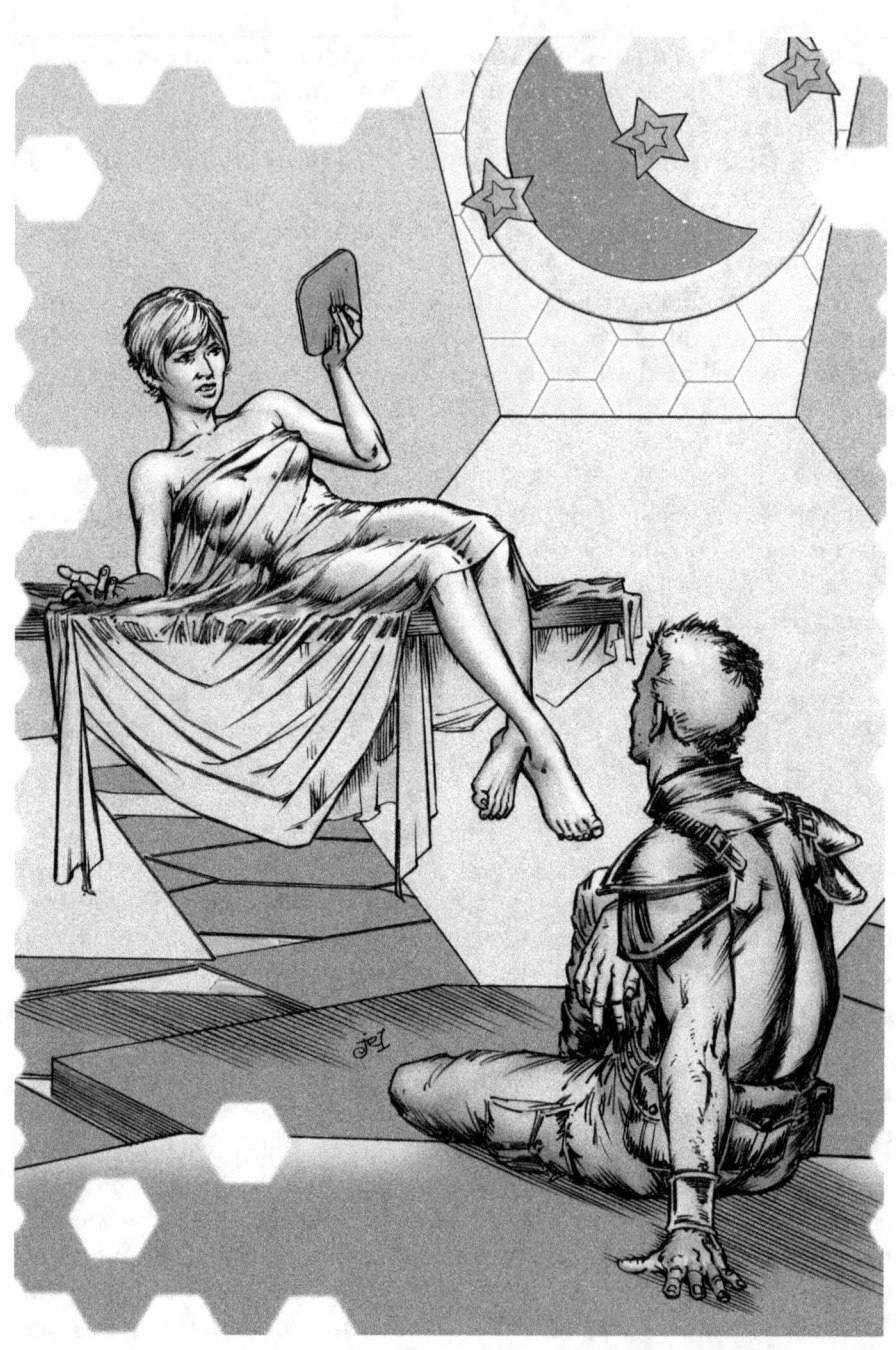

"I can't locate six out of nine names…"

"Turn that off. Quick!" Michaels said as he turned on Hannah.

He grabbed her arm and hauled her up as she closed her computer. His other hand snatched up his clothes. "Quick! Get dressed."

"What's wrong?"

"We've got to get outta here. You've used their network. They're triangulating our position."

"What –"

He shoved her coat into her hands and pushed her toward the steps. They ducked under the curve of the roof and began descending. He kept constant pressure at her back, urging her on.

"They're outside," he said. "They're triangulating to locate us. They've probably been monitoring your network use all along. Just like with Ringer. Only they knew where to find him."

She froze at the bottom of the steps, Michaels bumping into her. "Oh my God," she said.

In the shop downstairs, the tailor waited on a customer. Michaels burst in from the back room and took them in with a glance. They stared back. He looked through the front windows to see the pedestrians on the market street. The crowd shifted to provide a path for the Tz-en patrol. The soldiers walked steadily down the street. The one with the tracer motioned toward the tailor shop.

"Out the back," Michaels told the two El'arans. "Get out, quick!"

The tailor glanced to the street, where he had seen Michaels looking. He gently took his customer by the arm and led him through the back room. Michaels followed, wishing they would move faster. Hannah already had the rear door open.

"They're coming," he said.

The tailor and his customer hurried across the narrow alley to a neighboring shop. Michaels pulled a metal trash bin in front of the door. Then he and Hannah ran down the left branch of the alley.

The street drew closer ahead of them. Once they rounded the corner, they could vanish in the crowd, maybe make their way to a place where they could steal some transportation and get out of Khadeej.

He heard the trash bin hit the ground behind them. Someone had come through the tailor's shop. He felt their eyes on his back. Their weapons would be raised, taking aim.

"Keep going!" he told Hannah. "Get away!"

Energy bolts sizzled through the air. Explosions flashed across the walls, dumpsters, the cobbled alleyway.

A flare of orange blossomed across Hannah's back. Her arms flew out and she sailed over the cobbles. Michaels tried to catch her. He reached out for her arm, but she pitched forward and skid across the ground. Her computer flew toward the left wall and shattered on impact. Hannah slid to a stop, her arms and legs limp and sprawled.

Michaels stopped, overshot her, then scrambled back. Bolts tore into the street around him.

Four Tz-en ran down the alley.

He fired twice, and two Tz-en tumbled over the cobbles. Three more shots brought down a third man. The forth dropped behind the cover of crates against one wall. He shot back. Michaels kept firing until the crates crumbled and his bolts found the man behind the debris. Heat from his blaster burnt his hand.

Kneeling beside Hannah, Michaels reached out for her. His hands shook. He stared at the burn that covered her back, blending clothes with skin and muscle. He couldn't tell how deep the burn went. Too deep, he realized. She wasn't breathing.

He turned her over and searched for a pulse. First at her neck, then her wrist, then neck again. Nothing. He remembered hearing that some people died from the shock caused by blaster wounds rather than the damage itself. If they were resuscitated in time ... He pulled open her lips and breathed into her lungs. Her skin felt so cold. He tried everything he could remember. Nothing brought back the beat of her heart. Nothing chased away the coldness of her touch.

What else could he do? He sat and stared and cradled her in his arms. Her face paled as he watched it.

His eyes stung.

"I'm sorry," he said. "I'm so sorry." His voice cracked. His heart thundered in his ears. He should never have gotten her involved. This was his fault.

He was unaware of others around him until someone spoke.

"Michaels, there's nothing more you can do. Come with us."

He looked up. His vision blurred, but he recognized Jiin's voice.

"No. I need to stay."

Her hand took him under the arm and lifted him. He laid Hannah down gently, her hand slipping from his fingers. Jiin wasn't alone. A squad of Tz-en surrounded her. He didn't care. Let them kill him. It didn't matter any more.

One of the Tz-en bent down over Hannah. Michaels struck out and kicked him across the side of his face, sending him backward on the cobbles.

"Don't you dare touch her!" His voice echoed down the canyon of the alley. He felt Jiin's grip tighten on his arm.

Jiin shook her head, and the soldier backed away.

Another soldier drew near, a twisted piece of metal and plastic in his hands. He held it out for Jiin's inspection.

"We found this, Commander. It must be the computer we traced. I have extracted this data wafer."

Jiin took the wafer and placed it into a pocket of her uniform.

"Take Michaels to the prison," she said. "To ensure he doesn't escape in transit, give him an injection."

Michaels felt the sting as a hypo hissed into his shoulder. He looked into Jiin's eyes. He couldn't read what lay beyond them. Would she help him again? Looking into her hard-set features, he doubted it. Why was she even here? Her cold touch over his arm made him think of holding Hannah's hand. Cold in death.

The alley started to swim in circles around him.

He looked at Hannah's body. Then blackness swallowed her.

CHAPTER FOURTEEN
THE FACE OF THE ENEMY

Through a mist, Michaels saw the prison. He couldn't feel the hands that pulled him and threw him into the dark cell. He floated across the filthy floor, never touching the ground. At least, he thought he did. Somehow he ended up laying flat, staring up at the faint, bare bulb that shed its meager light into the room. He could hear distant noises, but made little sense of them.

When men came and dragged him out into the light, he began to feel the pain. First and foremost, his head hurt. The light stung his eyes. By the time they reached the surface, he could feel the sting of a binder field over his wrists, holding his arms behind his back. When the guards tossed him into the back of a security van, he was aware of an assortment of bumps and bruises.

"Hello, Tony."

He struggled to sit up. He'd been shot before, and stabbed, broke bones and ruptured organs. He'd been cut and bruised and beat. Nothing ever felt like this ache that tore him in half. Hannah.

Sitting on the bench against the van's wall, he shook his head to clear his vision and looked across at the man who had spoken.

"Together again," he said to Perry.

"It would seem. Though I had my doubts that we'd end up together in this little adventure. Mind telling me how you wound up on the wrong side of the Tz-en?"

"Whenever the planet stops spinning."

"The truck's moving," Perry said. He looked out the small window in the rear door of the van, leaning awkwardly with his hands cuffed behind him. "We're getting the one credit tour of Khadeej."

"Well ... I kept my promise."

"Which was ?"

"I gave my word Mar'a would be released."

"Is that why you're here?"

"Not entirely. But it's a start. While you've been taking it easy in Khadeej, I've been busy."

Michaels became aware of Perry's intent stare.

"Where is Mar'a?"

"As far as I know," Michaels said, "back with her people. As safe as anyone in Khadeej, I guess. Jon ... they killed Hannah."

"I'm sorry, Tony."

"I should have ..."

He laid his head against the bulkhead of the van. His eyes quivered shut, but he still saw Hannah's face as she lay in the alley.

When he awoke, he immediately noticed the stench. Worse was the realization that the smell came from him. His stomach grumbled.

"We're on the river road," Perry said.

"Are we near Achari?" Michaels asked.

"Twenty minutes ago."

"Then we'll be at Jhamrahl soon."

"You've learned the territory. That's good. Now, mind starting at the beginning and telling me what happened to bring about your fall from grace?"

"Don't be so smug, Perry. I wouldn't be in this mess if it wasn't for you."

"True. But you had a choice. What changed your mind?"

Michaels began with his going back to Jhamrahl. Perry sat and listened, not interrupting during the narration of Hannah's discovery of the faking of the broadcast confession. Michaels went on, eventually describing the nighttime visit to the Deltan estate. The shadow of a smile pulled on

Perry's beard and wrinkled the corners of his eyes. When he finished with the encounter at the archeological excavation at Achari and his flight to Khadeej, he felt the van turn off the main road.

"We've turned off before Jhamrahl," he told Perry.

"We're headed toward the palace."

The road played out behind them. Michaels watched the familiar scenery, his mind rolling over the last time he traveled this way. Hannah's image kept creeping in. Their exploits played through his thoughts.

The van stopped.

The rear door opened. About twenty carbines and blasters leveled at them. One Tz-en officer motioned him and Perry out. He stepped down and looked around. They had parked at the rear of the mansion. The very place he and Hannah had used to sneak into the building. They had parked their vehicle over there. Other Tz-en held positions at various places in the lot. At the rear door to the palace, a Human security man stood and beckoned them in.

"Why are we here?" Michaels asked the security man.

"You'll be taken to a room to clean and change. Do it quickly. The cuffs will be replaced afterward. Don't try to escape. You'll be monitored every second. Any move that could be considered inappropriate could cause your immediate death."

"Stepped up your security, eh?" Michaels asked, flashing a wry grin.

The Tz-en shoved them through the doorway, down a narrow hall, to an unfurnished room. Ten soldiers crowded into the room and waited with leveled weapons. The officer deactivated their binder fields and stepped back.

Michaels rubbed the tingling from his wrists and looked down at a pile of civilian clothes. In front of him was a shower stall. Considering the smell he acquired from the prison, he wasn't about to argue with the facilities. He turned his back on his audience and began stripping off his stained and torn clothes. The hot water of the shower revived him, chasing away the last vestiges of the drug and easing some of the physical pain.

Within minutes he was dressed in black slacks, white shirt, and black shoes. Perry had similar clothes. They took some of the wildness out of Perry's appearance.

The cuffs were replaced and they were led from the room.

The route they traveled led through various intersecting corridors. Michaels tried to remember the way, overlaying it on his memory of the building's plans. They were in the main wing, headed forward. With a bend in the corridor, they came to the entrance to the former throne room.

Jiin stood at the large doors, with two soldiers on either side. She nodded to the officer.

"I will take charge of the prisoners," she said.

The officer nodded and stepped back.

The security man opened the doors.

She walked behind him, gabbed hold of the binder rings on his wrists, and jerked them up and forward. She propelled him through the opened door, into the great chamber, before he could wiggle free.

Pieter Tabor sat at the far end of the long conference table. An old Tz-en occupied the chair on his left.

"We can finally wrap up this irritating little business," Tabor said. "Do you have the data wafer?"

Jiin slipped the wafer from her uniform pocket and placed it on the polished table, where it seemed to float over the glazed surface. She pushed it, sending it gliding across the table. Tabor snatched it up as it reached him. Holding it between thumb and finger, he turned it over as he examined it. Then he slid it into a slot in a terminal on the desk. The small holographic screen flashed in the air in front of him, and he scrolled through the material.

"Good," he said. "This could have proven damaging if the wrong people received it. I understand the person who downloaded the data is deceased. That ties one loose end. Now we can tie off the others and make an end of this."

He popped the wafer from its slot and bent it in half with the sound of a crushed bug.

"I suppose you know nothing of what was on that wafer?" he asked.

Michaels had the feeling anything he said would not alter his ultimate fate, which looked pretty dismal. "Suppose I told you that copies of that wafer have been transmitted off-world."

Tabor's grin chilled the air. It was cunning and malevolent. "I would say you were a liar, Mr. Michaels. We've monitored off-world transmissions. We always do. Nothing of that nature has been sent. We also monitor network inquiries, which is how our people traced your position. I understand you do not have a very computer literate background, so the work was confined to your late associates. Do you happen to understand the significance of their investigations?"

"Yes, but I don't really give a damn that you're running this planet with shadow companies. I don't care that you own all the businesses and that you get all the profits."

"Not all of them, but a sizable percentage. In cooperation with Tung-Cho." He motioned to the Tz-en beside him.

Now Michaels recognized the old man. Funny how quickly the Tz-en age. He hadn't lost that sadistic curl to his thin lips, which tended to expose his left canine.

"Do the Tz-en see any profit?" Michaels asked.

"The Tz-en government receives a modest amount."

"But it mostly goes to you."

Tabor shrugged. "Deltan Technologies made a great investment over ten years ago. You both should recognize that. It is only fair we receive the advantages of our endeavors."

"Yeah," Michaels said, "but I bet Deltan isn't wise to the shadows you've installed. I bet they lead to you, not Deltan. A few special bank accounts in a few scattered systems."

"You're very astute, Mr. Michaels. Yes, I'm afraid that the main offices of Deltan would frown on certain activities in this sector. Not to mention the Trade Consortium as a whole. But none of that information has escaped and you are not likely to carry it beyond this planet. Even if it was passed on to some of the erstwhile revolutionaries, it will go no further. We already have a full fledged plan discrediting the indigenous Human population."

"How long do you think you can hide the origin of the Tz-en?" Perry asked.

"Indefinitely. Soon we will have all of them transplanted. Their homeworld is of no consequences. It will be obliterated. No trace will be found, and the galaxy will accept that the Tz-en are the original inhabitants of El'aris. Marketing is the key. The masses will believe anything you tell them, especially if you play on their sympathies. The poor Tz-en minority; overrun and displaced by the evil colonizing Humans. It's happened before, why wouldn't they believe it happened again?"

Michaels shot a sharp glance at Jiin. "So," he said, "they really aren't from here. Then they must have come here about the time we came to train them. That's why we never saw any towns, just temporary settlements. You brought them here and created the story of the poor miserable minority."

"You catch on slowly, Mr. Michaels. I imagine your associate, Mr. Perry, discovered the truth some years ago, though he had the help of those barbaric Shir'ka."

"I wonder," Perry said, gazing up at the masterpiece of creation on the dome ceiling, "who is the more barbaric? An honorable people who fight for their freedom or the deceitful people who steal that freedom away? Is it a way of life or what is in the heart?"

Tabor laughed. "Be as philosophical as you like, Mr. Perry. That does not alter the fact that I own this planet. I control it."

"On the blood of Humans as well as Tz-en," Perry said. He looked over to Tung-Cho. "You accept this man's truth? You sacrifice your homeworld to live under his control? Maybe you believe you control El'aris and its people. You turn the El'arans into slaves or menials. Do you see the parallel with what Tabor has done to you? This planet will never replace your homeworld. You'll never control it, never master it. And you'll never be free from Tabor."

"I am disappointed with you, Mr. Perry," Tabor said, shaking his head. "Trying to turn us against each other. Not very original. You see, Tung-Cho would not be in his present position, both influentially and monetarily, without me. He and his people rule El'aris. I merely assist in certain decisions, especially those dealing with the economy. Tung-Cho hasn't had exposure to such sensitive situations. We have an excellent partnership, and soon the El'arans will no longer be in a position to interfere. The revolution in Khadeej will be swiftly put down. A few thousand more Tz-en will arrive from their former homeworld, secretly unloaded in other parts of the continent to avoid media coverage. When the placement of new satellites is completed, the Shir'ka will no longer be able to hide. Some more aircraft and the Tz-en can purify the desert."

"What about the Tz-en who don't want to be here?" Michaels asked.

"When their homeworld is destroyed," Tabor said, "they will have incentive to work with the government."

"Better to be rulers in hell than servants in Heaven," Perry said.

"I believe you have some things backward, Mr. Perry. This is hardly hell. This planet is a veritable paradise. No sparsely populated planet such as this exists anywhere. It's a gold mine."

"Is that a pun?" Michaels asked.

Tabor lost his smile. "I am not going to defend my actions against you two. You are here only as a final courtesy. Even as we speak, a story is passing on to the media. Two mercenaries have been captured by Tz-en officials and found guilty of terrorism. They will be executed by the time the story is broadcast. No one will ever hear of the short revolution, though. We have sent troops from Achari and Jhamrahl to join those in Khadeej. When Mr. Perry's friends try to rise up and take over the government complex, they will be surrounded by thousands of Tz-en soldiers and immediately put to death. No El'aran will ever think of raising so much as a finger against any Tz-en ever again. And we owe that advantage to Mr. Michaels and his informant. It only saddens me that the information had to come from the late Mr. Vindal, rather than Michaels. I had hoped that there would be some loyalty to an employer. Perhaps his greater loyalty lay with his former friend."

"Damn right," Michaels snapped.

"Of course, the media is helpful in raising support for the Tz-en. The excavation site at Achari is a fabulous tourist attraction, for Humans as well as non-Humans. It amazes me how quickly Humans will turn against their own in favor of a poor, subjugated race. Even before the construction of the resorts, the Tz-en received hundreds of offers for aide from sympathetic off-worlders."

"It's called compassion, Tabor," Perry said, "Something you wouldn't understand. They didn't turn against their own. Although the Human race has had a long history of such opposites as saints and people like you."

Tabor's lips drew into a straight line. "You know, I may even come to your execution. I would enjoy the spectacle. It won't be particularly long, though Tung-Cho argued that torture would be good for his people's morale. I suggested it be quick, though degrees of pain were optional. I just want both of you gone as soon as possible."

Perry shrugged, straining against his binder field. The binder's hum warbled softly. "Why not do it here? Just have one of them shoot us. I'm sure Tung-Cho wouldn't mind."

Michaels leaned toward Perry. "Don't give them any ideas." He felt the sting of his binder field as he pulled against it. His wrists parted, stretching the field

"That would not be appropriate," Tabor said, shaking his head. "Even though we have a great deal of influence over the media, we do not want to have to explain two dead bodies in the corporate offices. Not that a story couldn't be devised, but we will stay within the confines of the plan already formulated."

Lights around the dome flickered, then went out. The affect was hardly noticeable, since El'aris's bright sunlight cut through the slit windows over the dome itself. But Tabor's expression as he looked down at his computer terminal showed a greater disturbance. He pressed the keypad several times, then turned to a comlink panel just to the right of the terminal.

"Security."

No response came.

Tung-Cho leaned toward him. "What is wrong?"

"Power malfunction of some kind."

Tung-Cho motioned a hand toward Jiin. "Send someone to see to the problem. This is most inconvenient. I want a transport ready to take these two into Jhamrahl for the execution."

"Yes, First Minister," Jiin said. She turned to one of the escorts and gave him a quick order.

The man bowed his head and retreated. As he passed through the doors, Michaels could hear thunder in the distance. He didn't look forward to a rainy day for his death. He always wanted to die with the sun on his face. He'd seen too many comrades die in rainstorms, ice storms, or just plain dreary days. He glanced up at the dome. The afternoon sun blazed through.

"You don't seem to understand," Perry was telling Tabor. "You can't stop the will to be free. The El'arans and the Shir'ka will fight back, one way or another. They won't lose their planet to you."

"Then they'll all die, because the Tz-en won't give it up. Most of them won't go back to their homeworld and soon they won't have the choice."

"And some day the Tz-en will get tired of you. You can't win, Tabor."

"Eventually, I won't need to be an influence here. I'll retire in comfort, and the Tz-en will be free to ruin the delicate economy I've set up. They will have their new world all to themselves."

Perry laughed. "As if you could take your hand away. Your greed won't let you. No matter how much you have, you'll still want more. More power, more control. You're a servant to your greed the way the Tz-en are servants to you. You're deceiving yourself if you think you could just walk away from El'aris."

Tabor's face flushed. He gave a quick glance to Tung-Cho, whose eyes narrowed.

"Enough of this," Tabor said. He pushed his chair back and stood. Walking around the table, he came face to face with Perry. "Perhaps I will take your advice and dispose of you now."

Perry sneered at the man. "You don't have the guts."

Tabor's face darkened. He turned to the Tz-en nearest to Perry and snatched the blaster from his holster. He thumbed the activator and pushed the muzzle under Perry's chin.

Michaels moved toward Tabor, but the soldier on his right anticipated the attack and grabbed his arm, pulling him back. Michaels strained against the binder field, which tingled rather than stung. His wrists came free of the field and the binders fell clattering to the tiled floor. Both Michaels and the soldier stared down at them.

Michaels hit the soldier full in the face. The man fell back, losing his grip.

"Not a step further, Mr. Michaels," Tabor said, his voice tight as he held the blaster under Perry's chin.

Jiin slowly circled them, her eyes and weapon trained on Michaels. The other Tz-en in the room stood on guard, except for Tung-Cho, who folded his arms and patiently waited at the far end of the table.

Too many guns, Michaels knew. But at least he'd die fighting, and take a few of them with him. He watched how Jiin placed Perry and Tabor between them and wondered what she was up to.

Jiin's eyes narrowed and her head shook a mere fraction of a centimeter.

He paused, contemplating what that little expression meant. He heard the thunder, closer than before. The floor vibrated.

"If either of them moves," Tabor said, "shoot them." He stepped away from Perry; his face still flushed a deep red. His breath came in shallow puffs. "Both of you have caused us enough trouble. You will be taken now to Jhamrahl or executed right here in your failed attempt to assassinate the First Minister and myself."

He flipped the blaster around and held its butt for Jiin to take.

She kept her own weapon aimed at Michaels and took the blaster from Tabor with her other hand. Then she tossed it through the air – at Michaels.

As the blaster spun, Jiin turned and fired three short bursts that sent two of her own men sprawling with holes burned through their shoulders.

Michaels caught the blaster.

Perry's hands came free, his binder rings flying across the room. He grabbed Tabor by the throat and lifted him off the floor to throw him heavily onto the broad table.

Michaels caught Tung-Cho's movement out of the corner of his eye. The old Tz-en leaped from his chair and drew a small blaster from beneath his coat.

"Traitorous –"

A bolt from Michaels' blaster bore through the First Minister's forehead. He dropped dead onto the floor, what was left of his face smoldering.

Michaels turned on the remaining Tz-en, but Jiin reached him and pushed his hand down before he fired. A bolt melted one of the floor tiles.

"No. These men are with me," she said. "The other two were not, which is why I had to wound them."

Heat flowed across Michaels' flesh as he glared into her pale eyes.

"Just because our leaders, like Tung-Cho, are corrupt," she said, the lines of her face softening, her eyes reflecting a passion, "does not mean that all Tz-en are. I could not help you until now, when I lowered the intensity of the restraining fields. I was not there to prevent your friend's death, or I would have done so. Many of us are weary of being servants for this Human. We want freedom just as much as the El'arans."

"Don't be a fool!" Tabor shouted, his voice hoarse. He lay half across the table, grasping at its smooth surface with one hand, holding his bruised throat with the other. "You two will be killed as soon as you step through that door. Commander, you'll be tortured as a traitor. Take charge now, and we can overlook this incident. The Tz-en are not going to give this world over to the El'arans, no matter how many are unhappy with the arrangement. Do you want to go back to your homeworld?"

Another peel of thunder shook the floor tiles. Not thunder, Michaels realized. He hadn't been paying attention, or he would have recognized the sounds.

"I believe you have greater worries than us," Perry said. He had taken weapons from the wounded Tz-en while their comrades saw to their injuries. Without raising a weapon, he stepped toward Tabor.

The Deltan executive drew back, eyes flashing with terror. Perry grabbed the front of his coat and dragged him to his feet.

"Listen!" Perry barked. "What do you hear?"

"A storm." Tabor's voice cracked.

"Yeah, a storm," Perry said, a smile spreading across his beard.

The doors to the audience chamber crashed open. In ran security men and a dozen Tz-en.

Perry pushed Tabor away, and he and Michaels turned toward this new threat. But they were ignored. Shouts and the sounds of explosions and blaster fire rang through the hall outside. An energy bolt sizzled through one of the security men. Tz-en returned fire down the hallway.

Michaels glanced at Perry. Then at the conference table.

Without a word, Michaels knew Perry had grasped the same idea. He went to one end, Perry the other.

"Get behind the table!" he shouted to Jiin.

Jiin and her two Tz-en circled the table. Together, they managed to tip the massive piece on its side, spin it a few degrees to face the doors, and drop behind it for cover. Stray bolts burned across the polished surface.

Tabor staggered to his security men. He waved his hands, screaming about Michaels and Perry. And was promptly shoved out of the way.

The Tz-en had no cohesion, no strategy. They fired blindly down the hall. The three remaining security had no military training. They hung back, shooting with their smaller weapons. They had no chance against any kind of organized attack.

And the attack came like a raging bull.

A huge figure in full battle armor, a blaster in each hand, stormed into the audience chamber. Energy bolts cut into the armor plating, discharging in a wash of blue plasma. His blasters glowed red from constant activation, bolts tearing into the Tz-en.

Michaels knew that armor. Thatcher had it for as long as he had known the big man.

What was Thatcher doing here? Michaels expected him to be in another system by now. Did he expect to fight all of the Tz-en to rescue Michaels? Touching, but stupid.

But Thatcher wasn't alone.

A dozen figures in rust colored robes raced into the room. A blur of red, accented by blasts from weapons.

The Shir'ka cut through the remaining Tz-en before Michaels or Perry could lend their weapons to the battle.

One security man left standing threw his pistol aside and fell on his face, hands over his head.

Two Shir'ka dragged Tabor from behind a pillar. He cowered and screamed.

"Don't kill him!" Perry called out.

As he and Michaels stood from behind the cover of the overturned table, dozens of blasters snapped up to aim at them.

Michaels raised his hands, trying to make the blaster in his hand look non-threatening.

"Geoff! It's me!"

Jiin stood up beside him, and Thatcher's blaster fired.

Michaels turned and encircled Jiin in his arms, pulling her down. He felt the heat of the bolts flash by, felt the burn across his shoulder. They fell hard, but they were both alive.

He winced and stuck his head over the edge of the table. "Damn it, Geoff, she's on our side!"

Thatcher unlatched his helmet. He glared at Michaels and shook his head.

"Perry!" called one of the Shir'ka. He pulled away the headwrap, revealing an older bearded face.

"To'mahs!" Perry said, coming around to greet him. "So you changed your mind."

To'mahs nodded his head toward another Shir'ka. "I was convinced."

The other man tugged down his headwrap, revealing the face of the young man.

Thatcher led some of the Shir'ka and a couple El'arans toward Michaels. They weren't happy with Jiin and her comrades, but at least their weapons were pointed down.

"Just stick with me," he told Jiin. "I'll take care of you."

"And Hiun and Chyn?" she asked of her men.

He nodded. They were no longer armed. He'd make sure nothing happened to them.

More blaster fire could be heard from other areas of the palace. The fighting was far from over, and most of the Shir'ka left to continue the battle.

"Geoff, what's going on?" Michaels asked. "I thought you'd be long gone."

Thatcher grinned at him. "You wouldn't have left me, would you? Besides, a bunch of us got offers to lend a hand. Turns out this is a pretty rich planet. The bid was pretty high for some light work. Yeah, the gold was stolen, but it spends just as well in any system. Besides, once the El'arans take the planet back, it won't be stolen no more."

"Oh, yeah," Perry said with a glance toward him, "that ship we sank in the river? The reason we sank that particular one was that its cargo already lacked a few thousand pounds of gold. We figured sinking it would delay that discovery."

"And it helped pay for some off-worlder help," the young man in the Shir'ka clothes said. He held up the weapon in his hand. "Like these blasters."

"Courtesy of Harry Capetti," Thatcher said. "He's been smuggling them in for months."

"Yeah," Perry said, "I worked that out with him some time ago."

"I thought the attack was going to be in Khadeej," Michaels said.

The young man smiled. "You were meant to believe that. We hoped that, if they believed Khadeej was our target, they would transfer troops and leave Jhamrahl vulnerable. We were disappointed you didn't immediately tell the Tz-en. We would have had to devise another plan if they hadn't been listening to your conversation. The boy who had helped you had a change of conscience. Apparently, so did you."

"Just who the hell are you?" Michaels asked.

"Dh'vid." He looked up at the dome, the light bathing his face. His eyes lost their gleam and filled with a sadness.

"Those troops they were sending to Khadeej," Thatcher said, "their transports met with an unfortunate accident … about now. We stole some of the fliers from the spaceport. Grips and a couple other old pilots should be strafing those troop carriers as we speak. And Jhamrahl's military targets were hit the same time we raided the palace. Boy, Mick, you should see these Shir'ka fight."

Perry approached the bound figure of Tabor held between two Shir'ka. "I think Mr. Tabor will cooperate in your taking control of the Tz-en population. I also believe that some media coverage will bring in off-world support."

Jiin pulled a data wafer from her pocket and placed it in Michaels' hand. "This might be of help. It contains the information the man Ringer was killed over, and which led to Hannah O'Brien's death. It was removed from her damaged computer."

"I thought you gave that to Tabor," Michaels said, looking at the square plastic in his palm.

"No. I gave him a copy, with the same data in case he might examine it. I intended for the real one to be delivered to appropriate authorities."

Michaels closed his fingers over the wafer, thinking of Hannah. Her and Ringer, dead because of what was on this. He would not let their deaths be in vain. "We'll get this to the media. It will destroy any influence Tabor has over them. When the story spreads, we'll get off-world support. The Consortium will get involved and start their investigation. When the dust settles, El'aris will be a free world."

El'aris's sun bathed the spaceport with golden morning light. Michaels, enjoying the shadow under the *Crazy Eight*, watched one of the large transports lift off. The ground beneath his feet rumbled. Hundreds of Tz-en went streaking into space, homeward bound whether they wanted to or not. Those who never wanted to leave their planet would be happy. Those who didn't want to go back had little choice. The Tz-en who had survived the liberation of El'aris had to leave immediately, never to return, as decreed by the new M'ji and his fledgling parliament. Any formerly influential Tz-en no longer had enough credits to buy a berth on any outgoing cruiser. They were literally in the same boat as a lowly clerk. A few, Michaels had heard, had talked their way onto private ships whose owners or captains were willing to have another deckhand at bottom pay rate. Michaels couldn't feel sorry for them. He never liked them, on the whole.

"About ready?" he asked.

"Yes," Jiin said.

Standing beside him, she watched the departing ship too. She was an outcast. He understood that feeling.

"Are you certain you want to do this?" she asked.

She studied him, her eyes searching his. He saw the fear in them that his answer might be different.

"Are you kidding? I take care of my partners, never forget that. Geoff's moving on, already used his sizable fortune to buy a bar on a beach he knows in this quiet system with only one planet, so I need someone to watch my back."

Harry Capetti slid down the ramp from the ship's underbelly. "I thought you were retiring, Mick."

"You bet. Taking your lead and buying myself a little ship like this, soon as we make one of the bigger systems. Jiin's a darn good pilot herself. She'll make a great partner."

"Good for you. We'll be ready to leave in about fifteen minutes," Harry said. He climbed back inside.

Across the tarmac, Perry walked from the main terminal. Instead of the rust colors of a Shir'ka, he wore the brighter clothes of an El'aran. His long strides brought him into the shadow of the freighter. As he drew close, he held out his hand. Michaels gripped it.

"Sure you won't stay?" Perry asked.

Michaels glanced at Jiin. She stepped back, near one of the landing struts, as though to give them some measure of privacy.

"I'm sure. Jiin gave up a lot for me. I owe her. Besides, you don't need me around here. I thought the new government was trying to get rid of all the undesirables."

"Executives from Deltan have been storming the port. They're trying to get out before the Consortium investigators arrive. We've been trying to stop them. One or two might have sneaked out with the Tz-en deportees, but then that's their problem now. A lot of Deltan employees just never knew what went on, but they panicked anyway. There will be a lot of data to sift through. Tabor won't be leaving El'aris for a long time. Right now, he's a guest of the old prison in Khadeej. I arranged for him to have the cell of a friend, named Jor'm. Thanks to Jor'm I was able to track down Dh'vid."

"So that's what you were up to. I had a feeling old Jor'm was hiding something. So he was behind the M'ji heir?"

"And Dh'vid seems well suited for the position."

As he glanced over the busy port, he thought of Hannah. He missed her. Dh'vid had insisted on a resting place on the estate grounds, with honors for service to the people of El'aris. He would have buried Ringer next to her, but he had family somewhere. So Hannah received all the honors. Imagine, a hacker from Helbent becoming a hero, sharing a place with royalty. He smiled, wondering what her retort might be. It was a beautiful grove, surrounded by shade trees and native flowers that bloomed all year long. There was even talk of a statue. He'd come back, visit Hannah. Maybe get to tell her about his newest adventures.

He'd be back.

THE END

ABOUT OUR CREATORS

WRITER

WAYNE CAREY—A life-long fan of science fiction and pulp fiction, Wayne Carey grew up reading Edgar Rice Burroughs, H.G. Wells, Isaac Asimov, H. Rider Haggard and all the grand masters, which guided him toward a career in science with degrees in biology and education and provided the desire to write from an early age. A love of classic and noire films, such as *Casablanca* and *The Maltese Falcon*, also influences his writing. He is the author of *The Nanon Factor*, a young adult contemporary science fiction thriller that blends a murder mystery with cutting edge technology, and has appeared in a variety of anthologies such as *Legends of New Pulp Fiction*. He and his wife Brenda live in the wilds of Central Pennsylvania with their three children, who provide a great deal of inspiration for his work. Email him at wgcarey@1791.com.

INTERIOR ILLUSTRATIONS

JAMES E. LYLE - is a native of western North Carolina, having been born in Asheville in 1963 and raised in the mountains near Waynesville. In the sixth grade he decided that being an artist was what mainly interested him. James has been a professional cartoonist and illustrator for the past thirty years, working primarily as a freelance but occasionally dabbling in full-time employment.

He has been published by such companies as Acclaim/Valiant Comics, Caliber Comics, Now Comics, and Zenescope Entertainment. He contributed a number of illustrations to the Weekly Reader line of magazines, he has created illustrations for Jones Soda Co., Ron Jon Surf Shop, J.C. Penny Apparel and other major companies. James has also designed CD art for recording artists like Todd Rundgren and Sloug Feg. He also finds time to give private art lessons, creates commissioned artwork, and also plays music with Gypsy Bandwagon.

In 2013 James was elected Chairman of the Southeast Chapter of the National Cartoonists Society after serving two terms as Vice-Chair to that group. James still lives near Waynesville with his wife, Karin.

COVER ARTIST

TED HAMMOND - is a Canadian artist who has been creating amazing art for over twenty years. His work has appeared in magazines, ads, books and graphic novels just to name a few. Go to (www.tedhammond.com) to contact him and check out more of his work!